"It's a body!"

"A body," she said. "Then get the hell away from there."

I stepped into the water and gasped at how cold it was. I flashed the little bitty light at the man's head and it illuminated the features enough for me to see that it was Jacob Lahrs. A dark red stain ran down the side of his face—blood, I assumed.

"It's Jacob Lahrs!" I said.

"Is he alive?" she asked.

"Mr. Lahrs," I said. "Mr. Lahrs, it's Torie O'Shea."

No response. He was either unconscious or dead. I stepped a little closer, and when I did, I must have stepped on part of the wreckage. My foot sank into it, and I felt wood scraping my skin. A creaking noise was the only warning I got, and not soon enough for me to move. The whole thing tipped and Jacob Lahrs just sort of spilled on top of me.

I screamed.

———————— ★ ————————

"For fans and readers who enjoy cozies."
—*Library Journal*

Forthcoming from Worldwide Mystery by
RETT MacPHERSON

IN SHEEP'S CLOTHING

BLOOD RELATIONS

Rett MacPherson

W☉RLDWIDE®

TORONTO • NEW YORK • LONDON
AMSTERDAM • PARIS • SYDNEY • HAMBURG
STOCKHOLM • ATHENS • TOKYO • MILAN
MADRID • WARSAW • BUDAPEST • AUCKLAND

To Kathy Gore, Jackie Mikel and Suzie Potts,
the girls I've danced with, sang with, cried with and
slew dragons with. As the song says, "We are family."

BLOOD RELATIONS

A Worldwide Mystery/February 2005

First published by St. Martin's Press LLC.

ISBN 0-373-26519-0

Printed in U.S.A.

Acknowledgments

The author wishes to thank the following people who helped bring this book to publication:

My agent, Michele Rubin. My editor, Kelley Ragland, whose editorial suggestions made this a much better book. The usual suspects: Tom Drennan, Laurell K. Hamilton, Deborah Millitello, Marella Sands, Sharon Shinn and Mark Sumner for endless support, friendship and, last but not least, delicious food; and my husband, Joe, and the kids for their patience.

A special thank you to Janie Pecarina, Lee Estep, Donna Burgee and the people at the Booksource for promotion beyond the call of duty.

ONE

"THE GAHEIMER HOUSE is one of the oldest houses in New Kassel, dating back to the mid-1860s," I said. I was back to giving tours of the house, and I could finally fit into all seven of the reproduction dresses that my boss, Sylvia, had made for me several years ago when I started this job. I wish I could say that having a baby last year had added the extra pounds to my rather short frame, but it really hadn't. It wasn't my son's fault that I had eaten too much and reduced my exercising to chasing my chickens around the backyard. No, it was mine. All mine.

But a year later and about thirty pounds lighter, I could fit into the reproduction dresses and was giving tours twice a day. I wore my favorite, the 1870s deep-blue polonaise gown with an open front that revealed an underskirt of the same color. It was trimmed with chenille-ball fringe in a deeper, almost navy blue.

I moved the tour of about eleven people into the dining room, my stiff and itchy crinolette swishing as I went. "For those of you who aren't from the eastern Missouri area, New Kassel was founded by a group of German immigrants in the 1830s. The Mississippi River was an excellent way of importing and exporting, and the town was located not too far from the Missouri River junction. The Missouri River is important because before the great railroads were built west of the Mississippi, the Missouri was the main route west. Unless you went by wagon."

On this particular tour, I had a young couple with twin girls, an elderly couple, a threesome of mid-forties women, an ancient-looking man who could have passed for a mid-western version of Rasputin, and a solitary female about thirty.

"I want to remind everybody as we enter this lovely room filled with delicate china and silver that all of the items in the Gaheimer House are antiques, so we ask that you refrain from touching them," I said, more for the couple with the twin girls than for anybody else. I'm the mother of three kids; I know how things accidentally get broken. Kids are great. I had been thoroughly amazed at how much I could love a little creature when Rachel was first born, but that didn't change the fact that kids live to touch things expensive, old, or irreplaceable. And if the twins on this tour were anything like my middle child, Mary, something would get broken.

"The wainscoting that you see here is made of sycamore. Mr. Gaheimer went to Connecticut on business in the late 1880s and brought back this dining table, which seats twelve. If you'll notice, the chandelier matches the gilt convex mirror...."

I could say this stuff in my sleep. I've been doing this for almost ten years. I'm also the archivist for the town, compiling things like marriage and land records for Granite County. Sometimes I even write biographies, and I'm usually the one in charge of any displays we put up, as well. I know this town inside and out, and I know the job inside and out. Every now and then, though, if something distracts me, I forget my monologue and end up staring out at the tourists, stammering and stuttering. Just like today.

The solitary female, whom I mentioned before, was staring back at me. Not staring at me like you'd expect someone might when listening to a tour guide, but *really* staring at me. She was about my height, maybe an inch taller, and had brown hair and hazel eyes. Something about those hazel eyes disturbed me, beyond the fact that they were boring through me as if she were trying to read my soul. There was a…familiarity, but I couldn't place it. Dark lashes and eyebrows stood out against her rather pale face. She hung on my every word, my every gesture. And soon it became very difficult for me to speak.

"And uh…um, this punch bowl at the end of the room was a gift from…from…" Who was it a gift from? I couldn't remember.

"Torie," somebody said.

"No, not Torie. Susan B. Anthony, that's it!"

"Torie," the voice said, more persistent now. I snapped out of my stupor and realized that *my* name was Torie and somebody was calling me.

"What?" I looked over to the entrance, where I saw my boss, Sylvia Pershing, standing there. Sylvia must be close to a hundred by now. Of course, I've been saying that for the last twenty years. I just knew that she was old when I was a kid, and now she seems immortal. She's thin, frail, bony, and full of piss and vinegar. She has never cut her silver hair in her life, and she braids it into twin braids every morning and wraps them around her head. She is the president of the Historical Society, where I am employed, and she owns half of the town, including the Gaheimer House. Her sister Wilma died last year, and Sylvia has not been quite the same since. She can still do more than half of the people in the town, and she can still cut you with her razor-sharp tongue, but it's as if she doesn't enjoy it anymore.

"Yes, Sylvia…what is it?"

"I hate to interrupt the tour, but when you're finished, you need to call the school," she said with a slight tremor caused by age.

"Oh, all right," I said. I resumed the tour, wondering just what Mary had done that would require me to go and bail her out. The rest of the tour went much like the first part had, with me stumbling over words and finding myself stealing glances at the woman staring at me. I found myself doing things like wiping at my nose to make sure there were no errant boogers, and cleaning my teeth with my tongue. I mean, was there something gross about me? What was her problem?

Finally, the tour was over. I headed down to my office as fast as I could. I put sixty cents in the soda machine, got a Dr Pepper, and went to my office. I shut the door and took a long, fizzy sip of my soda. Then I dialed the school, whose number I've had memorized since Mary started kindergarten.

Of course, New Kassel is a tiny town. There's one school for kindergarten and all twelve grades, and the graduating classes have about forty students each. And so when Francine answered the phone and I said, "Hi, it's Torie," she knew exactly who was calling.

"Yeah, Torie," Francine said. "We got a problem with Rachel."

"Rachel?" I asked. My oldest. This, I hadn't expected. "Are you sure?"

She laughed a little. "Of course I'm sure."

Rachel. Hmmm. "W-what's the problem?" I asked. I would have sat down, but you can't sit down in a dress like the one I was wearing. Potty breaks are an event that take as much organization as the invasion of Normandy. And nearly as much time.

"She got into a fight," Francine said.

"A fight?" I asked. "Francine, this is Torie O'Shea. Are you sure you got the right kid? Rachel O'Shea. You're sure?"

"Yeah, I'm sure. She gave Davie Roberts a bloody nose because he flicked her bra strap."

"Oh jeez," I said. Yes, it had been one of the great emotional moments of my life when my prepubescent daughter became pubescent and had to go out and buy her first training bra. She was still a kid, for crying out loud, but boobs are boobs. She was humiliated beyond belief, no matter how many of her friends I could name who were wearing training bras already. It also didn't matter when I pointed out that usually she couldn't wait to wear what everybody else wore, so why was this one item of clothing any different? But it was, and she didn't see my logic at all.

"It's pretty bad," Francine said.

"What do you mean, 'pretty bad'?" I asked.

"I mean, I think she broke his nose. His eyes turned purple within twenty minutes."

My first reaction was to say, "Well, then Davie should keep his hands to himself," but that didn't make what Rachel did right. I don't know how many times I've told my kids, "I don't care who throws the first punch, it's the kid who throws the last one—the one who retaliates—whom I will punish." Yes, Davie should have kept his little twelve-year-old perverted hands to himself, but Rachel should not have broken his nose. "I'll be right there," I said to her.

"Okay," Francine said.

"But, hey…are you guys going to do anything to Mr. Frisky Hands?"

"Yes, he's getting detention. That is, as soon as he returns to school."

"Oh jeez," I said again, wondering just what Davie's mother was going to say to me at the next PTA meeting. There was a knock at my office door just as I said good-bye and hung up the phone.

"Come in," I said.

The door opened and in walked the woman from the tour. The one who had kept staring at me. I was a little surprised, but yet…was I really? "Can I help you?" I asked. I sounded a little defensive, maybe even hateful. The woman flinched.

"Um, I was wondering if I could...I can come back at another time," she said.

"No," I said. "I'm sorry. It's just that I have to go to the school to get my daughter. There's been a...disagreement with one of her classmates."

"Oh."

"Could you...I'll listen to you, if you'll help me out of this stupid dress," I said, turning my back to her and exposing the buttons.

"Oh, sure," she said, and began undoing the buttons. There was an underslip, chemise, and crinolette, so I knew she wouldn't actually see any flesh. Women in the nineteenth century were packaged in layer after layer, so the only person who could ever glimpse their bare skin was the person who was supposed to. A satin and lace prison, if you will.

"What can I do for you?" I asked as I unbuttoned the sleeves.

"I understand that you trace family trees? You are Torie O'Shea, correct?"

"Yes," I said. "I wouldn't wear these tombs if I weren't."

"Well, I was wondering if I could hire your services?" she asked.

It was January. No major holidays or projects coming up. No marriages or births. There was no reason I couldn't take on this job. I just wasn't sure I wanted to, though. I always react this way. I am a historian. A genealogist. And yet when somebody actually asks me to do my job, I always balk.

"It might take me awhile. And even then, I can't say that I'll have every branch fleshed out as far back as it will go. What I'll do is establish a certain number of generations and try to fill that in. If I get more in the time allotted, then that's a bonus for you."

I turned around and began looking for my car keys.

"How many generations do you go back to?" she asked. "When were you born?"

She looked around the room, self-conscious suddenly. It was as if she wasn't sure if she should answer. How could I trace her family tree if she wasn't even willing to give me her birth date? "Nineteen seventy."

"Then I'll try and finish eight. That's about two hundred years. Is that okay with you?"

"Sure," she said, and shrugged.

"All right," I said. "What's your name?"

Again, that semifrightened bunny-rabbit look. Her eyes darted from the Rose of Sharon quilt hanging on my wall, to the window, to the poster advertising all of New Kassel's charms, to the floor. Finally, she spoke. "Stephanie."

"Stephanie…" If I hadn't been so rattled over Rachel, I would have asked her more questions, like why she had been staring at me so intently during the tour and why she was acting so weird over simple things like her name and age. But my anxiety about Rachel mounted with each moment that passed.

"Connelly."

"Nice to meet you, Stephanie Connelly," I said, my dress hanging on my shoulders. "I'll leave you a form to fill out as best you can. And my rates are on there as well, so you can see how much this is going to cost you. But right now, I need to get down to the rest room and change my clothes so that I can go and pick up my daughter."

"Okay," she said, putting her hands in her jean pockets.

I pulled a form out of the top desk drawer, set it on my desk, and put a pencil next to it. "Just fill it in, leave me your phone number and e-mail address, if you've got one, and I'll get back to you. I'm sorry. I have to go."

"Sure, that's fine."

Realizing that my keys were in my jean pockets—where

they always were—I picked up my jeans and shirt and tennis shoes from the chair next to the door. "Thank you so much for undoing these buttons. You have no idea how difficult it is to get in and out of this dress."

"Oh, you're welcome," she said, and smiled brightly.

Immediately to the right was the kitchen. I walked through it to the rest room that Sylvia had built for staff use. Nobody could see me walking through the kitchen with the dress unbuttoned to the small of my back, unless Sylvia happened to be there. But since Sylvia was usually the person to help me out of the blasted things, I didn't really care if she saw my slip-covered back or not. As soon as my clothes were changed, I was out the door and on my way to the school. But I couldn't help feeling a little weird as I left. I remembered an occasion a few years ago when a tourist had approached me after a tour and had hired me as a genealogist. She had ended up dead.

TWO

I JUST THINK you should say something to Rachel, other than 'Good shot, honey!'" I said to Rudy.

Rudy, my ever lovable and generous-hearted husband, was leaning up against the countertop in our kitchen. He was eating an Oreo, the inside first, and teasing our dog Fritz with any possible crumbs. He wore his long-sleeved blue oxford shirt and khakis for work, but he hadn't put his shoes on yet, so our wiener dog kept licking his toes, trying to find crumbs.

"And why are you eating Oreos for breakfast?" I asked, irritated in general.

"I'm not eating Oreos for breakfast. I had eggs and waffles for breakfast. I'm just eating the Oreos because I want to and I can eat them anytime," he said. "Lighten up."

"You know...our daughter broke another kid's nose."

"I know," he said, glowing.

"You're seriously missing something here, Rudy."

"What? Davie got too friendly with her and she put him in his place," he said.

"Look, I agree that I want our girls to be able to defend themselves in case they are ever attacked," I said. "But we shouldn't condone Rachel's actions because a kid flipped her bra strap. I mean, self-defense is one thing, but if we condone this, then who's to stop her when the next kid just *looks* at her breasts?"

Rudy stood up straight. "Hey, that is my daughter you're

talking about. And I don't want to think about any kid *looking* at anything but her face.''

Rudy was having a difficult time dealing with the fact that Rachel *has* breasts, much less that they are growing. He had equal difficulty with the fact that she was no longer that little girl who used to wear ribbons in her hair and big pleated dresses with gigantic bows. Now, she wears bell-bottom jeans with yin/yang symbols on the rear-end pockets, and her straight hair is parted in the middle—a *crooked* part, for that's the in thing—and hangs shaggily around her shoulders. She is still a kid in many ways. She still loves boy bands and Harry Potter, and on occasion, if nobody is looking, she'll still play Barbies with her sister. But in another year, she'll be a full-fledged teenager, complete with pimples and boys. Rudy was in denial.

''Boys are going to look at her, Rudy. And someday they'll—''

''Don't go there!'' he said, and held a hand up and shut his eyes. ''I can't deal with this.''

''Why not?''

''Because I was one of those sweaty, hormone-driven teenagers once, and I know what I used to... She's not dating until she's thirty. That's that. Can I just enjoy my cookies, for crying out loud?''

''Look, we don't have to worry about her dating, not just yet anyway. We've got a few years. My point is, she'll be leaving broken bones in a path from here to Arkansas if we don't do something about this now.''

''And there's a problem with that?''

''Rudy!''

''All right, all right,'' he said. ''You're right.''

''I'm just saying that she should have gone to the teacher or the principal first, and then if he did it again, she could have taken more drastic actions, but we can't just condone the violence. Because if we condone it enough, someday she'll be the aggressor and we'll be getting phone calls from the school telling us to come get our bully. Not to mention we'll have to deal with the parents of all the wounded children. As it is, I'm not looking forward to seeing Davie's parents anytime soon."

"I think you're overreacting," he said.

"Probably. But, I just—" I took a deep breath. "One of my New Year's resolutions was to be more tolerant and accepting. And to be kinder, more forgiving. In this world where people shoot other people for having a soda bottle in their hands, we need to practice and teach tolerance and forgiveness."

"Okay, I hear you," he said, putting his hands up in surrender. "Did *you* talk to her?"

"Yes," I said. "I let her know that I was happy that she could take care of herself and that Davie was a jerk. But I also told her that if she ever busted a kid's nose again for something like this, I would ground her until her wedding day. I mean really, Rudy, was his behavior that bad?"

Rudy shrugged. "I used to do the same thing." He blushed. "Sometimes worse."

"Exactly. Davie's parents need to teach him to keep his hands to himself, and we need to teach Rachel not to take any crap. But not to go beating people up over every little thing. We're lucky she didn't get suspended. If it hadn't been for the fact that she's never been in trouble a day in her life, they probably would have suspended her."

"I know," he said. "But I was just so proud of her."

I couldn't help myself. The thought of my waiflike daughter hauling off and slugging Davie Roberts was just too surreal for me not to laugh. "Me, too," I said. We laughed together a minute and then I straightened up. "But only for a moment."

My son, Matthew, came toddling into the kitchen with his sippy cup in one hand, a plastic velociraptor in the other.

He wore his Batman pajamas, but the cape had come off somewhere in his bed. Rudy picked him up and gave him a big hug. "No flicking bra straps when you get older," he said to him with a stern face.

Right, like that was going to work.

"I gotta go," he said, giving me a kiss and handing off Matthew. "I'll talk to her tonight."

"Okay," I said.

I WAS LATE getting to my office. First, I had taken Matthew to my mother's house for the day, then dropped Rachel and Mary off at school, where I'd had a talk with the principal about yesterday. I'd asked him to please stress to Davie's parents that their son's behavior wasn't entirely acceptable, either.

I had barely sat down, when there was a knock at my door. "Come in," I said.

"Hi," a woman said. I stared at her for the longest time and then realized that she was the woman who had been on the tour yesterday. Stephanie...Connelly. Surely she didn't think that I had her family tree finished already.

"Ms. Connelly," I said, and stood.

"I was just wondering if you had a chance to look over the form I filled out."

Well, she was certainly a tenacious one, I'd give her that. She wore jeans and a pink sweater, no jewelry except a wedding band, very little makeup. "No," I said. "I just got in. Ms. Connelly, I won't be able to have anything for you to see for at least a week."

Her expression fell. "Oh, well, I know that. I just thought you'd at least have looked at the paperwork."

"No, not yet."

The phone rang then. I held a finger up to her as I answered it. It was my mother. "Hi, Mom," I said. Mom's voice was pleasant on the other end of the phone, asking me if we'd come to dinner later that evening. "Sure. I don't think we have anything else going on. We'll see you about six. Look, I have to go. There's somebody in my office. Love you, too. Bye."

Stephanie Connelly just stood there, picking at her thumbnail with her fingernail and biting her lower lip. What was her problem? Her gaze fell to the photograph of my children that I had sitting on my desk. It was one I had taken just two weeks ago—all three of them out in the snow with the lopsided snowman they'd spent the whole day making. Rosy cheeks, red noses, glistening eyes. They looked the picture of happy, healthy children.

"Are those your children?" she asked.

"Yes."

She just smiled and leaned a little closer to get a better look.

"Ms. Connelly—"

"Could you just look at my paperwork?" she asked. "It took a lot for me to come here and actually do this, and…I want—no, I *need* for you to at least look at it."

I fished out the Advil from the top drawer in my desk and put two in the palm of my hand. It was going to be a long day. "Just a minute," I said. I went to the soda machine and got a Dr Pepper, then chased down the Advil with one swallow. Back in the office, I seated myself, cleared my throat, and made a big production of retrieving her file from the top of my desk and opening it.

Name: Stephanie Anne Webster Connelly.
Birth: 26 June 1970, St. Louis, Missouri.
Married: Michael Norman Connelly on 10 May 1995, St. Louis, Missouri.
Children: Julia Victory Connelly, born 5 October 1996.
Mother: Julia Anne Thatcher.
Father: Dwight Keith.

I read that last line again. Dwight Keith. I looked up at her sharply, and she flinched. Then I looked back at the paper and read her daughter's name again. Julia *Victory* Connelly. My name. Victory is my real name; Torie is my nickname. Dwight Keith is my father's name. A chill settled in my chest as I looked up at her once more.

"Is this some kind of joke?" I asked. "I...don't understand."

The phone rang again. I picked it up. It was Eleanore Murdoch. "Not now," I said. "No, no, Eleanore, I'll talk to you later. Bye."

Tears welled in Ms. Connelly's eyes as she shoved her hands as deep in her pockets as they could possibly go. "I shouldn't have come," she said, and turned to leave, but I didn't let her go.

"What is this all about? What's the meaning of this?" I asked. What was she trying to say? What was she trying to accomplish by filling out her forms falsely?

Taking a deep breath, she just blurted it out. "I'm your sister."

I took another two Advil.

I didn't know what to say to her. I mean, it was preposterous. My father...

My father.

No, it was silly. I would have known if I had a sister, for crying out loud. I just sat there, blinking, not really sure what to say to her. She obviously expected something from me, but I didn't know what. And I'm sure my silence was not at all welcome.

"I...I think there's been a mistake," I said finally.

"No," she said. "There is no mistake. I am Dwight's daughter."

I am Dwight's daughter.

Her words echoed around in my head. My mind reeled and spun. A roaring in my ears blocked out all sound, so that I found myself in a vacuum, silent except for her words bouncing around. It was my turn to fight back tears. The familiarity in her eyes... They were my father's eyes. She was looking at me with my father's eyes. *My* eyes. But then, that could only mean...

My parents hadn't divorced until I was twelve. She was only five years younger than I was. The betrayal was like a bitter pill, too big for me to swallow. I felt as if a knife had been shoved in my heart.

"You can call him and ask him," she said.

Call him and ask him? Then that would mean that he knew about her. The fact that he would know about her and not ever have told me hurt me even more. How could he keep this from me for thirty years? Knowing how I felt about family, knowing I hated being an only child. When I was a kid, I would ask Santa for a sibling. Every single year. Wasn't it just like him to keep something to himself that I had always wanted? It was as if somebody had just twisted the imaginary blade that had penetrated my flesh moments ago. Just call him and ask him. That simple. With one phone call, shatter my whole world.

"I don't think so," I said.

Call him and ask him. Did she know his phone number?

"But..." she began, unsure of what to say. "I..."

"You what? What do you want exactly?" I asked, trying hard not to be too angry.

"I want a relationship with my sister." She shrugged.

"Right," I said, pushing my chair away from my desk and then standing. "Well...I'm not your sister."

Before I could ask her to leave my office, Elmer Kolbe came bursting through the door. He's our fire chief, way past retirement age, and all-around good guy. "Torie, you gotta come see this."

"See what?"

"You know how the river's been down so low?"

"Yeah?"

"You can see the wreck."

"The wreck."

"*The Phantom*," he said. "The steamboat that sank back in 1919."

"You're kidding," I said. But I found myself at odds with how I wanted to feel. Any other time, I would have jumped over my desk and taken off to the river like Tom Sawyer or Huck Finn. The legend of *The Phantom* is something told on every bar stool of every pub and diner in New Kassel. I'd grown up with the legend. I'd grown up, like everybody else, wondering if there would ever be a time that Old Man River would be low enough that we could actually view the wreckage. And it had finally happened. But now, with Ms. Connelly standing there with her news so fresh in the air, I was just sort of numb.

I was happy for Elmer's interruption, I decided. Because it saved me from any further discussion with Ms. Connelly. It saved me from having to kick her out of my office.

"Come on," he said, waving a hand at me. "Come and look."

THREE

Ms. CONNELLY excused herself, and I followed Elmer outside and down to the river. I tried to shake her from my mind. I tried to shake her and her words. But they just kept echoing over and over as I walked along the sidewalk.

I am Dwight's daughter.

You can call him and ask him.

On one hand, the whole thing seemed so preposterous that I felt I could just dismiss her and everything that she'd said. How could my father have known of her existence for thirty years and not told me? Or my mother? And I knew he hadn't told my mother, or she would have told me. She wouldn't have kept something like that from me. It was such a ridiculous notion that by the time I'd reached River Point Road, I had myself half-convinced that Ms. Connelly had been lying.

But why would she lie? What reason would she have had to make up something like that? And then confront me with it? Maybe she didn't have a father and she'd just fixated on me for some reason and wanted to be a part of my family. Yeah, right. I was beginning to sound like the scriptwriter for a soap opera. She had no reason to lie. But she could be mistaken. Maybe there was a different Dwight Keith. Maybe her mother didn't know who her father was and so just gave her the name of an old boyfriend or something.

My father certainly would have been capable of having an affair. I knew of at least two that he'd had, in fact. He was a musician, and, well, all that drinking and playing music to the lovely women who would sell their souls to be with a musician might have been a little overwhelming for somebody not so happy with his own marriage. Or somebody without a conscience. At least that was how my mother had explained it to me. She was allowed to be a little bitter over that one. So having an affair was something I could believe of him. Fathering a child and keeping it from me was an entirely different matter.

And what was it about musicians, anyway? I mean, if Mick Jagger had been a shoe salesman, do you really think he would have had all the women, all the *beautiful* women, he's had?

So, maybe Ms. Connelly's mother had had an affair with my father. Maybe she'd had many affairs and just didn't know which man was the father of her child.

But then I remembered Ms. Connelly's eyes.

Not possible, I told myself, and concentrated on the things around me.

I have always loved my town, by the way. Most of the buildings on River Point Road are old, having been built prior to 1910 at least. Many are white clapboard with wraparound porches, some red brick with dark shutters and roofs. River Point Road is the center of commerce. This part of town, where all of our shops and restaurants are, attracts tourists from all around, who come to eat and sample the wares. Living in a historic tourist town can have its problems. Tourists park in our driveway because they can't find a better place to park. And then there is always the threat of things like the riverboat-gambling issue, which we've managed to beat—so far. But the mayor won't stop. He'll bring back the issue of riverboat gambling again. But for the most part, I love everything about New Kassel life.

As I came over the hill, I could see the Mississippi River in the distance. The Mississippi is everything. It allows the barges passage for supplies. For eons, it has provided food and water to the area. And when Mother Nature unleashes her fury, the river can wipe out everything in its valley. There was only one time in history that something else controlled the river, and that had been during the New Madrid earthquake in 1811. The earthquake had made such large waves upon the river that it looked as if the water were moving backward.

But this year, there had been a drought. Not just a drought here but out west and up north, too, so that the tributaries that feed the river before it gets to St. Louis had nearly dried up as well. There are dunes in various places on the river now. Illinois seemed closer to us than usual. And on more than one occasion this winter, the river had actually been bumper-to-bumper with barges and tugboats. Because of the drought, the vessels had been forced to stay in the deepest part of the river, which had been reduced to an area half the size they were used to.

In fact, the river and the surrounding area looked as if it had been the location of a recent battle. The sky was that dirty cotton-ball color that happens sometimes before a snow. Along the Illinois side of the river, the leaves had died long ago and fallen, so that the riverbank resembled a forest of tall switches. The grass was brown, the river gray and filled with more sludge than usual. It was as if the land had been stripped of life by some superior being who took its nourishment and then moved on to its next feast.

Just as I made it to where the old Yates house used to stand, I could see a crowd of people pointing off to the right. I stepped through the tittering crowd and down over the railroad tracks, until I was standing on the bank of the river. Sheriff Colin Brooke, who also happens to be married to my mother, was standing almost in the water, his hands on his hips.

"Oh my gosh," I said as I saw the pilothouse of the

steamboat sticking up out of the water. "It really is *The Phantom.*"

"I know," Sheriff Brooke said. A large, strapping man, he always has to look down at me, even if we are both sitting. "Pretty amazing, huh?"

Elmer Kolbe finally stopped short behind me and gouged me in the arm. "Told ya," he said. "Wish my dad had lived to see this."

I couldn't help thinking that my father might not live to see it, if Ms. Connelly was telling the truth. "Do you think there are bodies in there?" I asked.

The sheriff gave me a sideways glance.

"Nah," Elmer said. "Fish food a long time ago."

"You are both morbid," Sheriff Brooke said.

"Well," I said. "It's a natural thing to wonder about. You know, twenty-four people died in that wreck. And seventeen bodies were never recovered."

"I know," the sheriff said. "But I thought it was twenty-two who died."

"Twenty-four," I insisted.

"Don't argue with her," Elmer said. "You know she's always right about these kinds of things."

"Oh, yeah, if it involves a body count, Torie's the expert."

"Shut up," I said.

A sound came from the hill behind us. When I looked back, I saw a television crew pulling up and hauling its equipment out of a white van that had the news to watch. channel 6 news written on the side of it.

"That didn't take long," Sheriff Brooke said as we looked back out at the ancient wreckage. The water lapped up on the side of what had been the pilothouse.

"Never does," Elmer said.

"I wonder if anybody called that guy at the college," I said.

"What guy?" the sheriff asked.

"A man came by a few years ago and asked to be called if the wreckage was ever exposed enough that somebody could get to it without too much trouble. Can't remember his name. Jacob something."

"I don't know," Sheriff Brooke answered.

"You know what I'm thinking," a voice behind us said.

We turned around to see Chuck Velasco standing there with his Doc Martens covered in river sludge and the edges of his jeans damp from the water. His parka was open enough to reveal the gold-and-black flannel shirt that he always seems to wear. He must have bought every one that Wal-Mart had and really wears a different one each day. It makes me feel better to think that way anyway, because he owns the pizza parlor in town. I love to eat there. The idea of him wearing the same shirt every day is not very appealing.

"What's that?" Sheriff Brooke asked.

Chuck looked around and picked up a stick from the ground, then went about dislodging great globs of sludge from the bottom of his boots. "I'm wondering if we can get to the diamonds."

"You don't really believe that there were diamonds on board," the sheriff said, watching Chuck as he threw the stick down and smeared his boot on a rock. "Hey, you haven't been down there already, have you? Chuck, you can't go down there. It's too dangerous."

Chuck shrugged. "I just took a peek."

"What did you see?" I asked him.

"Down, Torie," Sheriff Brooke said. "Chuck, don't go back down there. It's the same as an abandoned building. It's not secure, and the wreckage could shift. I mean it."

"All right," Chuck said, holding up his hands.

Sheriff Brooke picked up the radio attached to his shoulder and called into the office, an expression of worry on his face. "Newsome, this is Brooke. Over."

"Newsome here," a voice over the radio said.

"I need you to come down to the river here in New Kassel. Bring some crime-scene tape. I want you to rope something off," he said.

"Sure thing. There been a crime?"

"No," he said. "I just don't want people meddling in this wreckage."

"Be right there. Over."

The sheriff then lowered his gaze to me. "And that especially means you."

I just rolled my eyes at him. He was like this before he became my stepfather. I hugged myself in the cold and turned to Chuck. "So you really think the diamonds are down there?"

"Why not? That's what the legend says, doesn't it?"

"Yeah, but legends aren't always right, you know. They are usually *based* on real events, but inevitably the one thing you want to be true in the fairy tale is usually the part that isn't," I said.

About that time, the Channel 6 news crew made it over the railroad tracks and down to where we were standing. I had seen the anchorman before but couldn't place his name. He was a spiffily dressed black man, and he was not liking the looks of what he'd just stepped in.

"That's far enough," the sheriff said. "Nobody goes any farther than this."

Before the sheriff could even blink, the camera light came on, and he had a large round microphone stuck under his nose. "Deputy—"

"That's *Sheriff* Brooke," he said.

"I'm sorry, sir. Sheriff, is this the wreckage of *The Phantom?*" the anchorman asked.

Sheriff Brooke looked irritated to say the least, but he

was a good sport and went about answering the question. "We can't say for certain," he said. "I will say that it does appear to be a steamer, the same type of ship that wrecked here over eighty years ago. But we won't know for sure until we get a team in here to look at it."

"So, you are planning to have it investigated?"

"Well, no. I'm not sure at this time. We may just leave it be and let the water reclaim it in the spring," he said. "I'm just saying that there's no way to know for sure what ship it is until it's been investigated."

"I see," the anchorman said. "But to the best of your knowledge, it is most likely *The Phantom?*"

"It probably is."

"Sheriff, what do you know about *The Phantom?*"

"Not a whole lot," the sheriff said. "In fact, this young woman right here behind you should be able to answer all your questions for you. Mrs. O'Shea…"

You know, there are times when I could just kill him, even if he is married to my mother. I glared at him as the camera swung toward me. I wore the most faded pair of jeans I owned. I also had on a T-shirt that said princess on the front, and a flimsy little sweater, which I now pulled tightly across my chest because I had run out of my office without my coat. My hair was flying all around and I was wearing absolutely no makeup. Great. Nothing like putting your best face forward for the camera.

"Torie works for the Historical Society, and she might be better equipped to answer your questions than I," the sheriff told the anchorman.

"What can you tell us?" he asked me.

I stared blankly into the camera for a moment, and then I cleared my throat. "Uh, well…in 1919, there was a steamer called *The Phantom* heading to Hannibal from Memphis. There were eighty people on board. We think…um…whatever it was that caused the boat to sink happened a little farther upriver, but the swift current probably brought the boat back south a little ways, until it sunk right there in that small cove.''

"Does anybody know what caused the boat to sink?'' the anchorman asked.

I had to think about that a moment, because I didn't really know. There were theories. For once in my life, I actually thought about what to say instead of just saying what I thought. "I'll have to get back to you on that one, if you don't mind. I don't want to give you the wrong information.''

"So you're saying that at this time nobody knows what caused the boat to sink, or you *personally* don't have that knowledge?'' he asked. The tone of his voice made me sound so stupid.

"I'm saying I'll need to read the file I have and let you know,'' I replied.

"All right,'' he said. "So, Mrs. O'Shea, were there any survivors?''

"Oh, yes. Fifty-six people survived and twenty-four died. Seventeen of those twenty-four were unaccounted for, including the Huntleigh heiress.''

"So, did the captain go down with the ship?'' the anchorman asked.

"That's the theory,'' I said.

"What else can you tell us about the boat?''

"Um…''

It had been so long since I'd thought about *The Phantom* that I couldn't come up with any of the specifics—such as when it left port, or even what it was carrying. Well, other than the rumor that there was a chestful of diamonds on board.

"And what of the heir to the Huntleigh fortune?''

"I just told you that her body was never found, either.''

"Uh-huh," he said, like he'd just discovered a new planet in the solar system.

"You have to understand," I said. "This was 1919. They didn't really have deepwater divers and equipment like we have nowadays. I think it's amazing that they recovered as many bodies as they did. Especially when you consider it was just the townsfolk here who pulled people out of the wreckage. It doesn't mean that there was a conspiracy of any sort. Nowadays, we quite possibly could have found all the bodies."

"Is there anybody else in town who might speak to us about this?" he asked. "Somebody who would have been alive when *The Phantom* actually sunk?"

My boss, Sylvia, would have been about fourteen at the time of the wreck. Wilma was gone now; she could have told about it, too. The only other person in town I could think of who was old enough to remember the wreck would be Harlan Schwartz. He would have been about ten when it happened.

Sylvia wasn't likely to speak to the media. And Harlan...well, he probably would have, but I wasn't so sure I wanted him to. The last thing we needed was a swarm of outsiders to come down here and try to fish souvenirs out of the water. The less mystery, the better for New Kassel. My gaze flicked to where Sheriff Brooke was standing. The expression in his eyes said the same thing I was thinking. No drama. No mystery. Get them out of here.

"No," I said. "I can't think of anybody."

"Thank you for your time, Mrs. O'Shea," the anchorman said.

When the camera was turned off, I was actually sorry to feel the warmth of the lights leave. Just as I was about to turn and walk back up the bank to town, the newsman grabbed my arm. "Can I make an appointment with you?" he asked.

"For what?"

"I'd like it if you'd review your files, or whatever it is you have, and then do another interview. Maybe then you'd be better equipped to answer more of my questions," he said. "Or maybe you could just turn the files over to me and I can glean what I need."

"Uh, well…"

"There's a time crunch, here, Mrs. O'Shea," he said. "I want to be the first one to break an actual in-depth story. Oooh, you wouldn't happen to have photographs of the wreck in 1919?"

He was like a kid on Christmas morning.

"What is today…Wednesday?" I asked. "Come back Friday."

"Tomorrow would be better," he said.

"Friday," I said, and walked up the hill.

I left him standing on the edge of the water, where the sheriff was guarding the wreckage. As I passed Chuck Velasco, I stopped. "If you talk to the reporters, don't tell them about the diamonds," I said.

"Why not?"

"Because, it's pure myth. Ungrounded theory. The last thing we need is people down here in the middle of the night in their scuba gear, looking for diamonds that aren't there, and have somebody end up dead. Plus, you know all the riffraff it would bring into the town," I said.

"Yeah," he replied, looking down at his boots. "I hadn't thought of that. Besides, the fewer people who know, the less competition."

He smiled brightly, as if it were all just a joke, but he'd already admitted earlier that he'd at least considered investigating the wreckage. "Chuck, stay away from that boat."

"I will," he said. "Jeez."

I climbed up the hill and saw Deputy Newsome's car pull up. He was here with the crime-scene tape. Sheriff Brooke's car was not around, so he must have been off duty when he found out about the wreckage. I waved to Newsome as I headed back to my office, and he waved back.

Aside from Stephanie Connelly, the one thing that kept niggling at the back of my mind was Eleanore Murdoch, the town gossip and ink-slinger. If the reporters got an interview with her—and she'd all but beg to be put on camera—every tall tale and wild myth in the county would be flushed out.

Sure enough, the next morning the following article appeared:

THE NEW KASSEL GAZETTE
The News You Might Miss
By
Eleanore Murdoch

For all of you interested in supporting the local 4-H Club, raffles are being sold at Pierre's. Just two dollars can buy you a chance at winning that beautiful Bears Paw quilt that was donated by Evelyn Walters, and help the 4-H Club at the same time.

Ned Buckholt wanted me to print this: If he had known you were going to cut down every tree in the yard, he would have never sold you his house. His wife went into spasms, fainted, and had to be taken to the hospital to be revived.

Father Bingham is holding a snowman contest after church this coming Sunday. The winner gets a gift certificate to the Lick-a-Pot Candy Shoppe and three free horseback rides out at the Lucas Stables.

And last, but not least, you have all probably heard by now that the Mississippi is low enough that the wreck of *The Phantom* can be seen. The sheriff wanted me to urge each and every one of you not to go investigating on your own. He says the wreckage is unstable and can shift beneath your weight. So, stay away.

Until Next Time,
Eleanore

FOUR

THURSDAY EVENING, I found myself staring off into the distance of my home office. It's actually part of the attic—where our bedroom is—and is not entirely sectioned off, so I could see into the bedroom from my desk. I was supposed to be researching the 1919 wreck of *The Phantom* for Bradley Chapel, the Channel 6 news guy. But sitting on my desk in plain view was the questionnaire that Stephanie Connelly had filled out for me, and I could read the name Dwight Keith written in her perfectly legible cursive.

I hadn't slept much the previous night. Every time I'd get comfortable, I'd see her eyes. And then her face would sort of morph into my father's without the eyes changing at all. Then I'd roll over, thinking that the new position would somehow keep my mind's eye from seeing. It hadn't worked. About four o'clock in the morning, sleep finally won the battle with my rebellious brain, and I dozed off for about two hours.

"Earth to Torie," Rudy said.

I snapped to attention now, realizing that half of the Tom Waits CD I'd been listening to was over, and I had no memory of hearing three of the songs. "I'm sorry. What?"

"How long have you been staring at our curtains?"

"God, I don't know," I said, and tossed my pencil at the computer screen.

"What's up?" he asked, crossing his arms and standing

in front of my desk. "You're listening to Tom Waits, so it must mean that you're wallowing."

I just gave him a grave stare, ready to take his head off for just asking. But he didn't know what was troubling me, so there was no use in being angry at him. "I'm...I have to research the 1919 wreck for Channel 6 news."

"I have never, in all the years I've known you, seen you this distraught over research," he said. "You thrive on it."

"I'm just distracted."

"Why?" he asked.

"It's Rachel—"

"Don't give me the Rachel and the violence spiel. What's really wrong?" he asked. "You skipped breakfast, you picked at dinner, and now you're staring at the curtains. Not to mention that you've barely said five sentences to me all evening. And there're two things I know as sure as the sun comes up tomorrow."

"What's that?"

"You love food and you love to talk even more."

I leaned forward and rested my head in my palms. I gave a great sigh and then looked up at him. There was nobody better than Rudy to share this with. I had to tell somebody or my brain was going to melt. "There's this woman," I began. "Stephanie Connelly."

He shrugged. "Don't know her."

"She took a tour of the Gaheimer House the other day. And then she came and asked me if I would trace her family tree," I said.

"Nothing unusual about that."

"She claims to be my sister."

Rudy's forehead seemed to move an inch as his expression dropped. His brown eyes grew serious. "Well...is it...is she... Do you believe her?"

"No," I said.

"No? Just like that?"

I said nothing for several minutes, and neither did he. He just looked at me, gauging my expression and what it meant. "We know she's not your mother's. So that leaves your father."

"Oh, she claims to be his daughter all right," I said.

"Did you ask your father about her?"

"No."

"Why not?"

"I can't."

"Then you'll never know if she's really your sister."

"That's fine with me."

Rudy looked shocked. "It is?"

"Yes."

"Why?"

"Think how this will hurt my mother."

"Will it really hurt her? She already knows about his affairs when they were married. She's forgiven him. They're good friends now. I think she's mature enough to handle it," he said. "Plus, she may already know."

"No," I snapped. "My mother would have told me."

He shrugged. "What's the real reason?"

I took a minute, staring at the *Far Side* cartoon taped on my computer. Could I really answer this? Yes, I could. And it scared me how angry I felt. "Because if I don't ask him, then I'll never have to know that my father has been lying to me for thirty years!" I said. I choked on a sob but then got myself under control quickly. I refused to cry over this. And I had to think: Was this anger, or was it just good old-fashioned hurt and disappointment?

"She's suggesting that Dwight knows about her?"

"Yes."

"Oh, I see."

"Do you?" I asked. "Do you really understand what this means?"

"I think so," he said. He stood for a moment longer

without moving or speaking. Then finally he came around my desk and knelt in front of me, taking my hands in his. "What does she want? Why did she contact you after all these years?"

"She says she wants to have a relationship with her sis— with me."

"Have you thought about what that must mean to her?"

"I don't care what it means to her," I said. I could feel my chin trembling, and it ticked me off. "Her world is still intact. Mine has been shattered."

"Torie," he said. "I think—"

"If you tell me I'm overreacting, so help me, I will divorce you right here and now."

The corners of his mouth turned up in a smile, but he managed not to laugh at me. "I think you should ask your father about her. One way or another, you have to know the truth."

"Why?"

"So you can deal with it," he said. "You are the woman who has to know everything. You have to know every single thing that has ever happened, every thought anybody has ever had. And you're telling me you don't want to know if she really is your sister?"

"No, I don't. Just think of what it will do to all of my genealogy charts," I said.

"Torie," Rudy said with a smile. "Just *think* what it will do to all of your genealogy charts."

"Yes, but shouldn't this be something that my father should tell me about? Voluntarily. Should I really have to drag it out of him?" I asked, infuriated at the thought of his cowardice.

"But he didn't tell you."

"No, he didn't."

"So, it's up to you."

"Like it always is," I said. And that was really what was at the core of it all.

FIVE

ON FRIDAY MORNING, I decided that one Stephanie Anne Connelly did not exist. She was a figment of my imagination and that was that. I would never think of her again.

I often do that—declare something is so, and then go about living as though it is, even though I know the delusion won't last forever. I am much too practical to be able to fantasize about anything for very long. But if pretending Stephanie Connelly didn't exist could get me through the weekend, then I would be happy with that. I was certain that Monday would roll around and the whole world would look different, and then I'd be in a better position to decide what to do about her.

Right now, I had a reporter who had to be part blood-hound sitting at my desk, wanting to know every little detail about *The Phantom*. It was funny how he was dressed in a silk suit but his cameraman was wearing a Rams sweatshirt, black sweatpants, and no socks on his feet, which were stuffed into sneakers that looked two sizes too small. I got the feeling that Bradley Chapel would not be caught dead in black sweatpants and a sweatshirt, even if he were the one behind the camera. And he would never go without socks unless he was wearing sandals. But then, I could never imagine Bradley Chapel in sandals, either. The camera was on, by the way, but Mr. Chapel assured me that not every word or every minute of film would make it in his "exclusive" spot on the evening news. Still, it was weird being conscious of every single word I said.

"Basically, the steamer was built around 1900, at the cost of ten thousand dollars," I said. "It was about one hundred and forty-three feet by thirty-one. Its engines were about ten inches in diameter of cylinders by four feet stroke. She ran the Arkansas-St. Louis-Hannibal route, carrying passengers, bumper crop, that sort of thing."

"I thought you said on Wednesday that the ship had just come from Memphis."

I just stared at him. "Yes, Tennessee is across from Arkansas."

"So, was this anything like the boat in *Showboat?*" he asked.

"Well, it certainly had the paddle wheel in the back, the two stacks, and the white trellis-looking things—called bull rails, by the way—but I don't think she was nearly as fancy as the one in that movie. She had two decks." I handed him a photograph of the boat taken in about 1905. "And then, of course, the crew could walk along the top, so that was sort of a third deck, but the top didn't have the railings."

"How fast could she go?"

"Hmm, that I wouldn't know."

"What kind of crew would she have had?"

"Well, a captain or a pilot, obviously. Leadman—"

"A who?"

"Leadman. He would use a sounding pole to judge the depth of the water, and then he'd call it back to the pilot-house. Water depth was very important. If they ran into shallow water, not only could they ground their boat, get it hung up on something, but it could do serious damage. Then who knows how long they would have been stranded with a cargo that might have been time-sensitive."

"Oh," Mr. Chapel said.

He had probably never been on a boat in his life.

"Who else?"

"Roustabouts, or deckhands. They worked under the mate on the deck of a packet. Um…a wood hawk."

"Who?"

"He would handle the woodlots on the boats."

"Okay," he said, more in a tone that said he wished he hadn't asked than one that showed interest. "What was she carrying when she sank?"

I supposed he didn't want to hear about the cooks and the other assorted crew. So, I responded to his last question, rather than add the rest of the crew. "Research indicates that this was mostly a passenger run," I said.

I handed him another photograph. "That is a picture taken the next afternoon."

"Gruesome," he commented.

Indeed it was. I had handed him a photograph of the seven recovered bodies lying in a neat row, covered by blankets. One was the length of a child. The sepia tone of the photograph made everything look dirty. But it had been winter, just like now, when the boat had sunk. So everything was sort of gray and desolate-looking to begin with. Standing to the left of the bodies was a man in a black derby. He sported a handlebar mustache. The chain of his pocket watch was clearly visible on his vest pocket. Sylvia had told me that the man was the town doctor, Doc Hallam. To the right of the row of bodies was a little kid, staring back at the camera, a look of shock frozen across his face. I wasn't sure if it was shock from the spectacle of death that lay at his feet or from the snap of the camera. Maybe it was a little of both. The river ran behind them, the top of one of *The Phantom*'s stacks barely visible, poking out of the water.

"What time did the boat go down?"

"Well, the time it actually sank in the cove was about four in the afternoon. So that picture was taken almost twenty-four hours later.'' I handed him another photograph. ''This one was taken about an hour after it sank. It was winter, so the sun was almost gone, but somebody thought to snap this picture. You can see the boat is slightly on its side. The top deck, pilothouse, and one stack can still be seen.''

He studied the photograph for a moment. ''I don't understand. If the pilothouse can still be seen, how come the captain didn't make it?''

I didn't follow.

''I mean, it's obvious. If you could still see the pilothouse in this picture, he should have had plenty of time to get off the boat before it sank.''

''I'm not sure,'' I said, shrugging.

''Are any of these people still alive?'' he asked. He gestured to the people standing all along the riverbank. Some were townsfolk who had come to stare in disbelief or to help rescue people. Some of the figures were people saved from the boat. One woman sat on a rock, soaking wet, staring past the camera with an expression that suggested she was reliving in her head what had happened.

''I doubt it,'' I said, knowing full well that one of the boys standing on a rock, looking out at the river, was Harlan Schwartz.

''Anything else of importance you can tell me?''

I got the sneaking suspicion that he had already heard about the diamond myth. Just by the way he kept pressing me, as if I should know more than I was telling him. Either that or he was just very intuitive and I was being unfair.

''Mmm, no, not really. I didn't have time to research all of the articles and interviews at the time to find out what the theories on the cause of the accident were. I mean, eyewitnesses said that she had flanked going upstream, then she was out of sight a few minutes, and then they saw her dead in the water, floating back down toward the cove, where she finally sank.''

'''Flanked'?''

"It means that the pilot had driven the boat hard, forcefully, toward the opposite bank, then set it back just as forcefully at the last minute and let the current swing the bow around.''

"Oh.''

No conspiracy in flanking, Mr. Chapel.

"When was it known to the New Kassel residents that the Huntleigh heiress had been on board *The Phantom?*" he asked.

"As far as I've been able to tell, nobody knew she was on board the boat until a few days later.''

"How did they discover that?'' Mr. Chapel asked.

"Well, I'm not sure. But some of her items washed ashore. I know that much. As to how they actually knew she was on board, I guess they must have looked at the manifest. I'll have to check on that.''

"Did her parents ever come to New Kassel?''

"Not that I know of,'' I said. "But I think they sent a private investigator. I really am not certain of these things. I'll have to do some checking.''

"Could I study your interviews and the articles that you mentioned?''

"It's all public domain, Mr. Chapel. You can find most of it at the library.'' If you know what you're looking for, I thought.

"If you don't mind, Kyle and I''—he pointed to his cameraman—"are going to stick around awhile.''

'''Awhile'?'' I asked.

"Couple days. We're going to stay at the…Murdoch Inn,'' he said, flipping through a brochure on my desk. "Just in case the sheriff might decide to do a little river diving.''

It's a free country. And why on earth would he need my

permission to stay? "Sure," I said. But deep down, I was already dreading the outcome of a news anchor staying at the very inn owned by the town's biggest gossip.

"Kyle," Chapel said. "Get some close-up shots of these pictures."

I watched as Kyle went about shooting video footage of the photographs that I had handed Mr. Chapel. Then Kyle gave them back to me with a nod of his head.

"So, how long have you worked for the Historical Society?" Mr. Chapel asked me.

"Too long," I said, and smiled. "No, I love my job. Um…about ten years, I suppose."

"Have you lived in town long?"

"Yes," I said.

"In your job as archivist, have you ever come across any old mysteries about this town? Anything juicy?"

If only he knew.

"Maybe," I said, and tried to stifle a laugh.

He smiled at me, showing perfectly capped teeth. "Where's a good place to eat in town?"

"If you're after something easy like pizza and beer, Velasco's is the best. Or the Smells Good deli. The Old Mill Stream offers a little finer dining. Fraulein Krista's Speishaus is my favorite place in town. Um…Pierre's is the place to go for breakfast. It's a bakery, wonderful teas and coffee," I said.

"Thank you," Mr. Chapel said.

"What about Burger King?" Kyle asked.

"If you want fast food, you need to head west out of town on the New Kassel Outer Road until you hit a place called Wisteria. The main road into town is fast-food heaven," I said.

"Forgive my cameraman," Chapel said. "He's so uncouth."

"It's all right," I said. "I hope you gentlemen have a nice stay."

"I'm sure we will."

As soon as Bradley Chapel and his cameraman left the Gaheimer House, I jogged through the kitchen, heading toward the back door. Sylvia just happened to be standing in the kitchen, of course, making herself a cup of black cherry berry tea. "Where are you going?" she asked without looking up.

"Eleanore's," I said.

"You're as nosy as she is," said Sylvia.

"No, I'm not. Be back in time for the next tour."

If Sylvia had anything else to say, I didn't hear it. All I heard was her spoon clanking against the cup as I stepped out the back door and began running through the alleys and yards to get to the Murdoch Inn before Mr. Chapel did.

SIX

THE MURDOCH INN sits on a slight hill at the south end of River Point Road, which means there is a gorgeous view of the Mississippi River from the front porch. Built in the 1880s by Alexander Queen, the house sports delicate latticework all along the porch and the trim of the house. It is white, with one turret, two stories, and a renovated attic, which has the cutest rooms in the inn.

Shivering from the cold, I looked around as I stepped up on the porch, hoping to be invisible to anybody who might happen to be looking. Entering the inn, I tiptoed past the front room, where tea was being served on silver serving sets to the guests lounging in the living room. However irritating Eleanore may be and however poorly she may dress herself, she displayed pretty good taste when it came to decorating the inn. The walls are a swirly cream and all the woodwork stark white. I peeked around the door to her office, where the patrons would check in, and I gave a sigh of relief that I had beaten Bradley Chapel here. I was half-convinced that he had gone on for lunch.

"Eleanore," I said.

"Torie! Come in, come in. Oh, it's just so exciting. I think I might bust a button from all the excitement," she said.

Eleanore is, at best, loud, obnoxious, and colorful, to the point of making one's eyes hurt. At worst, she is vainglorious and hasty, and quite often when trying to impress somebody with her vocabulary, she speaks like a thesaurus on acid. All of her jewelry is plastic or metal and comes in colors not found in nature. Today, she wore bright-yellow banana earrings and a necklace of big orange beads. She is also top-heavy and has an extra chin, and I do worry sometimes that she is going to drop dead of a heart attack someday. Well, I worry about her health when I'm not wishing one of the plagues of Egypt would set upon her.

"What?" I asked. "What's all the excitement?"

"The inn is full, thanks to that stupid shipwreck eighty years ago. I've got that crew from the college here, and Mr. Chapel from Channel 6 news called and made a reservation. Oh, you simply must find old shipwrecks more often!"

I stepped all the way into the room and shut the door behind me. "I'll try," I said, a little off balance. I sat down in the chair.

"What is it?" she asked. "Aren't you excited?"

"I'm certainly glad your business is doing well, Eleanore, but I have a problem."

"What?" she asked.

"Has Mr. Chapel checked in yet?"

"No."

"When he does, you must not mention the diamond lore to him."

"Why not?"

"Because the sheriff doesn't want people to come down here looking for nonexisting diamonds, that's why. He wants to maintain some sort of control," I said.

"Oh pooh," she said. She waved a hand at me, a big ring on her hand catching the light as she did. "If Sheriff Brooke thinks he has control over things in New Kassel, he's as deranged as the mayor."

"It's important," I said. "Somebody may go looking for the so-called diamonds on board and get hurt in the process.

Then we could get sued, people would stop coming, and your inn would be empty."

"Oh dear," she said, clearly not having thought to translate the danger to something that would affect her. Now that I'd helped her to see what damage could be done to her business, I had her undivided attention. "But the guys from the college…"

"What guys from the college?" I asked, and then remembered. "Oh, the guys from the college."

"Mr. Lahrs is upstairs unpacking as we speak. He's going diving later. He already knows about the diamonds," she said just as Mr. Chapel opened the door.

"What diamonds?" Bradley Chapel asked.

"The diamonds that were on board *The Phantom* when it sank," Eleanore said, wide-eyed. Well, so much for her keeping her mouth shut. If I had a dollar for every time I've been right about something, I'd have a mountain of money.

Bradley Chapel leveled his eyes to mine. Without him having said a word, I understood exactly what he was thinking. Surely the town archivist and historian would know a thing or two about diamonds in the wreckage of a steamer. "Mr. Chapel, nobody knows for sure if there were diamonds on board that ship," I said.

"Go on," he said, folding his arms.

"There's a diamond mine in Arkansas," I said. "Supposedly one of the passengers was carrying a case of uncut diamonds from the mine to St. Louis when the steamer went down. But nothing was ever recovered, not so much as even one sparkly looking rock."

"Why did you keep this from me?" he asked.

"You have to understand, Mr. Chapel. New Kassel relies on its tourism to survive. Sure, a bunch of people coming to our town to go diamond hunting would be good for business at first, but if somebody were to get hurt, it could do way more damage to us than good," I said. "The sheriff and I were just trying to keep the hysteria to a minimum."

"How much were the diamonds worth?"

See? Already the dollar signs were rolling around in his eyes.

"We have no way of knowing. First of all, they were uncut diamonds—straight from the mine. Second, we don't know if they were in a matchbox, a bread box, or a cedar chest, so we have no way of even knowing how many there were. None of the survivors had actually seen the diamonds; they'd just heard that they were on board," I said.

"And you're convinced they didn't exist?"

"What I'm saying is, nothing has ever washed ashore to indicate that there was anything on that boat other than people and some corn."

"But the box could have been sealed. That would explain why nothing washed ashore. They could still be sealed in there."

"Could have been," I said. "But wood rots eventually. So they would have to have been in a metal box."

"Nobody's ever thought to go down there and look?"

"Well, I don't know. Seems to me there was one guy who dived down there in the sixties, and he said there was nothing but rotted wood," I said. "And I think Sylvia said that several people dived down in the thirties."

"Did they know about the diamonds?" Mr. Chapel asked. "I mean, was that what those divers were looking for?"

"I'm sure they'd heard the rumors, the same as all of us have," I said.

He just shook his head. "Those diamonds are down there," he said. Then he looked at Eleanore. "I'm Bradley Chapel, by the way. I'm here to check in for my cameraman and me."

That was it. He'd dismissed me just like that. I'd failed

on my mission. Now all I could do was watch the way the pieces would fall and hope that I could pick them all up and keep New Kassel safe. I turned to go.

"Mrs. O'Shea, those diamonds are there. And I'm going to find them."

Right. I couldn't see Mr. Chapel donning a wet suit and slugging through three feet of Mississippi mud for all the diamonds in the world. He was the type of man who probably wore silk paisley pajamas.

"Well, good luck," I said.

"You'll need it," Eleanore added. "Mr. Lahrs is here from the college, and he's the only one authorized to do any diving anywhere near that wreck. You'll get arrested if Sheriff Brooke finds you down there."

Mr. Chapel didn't look very happy about that. And I felt very juvenile at the moment. "Yeah," I said. It was the adult equivalent of sticking my tongue out at him.

SEVEN

I STOOD ON the porch of the Murdoch Inn, looking out over the Mississippi and at Illinois on the far bank. I often just stare out at the river. I have found that it's impossible to live this close to water and not be seduced by it. We have tourists who come into town just to park their cars and look out at the Mississippi for half an hour. There's something soothing about moving water; the ocean has the same affect on me. I sort of mellow out and get lost in thought, quite often wondering, What kind of secrets do you hold, Old Man River?

Many times, I have thought of the Native Americans who lived here before the Europeans managed to find their way west. What had the river meant to their lives? Granted, it is the giver of life. But it also holds the power of mass destruction. I have lived through one too many floods to think that the river is always generous and giving. It can also be the taker with a vengeance. And yet sometimes the river doesn't take at all. Sometimes it is as if man makes sacrifices to it. Like the idiots who decide to swim across it on a bet or to impress some girl. I've seen with my own eyes a person getting sucked under, never to be seen again. One year at the Fourth of July celebration in St. Louis, I saw some jerk riding a speedboat up the river, and it was almost as if an unseen arm just reached up and flipped that boat right over. It sank within seven seconds. And of course, on one sad day a few years ago, the performer Jeff Buckley fell victim to the river down in Memphis. That's the worst thing: The river *seems* placid. But go three feet out, and you're in more danger than you could possibly imagine.

What had happened to *The Phantom?* As a kid, I had wondered about the diamonds. And about what had happened to the very young and beautiful Jessica Huntleigh. But now, looking out upon the mighty Mississippi, I couldn't help but wonder what had caused the steamer to sink all those years ago. Was she overloaded? Was she running loaded flat? I'd seen pictures of steamers so full of cargo or people that they ran flush with the water. If the captain had flanked her, driven her a little too hard, and she were flush, it wouldn't have taken much for the water to overtake the boat.

"Mrs. O'Shea?" a voice asked.

I turned away from the river and saw a young man standing on the porch next to me. He was a good-looking chap. Probably about twenty-eight, fairly tall, with green eyes and a military-looking haircut. "I'm Jacob Lahrs," he said, extending a hand.

"Oh, yes, Mr. Lahrs," I said, and shook his hand. No surprise that he had an extremely firm handshake. I had taken his phone-call several years back when he had inquired about water levels and the wreckage. I wondered, momentarily, who had contacted him. "I'm sorry, but I forgot to call you."

"That's all right," he said. "I happened to be down here last week with my mother. It was her birthday, and we came down here to shop and have dinner. When I saw how low the river was, I had a feeling that it would be getting low enough for the wreckage to be visible."

"So," I began. "Why didn't you just dive down there before now?"

"The river is so polluted, you can't see a foot in front of your face," he said. "You also can't see when you're getting tangled up in anything. And believe me, there're tons of things to get tangled up in. You ever been out on the Mississippi?"

I shook my head.

"I got snagged on a '57 Chevy once. There are cars out there, refrigerators, you name it. I'd just as soon wait until it's shallower."

"And what exactly are you diving for?" I asked, as if I didn't already know. But he surprised me with his answer.

"I want to try to determine what caused the steamer to sink."

"Oh," I said.

"No, I'm not after any diamonds," he said. "I don't believe there were any on board anyway."

Finally, somebody with common sense. "Why's that?"

"The entire diamond myth came from one source only. A woman who survived the wreck," he said.

Professor Lahrs had a military build, too. He wore an olive green sweater under one of those winter windbreakers. Large, broad shoulders made one think that he worked out on a regular basis, and he just held himself like a lot of military people do—shoulders back, chin up. He was teaching at one of the local colleges, if I remembered correctly. Biology, I think.

"Are you sure?" I asked. "I thought there were many accounts of people saying—"

"People *saying* they *heard* about the diamonds. But only one woman said she actually *saw* diamonds. I just don't believe her," he said. "She was a woman of a questionable reputation, if ya know what I mean."

Prostitute. Showgirl. Something along those lines.

"I see," I said. "You sure know a lot about the steamer."

"I've read everything your Historical Society has on it. Plus, I've read the material at the library in Wisteria, and even some of the holdings up in St. Louis. It did make the

St. Louis papers at the time, and even Chicago and Memphis mentioned it,'' he said.

If there were uncut diamonds from a diamond mine in Arkansas on board, I would think that the Arkansas papers might have carried the news, as well. And the New York papers probably carried the news, too, what with the Huntleigh heiress being from New York.

"Did the Chicago and Memphis papers mention diamonds?"

"Yes," he said. "I believe they called it an 'ungrounded and unsubstantiated claim.'"

"Well," I said, "I wish you the best of luck in finding out what happened. The town would be grateful to you if we finally knew what happened to the steamer. Maybe we could even put up a plaque at the site."

Professor Lahrs's eyes lighted up. "Oh, would you?"

"I don't see why not. Sylvia's really good about spending money on that type of thing," I said. "We just never considered it before because we really didn't know what had happened. So, if you find out why the steamer sank, then we'll have a plaque made for it. Because when the river gets back to its normal level, you won't be able to see the wreckage anymore. It'd be nice if we had some sort of reminder as to what lies beneath the water."

"Oh, that would be so cool," he said.

Just then, two men came out of the Murdoch Inn and joined us on the porch. "Oh, this is my assistant, Jeremiah Ketchum," Professor Lahrs said.

"Mr. Ketchum," I said, and shook his hand. Jeremiah Ketchum was about forty, I'd say. He had smooth skin and blond hair, and I only guessed his age at about forty because he held himself like somebody who had been around the block a few times.

"And Danny Jones," the professor said. "A very promising student of mine."

Danny Jones, however, was young. Very young. I'd say about nineteen. His eyes were brown, and his hair was done in one of those two-tone styles that all the young boys were wearing. Although short and dark on the sides, the top was a little longer and bleached blond. He looked as though maybe somewhere way back on his family tree, there had been an island ancestor. Based on his hairdo and his baggy pants, my daughter would be in a serious swoon if she saw him.

"Nice to meet you," I said. "All of you."

"We'll try to do the least amount of damage to your town as possible," Professor Lahrs said.

I gave a small laugh, wondering how he had read my mind. "Well, good luck, again."

"Oh, I've got more than luck on my side," Professor Lahrs said.

"Oh?" I asked.

Danny Jones smiled. "His great-grandfather was the captain of *The Phantom,*" he said. "He thinks he's got help from his long-dead ancestor or some such supernatural crap."

I'm not sure why that particular tidbit of news bothered me, but it did. Maybe it was because Jacob Lahrs's great-grandfather had succumbed to a pretty gruesome death, and if it were me, I wouldn't have welcomed help from beyond the grave.

"The river is in my blood," Jacob Lahrs said, looking out at the Mississippi.

Maybe it's more like your blood is in the river, I thought.

EIGHT

FRAULEIN KRISTA'S IS the coolest place in the world. It's where I retreat when I want to get away from everything. Not that there are a great many things I want or need to get away from, but it seems to be the one place, other than the riverbank, where I can collect my thoughts and just veg. Part of it is because the owner watches out for me when I come in and tries to make sure that nobody bothers me.

On Saturday, I sat in my favorite booth, the one in the corner of the restaurant, which has a good view of the street and the tourists outside. And even though I could see what was going on outside, nobody could really see me in the restaurant, unless they were sitting right across from me, because the tall wood walls of the booth hid me from the other patrons.

Everything in Krista's is dark and rugged. Exposed beams on the ceilings, and dark wood, almost black, all around the booths and halfway up the walls. At the end of the bar, there is a stuffed grizzly bear that we'd nicknamed Sylvia. I'm not really into stuffed things, so I just tell myself that it is a pretend stuffed bear. But the best part about the restaurant is all of the waiters and waitresses hustling about in their green velvet knickers and dresses, serving beer in steins and food on pewter dishes.

"What's it gonna be, Torie?"

I looked up to see Krista herself, who always seems to know when I come in and who waits on me personally. She is tall and has blond hair, blue eyes, dimples. If I didn't know better, I'd swear that she is one of Tolkien's elves. She holds herself as one would expect a tall beautiful blonde to hold herself—like the world is hers for the taking.

"I'll have one of those things I can't pronounce, with the crumbly stuff on top, blackberry tea, and...I don't know.... Surprise me."

She raised her eyebrows and sat down across from me in the booth. "Feeling adventurous today," she said. "What's up?"

"I'm on my lunch break. Saturdays are always pretty busy over at the Gaheimer House."

She gave me one of those looks that said, Okay, whatever. Be in denial. That soon faded and was replaced with a golden smile and then an expression of concern. "Again, what's up?"

"Nothing," I said.

"How's the slugger?"

"Meaning Rachel?" I asked, glaring at her. "She's fine."

"And Half-pint?"

"Mary's good, too."

"Torie," she said. "There *is* something on your mind."

There was, but that didn't necessarily mean that I was going to share it with her. I love Krista. She's great. But my inner circle, the people with whom I share personal things, is pretty much limited to my mother, Rudy, and my best friend, Collette, who lives up in St. Louis.

"There's always something on my mind, Krista."

"So, did that Lahrs guy start his diving today?"

"As far as I know," I said, looking out the window. I couldn't see the river from where I was sitting, but I could imagine him down there in his scuba gear, looking all around. "I think he and Bradley Chapel have struck a bargain."

"The guy from Channel 6?" she asked.

"Yeah."

"How so?"

"I think Jacob Lahrs has agreed to let Bradley film him. Jacob gets publicity, plus a documentation of his discoveries, and Bradley gets the story he wants," I said. "At least I think that's what's going on, because I saw Bradley down there filming and talking with Jacob's assistant, Mr. Ketchum."

"Well, it'll be interesting to see what they dig up," she said. She stood then and put one hand on her hip. "I'll be right back with your crumbly thing and your tea."

No sooner had she left than Sheriff Brooke took her seat. He was in full uniform, which meant he was on duty. He put his hat on the seat next to him and clasped his hands in front of him. "Hey."

I was going to have to find a new sanctuary, because this one was just getting entirely too well known. I looked toward the door and wondered just how he knew I had been sitting here, since he couldn't have seen me from the entrance. I didn't have to ask him.

"You always sit here," he said. "And if you're not at the Gaheimer House or your own, this is usually where you are."

"Not true," I said, defensive at being so predictable. "Sometimes I'm at the library. In fact, I'm always at the library. Or the courthouse, or out with the kids. I am not always here."

"Okay," he said. "Then how'd I know that you'd be here?"

"Beginner's luck."

He laughed at that. The sheriff and I share a long history. Most of that long history has been filled with me despising him in different degrees. But he is a good guy, regardless of how much he irritates me, or how many times he has arrested me. And he makes my mother very happy. Sheriff

Brooke is about twelve years younger than my mother, which I found really hard to deal with at first. But they've been married over a year now, and I have to admit that they are really meant for each other. He is a much better husband than my father ever was, and that was my opinion *before* Ms. Stephanie Connelly came knocking on my door.

"What do you want?" I asked.

"Lunch," he said.

"Aren't you supposed to ask me if I mind if you join me?"

"Now, if I did that, you'd say no."

"Duh."

He just smiled. "You're awfully cranky. More so than usual."

"Go sit somewhere else, thank you very much."

"Did I say cranky?" he asked, putting his hands up in a defensive posture. "Nope, no cranky people at this table."

"What do you want?" I asked. "Besides lunch."

"Your mother says you've been…distant the last few days."

"Oh, well. If she's concerned, have *her* call me."

"She didn't send me here to find out what's up with you," he said. "She just mentioned it in passing, so I thought I'd come see if you're all right."

I just stared at him. Right. He was concerned for me. I believed that like I'd believe in a giant bunny rabbit leaving hard-boiled eggs all over my backyard.

"Okay, all right," he said. "I just want to know if there's something I should know about. Found any bodies lately? Do you think your neighbor is really Jimmy Hoffa? Confederate gold in your basement?"

"You know what? When Krista gets back here with my lunch, I'm going to have her throw you out on your ear," I said.

"Come on, Torie," he said, smiling. "I just want to know if there's anything I should know about."

"No. Nothing."

"Okay," he said. He smiled at Krista as she came back with my food and a cup of coffee for him. "I'll have the stew, Krista."

"Sure thing, Colin."

"What do you make of the wreckage? You think Jacob Lahrs is going to find out what really caused the boat to sink?" the sheriff asked me.

I shrugged, sipping my tea. "Maybe."

He looked at me long and hard for a moment. "Okay, snap out of it. The Torie I know would be down there in her own wet suit, looking for diamonds and daring anybody, including her ever-wise and all-knowing stepfather—me—to stop her. What gives?"

"You don't like the new and improved, all grown-up and mature Torie O'Shea?"

He took a drink of his coffee, contemplating what I had said. "I'm concerned," he said. "Because this isn't you."

"Oh, well."

"I bought a new fishing pole in Wisteria the other day."

"Oh yeah? Bet you can't wait for spring."

"This fishing pole is so nice, I'm thinking about putting on my battery-operated socks and going fishing this weekend," he said.

His stew came a few minutes later and we ate in silence for a while. He commented on the Rams; I mentioned the snowstorm we were supposed to get next week. He brought up a case he was working on over in Wisteria. I listened like I really gave a damn. I don't know what came over me, but I just couldn't hold it in any longer.

"Colin, if…you…"

"What?"

"Hypothetically speaking," I said. "If you found out you

had a sister or a brother you'd never known about, how would you feel?''

He just stared at me for the longest time. ''I don't know,'' he said. ''Weird, I guess.''

''Weird?''

''Yeah, like I was somehow responsible for them.''

''Huh?''

''You know, sins of the father sort of thing. My dad is dead. So if a sibling came to me and said that he was my dad's son, I'd somehow feel responsible. Like I should do something to make it all right. And that would be weird.''

''Who said it would be your dad's child?''

''I'm just assuming, since I spent every day of my life with my mother, that it wouldn't be hers,'' he said. ''Of course, I guess she could have had a baby before she met my father and had me, but I just assumed, in this hypothetical situation, that it would have been my father's. Why?''

''No reason.''

He nodded, but there was a questioning look in his eyes.

''So, you'd feel responsible,'' I said.

''Yeah, probably.''

''Would you be angry?''

''Depends.''

''On what?''

''What my relationship with my father was like.''

''Would you be jealous?''

''Of what?''

''Well, I don't know. Like you suddenly have competition. That when everybody finds out about your new sibling, they'll like him better. Especially your dad.''

''My dad's dead.''

''But if he wasn't.''

''Maybe a little,'' he said, and took a bite of stew.

As he reached for the salt shaker, I stopped his hand. ''Mom says you're not supposed to have salt.''

He gave me a slightly abashed look and set the salt shaker back at the edge of the table. He picked up the pepper shaker instead, then added a generous amount of pepper to the stew.

"Would you feel betrayed?"

"Depends. If Dad knew about the child and never told me, I might feel a little betrayed. It would depend on when the child was conceived."

"During the marriage to your mother," I said a little too hastily. He regarded me cautiously.

"Yeah, I'd probably feel a little betrayed."

There, the sheriff had agreed with how I felt. If he were in my shoes, he'd feel the same way. I felt better. Less guilty. Validated.

"Of course," he said, "if this were to happen, you know, hypothetically and all, I'd have to consider how that sibling must feel."

"What do you mean?"

"Growing up and never knowing his or her father. Must be pretty tough to have only one side of a family."

I said nothing.

"Makes you sort of happy that you've got the family you've got, doesn't it? I mean, you know all of your family and have a great relationship with all of them and everything. You'll never know what it feels like to be on the outside."

"Yeah."

"Kind of makes you feel good, doesn't it?" he asked.

"Oh, yeah, makes me feel wonderful."

NINE

THE SWIRLS IN the plaster of my office walls were fascinating as hell. I'd probably been staring at them for half an hour already, and it seemed like only a few minutes. I shifted my gaze to the appliquéd Rose of Sharon quilt hanging on the wall by the window. The quilt was soothing to look at, all done in different shades of pink.

There was a knock at the door, and for a moment my stomach lurched, as I thought it might be Stephanie Connelly once again. But the way I had behaved toward her, she would probably never show her face in this town again. Which I can't say bothered me all that much. For my own sanity, I thought it would be best if I never saw her again. I was in denial. And I intended to stay in denial for as long as I possibly could.

"Come in," I said.

The door opened and in walked my best friend. "Collette! Oh my gosh, what are you doing here?" I stood and gave her a hug and was immediately enveloped in a cloud of her perfume. The fragrance was a little strong and a little musky for my tastes, but that was Collette for you. She was worth navigating my way through a cloud of perfume for.

"I'm here for the story," she said. Collette is a reporter up in St. Louis. We'd been raised together, gone to school together, but she couldn't wait to leave New Kassel and find her destiny in the big city. All I had wanted to do was bury myself in the past and become a fixture of New Kassel, like

Sylvia had. I loved to travel and see things, but I had no desire to live anywhere else than where all of my family and friends were. It's the people who make a place home, not the buildings or the scenery. And my home was New Kassel.

"The story," I said.

Collette rolled her eyes. She is a full-figured gal, with big hair and lots of gold jewelry, and about the most magnetic personality I've ever encountered. "You know, *The Phantom*," she said. "The Huntleigh heiress. The whole thing."

"Oh Lord. You're kidding."

"No," she said, and sat on the edge of my desk. She picked up my page-a-day calendar and flipped the pages across her face, causing her hair to billow. "I'm here for the big scoop."

"Was this your idea or your editor's?"

"My editor's," she said. "You know I don't come to New Kassel anymore unless I have to."

Which was the truth. If I didn't live here, she'd probably never set foot in this town again. As it was, when we went out, I usually just met her somewhere up in the city.

"Ole baldy, my boss, said that since I was a hometown girl, I would have the 'inside' scoop," she said. "Dipshit. I don't know what goes on in this town." Why would he think I would know anything about what goes on here? He sees me almost every day. I'm always on assignment. When would I have time to learn what's going on in New Kassel?"

True.

"And why would I care? I stopped caring a long time ago about what went on in this town."

True again.

"So, I was wondering if I could bunk at your place while I'm here," she said. "Now if you don't want me to, just say so, 'cause you're not gonna hurt my feelings. I can get a room at the Murdoch.''

"Well, no, you can't get a room at the Murdoch, because Eleanore is booked.''

"You're kidding,'' she said.

"Thanks to *The Phantom*.''

"Well, I'll be damned,'' she said. "I can stay over in Wisteria. It's not like it's far away. I can be here in five minutes.''

"You can stay with us,'' I said. "It's not a problem.''

"You're sure?''

"Positive. I'll just stick Mary in bed with Matthew and you can have her bed. Of course, you'll have to deal with Rachel primping until all hours of the night,'' I said. "She's really into this brushing your hair a hundred times and all that before going to sleep.''

"Well, all right,'' she said. "We can primp together, because I've been brushing my hair a hundred times before bed since I was eight.''

"Really?'' I brush my hair when I get out of bed, and then again if I'm going somewhere. And Rudy rarely ever brushes his hair, but that's because he thinks the less he brushes his hair, the less likely that it will fall out.

"I'm cooking dinner,'' she said. "I insist.''

"Fine with me. Like you'll hear a mother of three complain when somebody else insists upon cooking,'' I said. I've always blamed the fact that I hate to cook on my kids, but it isn't really the kids. I hate to cook, period. Actually, I hate cleaning up more than anything else.

"DON'T YOU HAVE any Vidalia onions?'' Collette asked an hour later. She had changed from her Liz Claiborne suit to jeans and a sweatshirt. The red-gold hair that usually hits the middle of her back was now piled up on top of her head.

All of her gold rings were sitting in a cup on my table, resembling the treasure on a pirate ship.

"No, just plain old yellow," I said.

"I guess that'll do," she replied. "Garlic?"

I went to the fridge and handed her a jar of the precrushed garlic in oil. She looked at it as if it were a pile of cow manure. "Please, Torie. Fresh garlic. You don't have fresh garlic?"

"No, 'fraid not."

"How do you keep Rudy here? I mean, the way to a man's heart is through his stomach, girl. You're just pushing him out the door to find love in another's arms. I bet you cook Hamburger Helper, too, don't you? No, don't answer that question. I don't want to know. No fresh garlic," she said, still disbelieving.

I folded my arms and leaned up against the countertop. "I thought you always said the way to a man's heart was through his—"

"Mom!" a voice screeched from the kitchen door. It was my middle child. My wild child. The child with as much personality as an amusement park and as much energy as a roller coaster. "Matthew keeps hitting me with his T. rex, and I'm about tired of it."

"Mary," I said, "tell him you're not going to play with him anymore if he keeps hitting you."

"I'm *not* playing with him," she said, her green eyes sparkling. "I am sitting on my bed, minding my own business, reading a book, and he just whopped me upside the head."

"Well then, that's his problem. He wants you to play with him."

"No!" she exclaimed. "I'll just go outside and read."

She turned and disappeared down the hallway, then came back dressed in her winter coat and slippers, her book in her hand. "I'll just go out on the porch and read."

"It's twenty degrees outside," I said.

"I don't care," she snapped. "It's better than having to put up with *him!*"

The door slammed behind her as she headed out to the back porch. Collette looked at me and then laughed.

"I give her ten minutes," I said.

"God, were we like that?"

"Yup," I said.

"Except you never had any siblings to fight with," she said. "I had my sister, who hated my guts. We got over that, though. Funny how that works."

"Yeah, you're right. I never had any siblings," I said. My voice trailed off as I reached for a pan from underneath the stove.

"Oooh, I detect a shift in mood here," Collette said.

"Hmm? Oh, no, I'm fine," I said.

"No, having Hugh Jackman lick your toes is *fine,* darling. What you are is…distracted."

"Right," I said laughing. "I'm fine."

She said nothing and went about chopping up my inferior yellow onion. Collette is really good about letting me come to her with things, rather than prying. I can't say that I'm as good a friend. I usually pry everything from her. Patience is not one of my virtues. "So, tell me what you know about the wreck," she said, changing the subject.

"Well, funny you should ask. In between tours, I managed to get some reading done, although not nearly enough."

"Yeah? And?"

"Well, I think she might have been loaded flat. I've got a call into one of the historical societies down in Arkansas," I said. "I want to see if they've got a picture of *The Phantom* as she left port. We might get lucky."

"What good will that do?"

"Show if she was loaded flat. She may have had too

many people on board, so that when the captain flanked her, which the eyewitnesses said he did, the water would have swept up on the deck, probably knocking people off into the river right then and there. Then it would have been just a matter of her turning on her side and going under.''

"So…where's the mystery in that?''

"There isn't one. Except why a seasoned pilot of a steamer would flank his ship that hard, knowing he was loaded flat. That doesn't make sense.''

"What do you know about the pilot?''

"Not a lot,'' I said. "That's one of the things I planned on reading about tomorrow.''

"And Jessica Huntleigh?''

"You know, I don't really know that much. I'm going to ask Sylvia some questions about her when I get a chance.''

"What about…you know, the diamonds?'' she asked, stirring the pasta sauce.

"I'm going to read the eyewitness accounts over, too. Jacob Lahrs—''

"Who?''

"The college professor who's down there digging right now. He claims that the whole diamond myth came from one source only. I can check that out tomorrow, too.''

"One source?'' she asked, surprised. "Isn't that sometimes how things get started? So, what's the scoop on Jacob Lahrs?''

"Supposedly, he's the great-grandson of the captain.''

"You're joking,'' she said.

"Nope.''

"Huh,'' she said. "When can I get down there to see the wreckage?''

"Tomorrow, if you want.''

"Think you could get me an interview with Lahrs?''

"Most likely.''

"Great. And can I have access to all of your papers on the subject?"

I hesitated a moment.

"What?"

"I'm not going to tell you how to write your article or anything, but...Well, this whole diamond thing, could you play it down a little?"

She gave me an incredulous look. "And compromise good journalism?"

"Collette," I said. "It could do a lot of damage."

"I know, I know," she said. "Tell you what. If there's nothing to it—I mean if there is nothing to corroborate the eyewitness's story—then I'll just give it a two-sentence pass. All right? But if there is something to it, then I'm going to have to devote a little more column space to it than that."

My silence seemed more judgmental than I meant it to be.

"It's my job," she said. "I'm not going to exploit the town."

"No, I know that," I said. "I didn't mean to imply otherwise."

The front door opened in the other room. "What smells good?" Rudy yelled.

Collette winked at me. "Now let's see if we can't get this husband of yours to stick around awhile. No fresh garlic," she muttered.

TEN

SATURDAY NIGHT in New Kassel isn't exactly like Saturday night on the Landing in downtown St. Louis, or in the Loop, for that matter. No, Saturday night in New Kassel consists of bowling, families eating out, gathering at the Corner Bar, bingo at the KC Hall, or just hanging out at Chuck's. For a bit of a wild time, one can wander over to Wisteria or make the journey up to St. Louis. Of course, there's loads of fine dining here. And in certain seasons, we often have a Blue Grass Festival, hay rides, that sort of thing. But not in the middle of January, when it's colder than in the Yukon.

Collette was used to going out on Saturday nights, so I accompanied her to the Corner Bar. That was as crazy as she would get tonight. Even though she was just going out to have a beer in a dead-end town, she still had to dress up. She had changed into a pair of those low-rider jeans and a sparkly sweater. She had put on heels, more makeup and, yes, more perfume.

The Corner Bar is, well, your typical neighborhood bar. Nothing fancy about it. It is located on the corner—thus the name—of Jefferson and Western Road. Even the door opens directly onto the corner. Once inside, I had to adjust my eyes to see through all the smoke. The only lights on in the place were the lights behind the bar, advertising different beers, and candles on the tables. My dad once said that the reason the lights are so low in a bar is so that you won't realize, until the next morning, what an ugly woman you'd picked up. He was half-joking when he said it, but looking around the bar, I had to wonder if maybe there wasn't some truth to his philosophy.

The bar was directly to our right, some booths were to our left, and toward the back were the pool tables and shuffle board. A Bob Seger song played from the jukebox. "You'll Accomp'ny Me," I believe. I shook off the cold as we entered the bar, along with some of the snow that had started to fall. I waved to the owner, Hiram Gernsheim, who was standing behind the bar and laughing it up with a couple of regulars. He waved back, looking a little surprised, because this was not my normal hangout.

We sat down in a booth, and before our coats were even off, Hiram was standing at our table. "Hey, Torie. What brings you in from the cold?"

I pointed to Collette. "You remember Collette," I said.

He looked at her a moment and then recognition hit. "Lordy, I haven't seen you since you was right out of school. Whatcha been up to, girl?"

"Just working," she said. "Seems like that's all I ever do."

"I hear that," he said. "Can I get you ladies something to drink?"

"I'll have a Bud Light," she said.

"Jeez, Collette, I figured you'd have found a different beer by now," I said.

"What's wrong with Bud Light?" she asked.

"It's just so…Yuppie. And it gives you the farts," I added.

Hiram laughed and wiped his hands on his bar rag.

"I'll have…an amber bock," I said. "Schlafleys."

"Sure thing," he said, and walked away.

"I can't believe you grew up in a German—that's *German*—town and you drink Bud Light," I said.

"Well, *you* didn't have fresh garlic," she snapped.

"True," I said. "I guess we're even."

We were halfway through our beers, talking and catching up on things, when I noticed Collette was no longer listening to me. Her eyes had wandered toward the door, which I couldn't see because my back was to it. She made eye contact with me a few times and she'd say "Uh-huh" every now and then, but she was obviously deeply studying something or somebody other than me.

"And then," I said, "the baboons came down and ate all the ice cream that the aliens had left."

"Don't you hate when that happens?" she said.

"Colette," I said, giggling. "Yoo-hoo. Earth to Colette."

She snapped to then and blushed all the way down her neck. "Okay, I'm sorry," she said. "But that guy has a seriously cute butt."

I turned around in my seat to see who was the owner of the seriously cute butt. It was Jacob Lahrs. He was laughing and drinking. It looked as if he was celebrating something with his assistant, Jeremiah Ketchum, and his student, Danny Jones. Funny, I hadn't noticed Jacob Lahrs's seriously cute butt when I met him the other day. Maybe it was the angle at which Collette was sitting. Or maybe it was because I was married—one sort of conditions oneself not to look at the dessert one can't have.

"That's Jacob Lahrs," I said to her, smiling.

"Jacob Lahrs...the professor?" she asked, eyes twinkling.

"Yup. You want that interview?"

"Oh, do I ever," Collette said, grinning widely.

"Come on," I said, and motioned her over. We got out of the booth and walked over to the three men standing at the end of the bar. "Professor Lahrs!" I called.

He turned around and smiled when he saw me. He was wearing a black turtleneck and had pushed the sleeves up to his elbows. "Mrs. O'Shea," he said. "Never expected to see you in here."

"Yeah, well...my friend comes down from the city and I get all wild. Go figure. This is my friend Collette," I said.

"Nice to meet you," he said.

She purred back some response, and I just knew I was about to watch the master at work. Collette loves men. Lots of men.

"Call me Jacob," he said. "What brings you here, Mrs. O'Shea?"

"We just came out for a beer. Collette is a reporter," I told him. "And she was hoping to get an interview with you."

"Oh, you can't interview me tonight," he said, all serious.

"Why not?" she asked, batting her eyes.

"Never do interviews when you're under the influence, because you never know what you may say. I once promised a woman my grandmother's antique clock after having seven too many Bloody Marys. My grandmother was not happy, and neither was the woman. Especially since she'd had such an...uninhibited time the night before."

He winked at Collette, and I nearly puked.

I looked at Danny Jones, who was entirely too young to be drinking. In Missouri, a person has to be twenty-one to drink, and if Danny Jones was even twenty, I'd eat my hat. I took his glass from him and sniffed it. He looked a little shocked at first, but then he smiled at me. "It's just Pepsi," he said.

"Good. I'd hate to see Hiram lose his liquor license because of you."

"Don't worry," he said, placing his hand across his heart. "I didn't even *try* to get liquor."

"So, what's the celebration all about?"

"Celebration?" Jeremiah Ketchum asked.

"You all seem like you're celebrating."

"Oh, nothing," Jeremiah replied.

"Now Jeremiah," Jacob said, chastising him. "We can tell Mrs. O'Shea. I think I may have discovered how *The Phantom* sank."

"The captain flanked when he shouldn't have," I said. "That's how the boat sank."

Jacob's green eyes narrowed on me. "Are you suggesting my great-grandfather was responsible for that accident?"

"He was the captain. Are you suggesting that he wasn't?" I asked.

Collette jabbed me in the ribs.

"He never meant to hurt anybody," Jacob said defensively.

"I wasn't suggesting that he did," I said. "I'm just saying that he was in charge and he was in the pilothouse. Ultimately, he was responsible. What do you think happened?"

"There's a lot of damage on the side of the boat," he said. "I think he might have run into something in the water, or maybe something hit him."

"Could the damage have been inflicted after the wreck? I mean, it's been lying there for over eighty years. Maybe something else ran into it in the past eighty years while it was just sitting there," I said.

Jeremiah's gaze flicked to Jacob's face and then back to mine.

"There's always that possibility," Jeremiah said finally.

"I'm almost certain that the damage was done *during* the accident," Jacob said.

"Well, we can talk to the sheriff and get a forensics team in here and find out for sure, if you'd like," I suggested.

"No," the professor said. "I don't think that will be necessary."

"Have you found any artifacts?" Collette asked. Which meant, have you found any diamonds?

All three men exchanged cautious glances among themselves. "We found a shoe buckle," Danny said finally.

"Well, good Lord, you hit the jackpot, didn't you?" I said.

"Torie," Collette said, rolling her eyes. I knew what she was thinking. I was ruining her chances of snaring Jacob Lahrs in her web. Well, I didn't care how seriously cute his butt was. They were hiding something. I could feel it. Besides, the way Jacob Lahrs was behaving, all Collette would have to do would be to remain conscious and she'd snare him. Where's the fun in that?

"You find the diamonds, Professor Lahrs?" I asked. "You know that if you did find the diamonds, they are the property of the mine."

"If there were any diamonds," Jacob Lahrs said, "they would belong to the family of the one transporting them."

"How so?"

He said nothing. He obviously knew that if he did answer, it would prove that he knew a whole heck of a lot more about the wreck and the diamonds than he'd let on. He wanted to keep up his "I'm here for academic reasons only" act. How did he know that the diamonds weren't the property of the mine? How would he have known that the person carrying the diamonds had bought them, unless he had done some research? And supposedly, he wasn't interested in any diamonds. They were just a myth.

Something didn't add up.

"So...*did* you find the diamonds?" I asked again.

"Have another beer, Mrs. O'Shea," Jacob said. "Loosen up."

"No thank you," I said. I made a sweeping gesture that included all of them. "Well, gentlemen, it was nice conversing with you, but we've got to go."

"So soon?" Jeremiah asked.

"Afraid so," I said. I took Collette's arm and led her back toward our table, where our coats and leftover beer were waiting for us.

"Torie, I think he was interested in me."

"It's probably all the gold you're wearing," I said, laying a ten and a five-dollar bill down on the table.

"Well, gee, thanks," she said, her hand on her hip.

"I'm sorry. I didn't mean that as an insult to you; I meant it as an insult to him. Really, Collette, you can do way better."

"I know," she said. "But he had a great body."

"For casual, meaningless sex, you're right. He had a great body."

"Well, what the hell else would I want him for?" she asked as she picked up her coat.

"You know I love you, Collette. But that's the sort of behavior I despise in men. It's not very becoming on you, either."

"Yeah, yeah, yeah. You're right," she said. "I guess that shoots my interview down the drain."

We walked past the three men on the way out the door and waved to them politely. "Tomorrow will look different to Professor Lahrs and he'll probably forget all about what I said to him. I'm sure he'll let you interview him," I said.

THE NEW KASSEL GAZETTE
The News You Might Miss
By
Eleanore Murdoch

What's this? Do we have a possible lightweight champion in New Kassel? Rudy and Torie O'Shea, it has been rumored, think that little Rachel has quite a right hook and might make a fine addition to the Olympic boxing team.

On a darker note, it seems that the hoopla over the steamboat wreckage has brought people to our town who seemed to miss out on etiquette school. Helen Wickland said she caught a reporter counting the money in the collection basket at Santa Lucia's. And one notable fancy-dressed newsman seems to have a flatulence problem. Fraulein Krista requests that said newsman refrain from eating in her restaurant. And that's just scratching the surface. Tobias Thorley swears that a reporter stole the fairies from his garden. He warns that they have special powers and so the thief should return them as soon as possible.

Until Next Time,
Eleanore

ELEVEN

SUNDAY BROKE with a gray sky and not a sign of blue anywhere. The Weather Channel had said that we would get serious snow today, not just the dusting we had last night. I couldn't wait. I love snow. In fact, call me strange, but I like winter in general.

Today I was going to turn Collette loose in my office at the Gaheimer House, and then, after a nice breakfast with my husband and kids, I was going to see my father. I'd made the decision lying in bed last night, watching the lights from the tugboats and barges play across my ceiling. If I didn't talk to him, if I did not confront him over Stephanie Connelly, I might never sleep again. Not to mention that interacting with him was going to be weird as long as I carried this news inside of me. Once it was out, we could deal with it and move on.

So I threw on jeans and a flannel shirt, put on my coat, and headed north on Highway 55 in the minivan. I passed Festus and the ever-growing town of Arnold, with its weird water tower, which looks like a giant green upside-down flashlight. I passed Reavis Barracks and Carondelet, and finally got off at Loughborough. My father lives in south St. Louis, in a very old redbrick building of a type common in this area. Back at the turn of the century, Italian immigrants had come to St. Louis and begun working in the clay mines over on the Hill. That clay provided many bricks for the buildings of St. Louis. Now the area he lives in is fast being taken over by Bosnians. As the Bosnian immigrants pour into the area from their war-torn country, they all seem to gather in the same area. It makes sense. If I was going to move to Yugoslavia, I'd certainly want to live where other English-speaking people lived.

I knocked on Dad's door and waited a few moments for him to answer. It was before noon on a Sunday, so he was probably just sitting around in the kitchen with his coffee, his cigarettes, and his guitar. I'd even go so far as to say he'd be barefoot when he answered the door.

Sure enough, he opened the door wearing only jeans. He looked down on me, surprised and possibly happy at my presence. He quickly masked any pleasure at my unannounced visit with a blustery "Yeah, what are you doing here?" His dark hair was down in his face, and I knew just from the antsy way he moved that I had interrupted an intense session of him "shredding" his guitar. And oh, how he loves to shred. He is sort of like a country version of Stevie Ray Vaughn. Just as skinny, too.

Funny thing about Dad and his music: He still plays all those honky-tonk classics from the late sixties and early seventies on his guitar. On mornings when he is feeling particularly nostalgic, he'll reach back to the late fifties and play all of those songs recorded at Sun Studios by Elvis, Johnny Cash, and Carl Perkins. Today's music just isn't country. Or at least that's what he always says.

I couldn't very well tell him that I just happened to be in the neighborhood and had decided to stop by. I rarely come into the city unless Rudy and I are taking the kids to the zoo or the Science Center. I couldn't say, Well, I missed you. Because then he'd say something gruff and stupid to cover up the fact that it pleased him that I missed him. And I couldn't very well just say, Well, I'm here to talk about my sister. So I took the least logical and least intelligent opening.

"Just thought I'd come by and see what you're up to."

"Who died?" he asked, and ushered me into his house. It's an old house with high ceilings and large pocket doors, which Mary always plays with when we visit. His hardwood floors hadn't been dusted or mopped since God knew when, because I could see a path right down the middle of the room—the only places that his feet ever touched.

"Nobody died," I said.

"Who's in jail?" he asked.

"Nobody's in jail," I replied, and followed him into the kitchen.

"Don't say it like it's not a possibility," he said. "You've been in jail twice now."

"Yeah, well you've been in jail more."

He turned around quickly. "Hey, that one time I dropped ketchup on my shirt, I was not drunk while driving."

"Oh, but your blood-alcohol content disagreed."

"No, no," he said. "The cop even told me that my blood-alcohol content wasn't that high. I'd had one beer, for Chrissakes. But because I swerved while wiping the ketchup off my shirt, he said I should sleep it off in the jail anyway."

"Whatever," I said.

"Hey, and that time in Mexico wasn't my fault, either."

"And the other two times?"

"Those were my fault," he said.

I sat down at his table, which was covered with coffee rings and cigarette ashes. A pile of unopened mail was shoved toward the end of the table, at least two weeks' worth of bills perching precariously on the edge. He sat down and picked up his twelve-string and started plucking away at some tune that sounded like an Irish jig.

"You like this?" he asked. "I wrote it."

"Yeah," I said, and meant it. "I really like it. Sort of different from your usual stuff."

"I've been thinkin' how Dad used to incorporate all of

that Scots-Irish stuff in his fiddle music," he said. "That's all it was really. Just Highland music tweaked a little bit. So, I dunno, I just sort of came up with this on the guitar."

"I really like it," I said.

He played awhile longer, his foot tapping on the floor in time. He can't play if he can't tap his foot, just like I can't talk if you immobilize my hands. I know this to be true, because Dad actually had conducted an experiment one time. He had set me on a chair and tied my hands behind my back with my jump rope. He proved it all right. I couldn't get out a single sentence without stuttering. And may I just say that I hate it when my father is right? Not because he is right per se, but because he is so darn smug about it.

I can handle being wrong. Just don't rub it in.

He stopped playing halfway through another round of the song and looked at me. "What's up?" he asked.

You're a lying, cheating bastard. We trusted you. All of this time I wanted a sibling, and you kept her from me. Kept her all to yourself. And even though you're a lying, cheating, selfish bastard, I still love you, because you're my dad. And I don't want to love you right now. I don't want to forgive you for this. But if you say the right words, I will, because you're my dad.

Nope, couldn't say that.

I took a deep breath and tried to steady my shaking hands. "I...had a visitor the other day," I began.

The fingers on his left hand went to the neck of his guitar—his security.

"Her name was Stephanie Connelly. She had the most interesting story to tell me," I said, amazed that I'd actually gotten the words out of my mouth.

He surprised me by standing up and pouring himself a fresh cup of coffee, but the guitar neck stayed firmly gripped in his left hand. When he sat down, he leveled a gaze at me that I couldn't read. Was he upset? Was he waiting for my attack? His expression was just blank. Finally, he leaned back and put the guitar across his lap. "And how do you feel about that?" he asked.

"What? Did you turn into a psychologist overnight? How do I feel about it? How do you think I feel about it?"

"I wouldn't have asked if I knew the answer."

I told myself to be calm, but I couldn't. I rose to my feet, hands flailing through the air, the heat evident in my cheeks. "How could you have known about her and not told me!"

He said nothing.

"How *could* you?" I cried. "Does Mom know?"

He still said nothing.

"Does she know?"

"No," he said. "She doesn't know."

I gave a sigh of relief, grateful that only one parent had lied to me.

"You know," he continued, "I am an adult. I have the right to keep certain things from my children."

"No, you don't," I said.

"Don't you keep things from Rachel and Mary? And Matthew?"

"The only things I keep from them are things that I think they're not old enough to understand. Or things that will serve no other purpose than to hurt them."

He gestured toward me, shaking from head to toe. "You're obviously hurt."

No. Don't let him twist this around to suit him. I won't let him use my anger and my hurt to plead his innocence. I will not be his excuse.

"Your job as a parent is to teach me right from wrong. To give me shelter. To give me unconditional love. To prepare me for the future and teach me about our history. That's the job of a parent. And what better way to teach me right from wrong than to use your own mistakes as examples,"

I said. "Gone are the days, dear Father, when parents are these untouchable marble statues. Gone are the days when children are seen and not heard. Wake up, smell your damn coffee, and get with the new millennium. These are the days when parents interact with their children."

I was so angry, I could feel the top of my head jolting with every beat of my heart. "It's called being a family," I said. A tear ran down my cheek and I swiped at it quickly. "It's called blood is thicker than water. If you can't confide in your own family about the things you've done, who the hell can you tell?"

"A person is entitled to his own ghosts," he said.

"Well, guess what? Your ghost just came and knocked on my door! Can you imagine how I felt?"

He still sat there, irritatingly mute.

"You're entitled to your ghosts, Dad, as long as they remain *your* ghosts. If it can come out and interact with the rest of us, then we have the right to know about it."

I headed toward the door. I was ticked off and I would have nothing further to say. Well, nothing that would be logical anyway. I was already entirely too emotional.

He followed me through the house until I reached the front door. He put his hand on the door to keep me from leaving. "Just wait a minute," he said.

I turned and breathed deeply. "I don't want any of your martyr crap," I said.

"Fine," he replied, putting his hands up in surrender. "I didn't know about Stephanie until about six years ago. She came knocking on my door one day, just like she did yours. You gotta give her credit for having some big *cojones*. Not too many people will just go and knock on the door of a parent they've never seen."

This was true.

"Her mother...Julia and I had an affair when you were about five," he said. "It lasted a few months. Then I told her that I felt too guilty, and I broke it off. I told your mother about the affair. But I had no idea that Julia was pregnant.''

"What would you have done if you had known?'' I asked.

"I'm not sure. Would it have been right to leave your mother and you for another woman and a different daughter? No, but I probably would have given her some sort of monetary support. I would have tried to see her at least a few times. I don't know. It would have depended on your mother really. Knowing her, she would have accepted Stephanie, and we might have had a semirelationship with her. But it didn't happen that way. So when Stephanie was old enough, she asked her mother why she didn't look like her dad. Julia told her that even though she had his last name, that was really her stepdad. Then Julia told her who I was, where I lived, and why I wasn't around. Stephanie was twenty-four years old before she got up the nerve to come and see me.''

He didn't appear overly distraught about the story, but I could see that it affected him nonetheless, because he wouldn't make eye contact with me.

"And?''

"Stephanie was engaged to be married. She wanted to know if she ever had kids, whether she could bring them around to see me. She wanted them to know their grandfather,'' he said.

The fact that my father had known about her only for the last six years seemed to ease the pain a little. It didn't seem to be as big a betrayal. But still, it didn't take six years to say one sentence. Why hadn't he told me about her?

"And you told her what?''

"I told her yes,'' he said. "She was my daughter. I wasn't going to turn her away. We'd already lost twenty-four years.''

"So how did she find out about me?''

"Her mother had told her that I had a little girl. She asked me about you. I told her your name, where you lived. I even gave her a picture of you," he said. "She suddenly had a sibling. Somebody who was like her. That seemed to make her happy."

"That's all I've ever wanted," I said.

The silence that hung between us was so thick, it seemed to make the room heavy. Neither one of us said anything. I accused him with just a look. And he stood there, defensive as a stone wall.

"So why didn't you tell me? You've had six years to tell me."

"It never seemed like a good time" was all he could come up with. "I mean, the whole thing with the antique dealer had just happened. I didn't think right after you found a murdered woman that you'd want to learn about a long-lost sister. Then you were pregnant. Your mom got married…. There just always seemed to be something big going on in your life."

"That's no excuse. For something like this, you make time."

"Whatever," he said, and waved me off. "Okay, string me up. I'm guilty. Just get it over with and go home."

I walked slowly toward him, until I stood a mere foot away. "No, Dad, I'm not going to string you up. This is your sin," I said. "You live with it."

I stepped through his door into the gray world outside, the clouds heavy with snow. I felt better. I had confronted him and I hadn't let him give me any crap. I hadn't let him become a martyr, nor had I let him weasel his way out of any guilt. And I hadn't forgiven him, either. Because it would do no good to forgive him for a sin he hadn't actually taken responsibility for. Not yet anyway. He would, though.

And then I'd forgive him.

TWELVE

RUDY, COLLETTE, THE KIDS, and I had all just finished eating pizza at Velasco's, otherwise known as Chuck's. It was Sunday evening and the snow was coming down in big fat wet flakes, quickly accumulating on the road as well as on the grass. Collette and I stood at the window with the kids, looking out upon the fluffy white stuff, just as enthralled as the kids were, while Rudy took care of the bill.

"Let's walk home," Collette said.

"Yeah!" Rachel said, backed up by Mary, who was squealing with delight.

"No, Rachel, you were complaining about a sore throat yesterday," I said. "Not a good idea for you to walk home."

"Can I walk home alone with your mom?" Colette asked the girls. "I'd like some time to talk with her."

This was news to me. I wondered if she'd found something in the files at my office. I glanced at her quickly, but her expression gave nothing away.

"Oh, all right," Rachel said, her lower lip thrust out in a pout.

I looked back at Rudy just as he was waving good night to Chuck. "See you Tuesday," Rudy said to him. They bowl on the same team. Chuck waved to all of us as we went out the door. Rudy fished the keys from his pocket.

"Hey, why don't you and the kids go on home," I said. "Collette and I want to take a walk in the snow."

"Sure," he said. "Be careful coming up the hill."

"If the road is slick, we'll just walk through the grass. We should be fine."

He gave me a quick kiss, and then we loaded up the kids and he drove away. I stood there a moment with my face toward the sky, feeling the snow land on my cheeks, light as a feather. Snow is a good example of the power of numbers. Because just one snowflake is soft and harmless, but put a bunch of them together, and they have the power to grind civilization to a complete halt.

"So, what's up?" I asked her as we began walking.

"Nothing," she said. "I just wanted to walk home in the snow."

"Yeah, right," I said. "Collette, you hate the elements. You hate nature. You'd be perfectly happy if the whole world was covered in concrete and it was seventy-five degrees and sunny every day."

Our voices sounded weird in the muffled air. Everything was hushed and quiet because of the added insulation the snow provided. I heard the train go by, the usual seven o'clock freight train on Sunday evening, slow and methodical as it made its way up the tracks. A kid came by on his bike, a streak of metal, a flash of orange windbreaker, his wheels slipping and sliding on the snow as he fought for control of the bike.

"Justin!" I yelled. He looked back at me, an expression of bewilderment on his face. "Does your mother know you're out?"

He just kept on going, disappearing behind a snow-covered car.

"Do you know everybody in town?" Collette asked.

"I think so," I said.

"How do you do that?"

"Well, you know," I said. "My job is sort of a public relations-type thing. I'm involved with so many people in the town on a weekly basis, plus there're the kids and all the people they know. PTA, Rudy's friends, my mother, the sheriff. I mean, if I *didn't* know everybody, I would find that more peculiar.''

"Don't you ever just want to leave?"

"Leave?" I asked. "No. Why would I want to leave? Well, I could do without a few of the residents. The mayor for one. But I love this place."

Collette laughed because she knew the history the mayor and I had. In these parts, the feud we had had over whether or not I could have chickens was as notorious as the Hatfield and McCoy dispute. We turned the corner and headed toward the river. We weren't really walking straight home, by any means. We were taking the long way.

"So…I say again, why did you want to get me alone? And don't tell me it was because of the snow," I said.

"You're good at this, you know. You should be a reporter."

"No thanks," I said. "I have enough to do."

"I think there was more to Captain Thibeau than meet the eye."

"Captain who?"

"The pilot, the captain of *The Phantom*."

"You don't say," I said, pulling my gloves out of my pockets and proceeding to put them on. I don't usually bundle up, but I had a feeling we were going to be out in this for a while.

"I read one of the survivor statements," she said. "This was a child, mind you, so I'm not sure how accurate his memory would be. But he said that he heard arguing coming from inside the pilothouse just before the boat turned sharply and was overcome by water."

"Really," I said.

"I'm wondering if the captain was having an argument

with somebody and there was a struggle and that's why the boat turned so suddenly," Collette said.

"Could be," I said. "What about the other survivors? Did anybody else say they heard arguing?"

"Well, I didn't get to go through all of the statements. But at least two other people mentioned that just before the boat flanked and the water came up over the sides, they had heard what sounded like angry conversation. These, of course, were people who were either standing directly under the pilothouse or who happened to be up on the very top deck, next to the pilothouse."

I thought about the implications for a moment. "I'll take a look at the accounts tomorrow," I said. "The problem is, I'm not sure, since it occurred eighty years ago, if we'll ever really know what happened."

"Oh, I know that," she said. "It's just going to make a really interesting story. I'm thinking I might get the front page of the 'Everyday' section."

"Possibly."

"So, how's your mother adjusting to married life?" she asked, changing the subject.

"You know, she'd been single for so long, I think it was a bit of an adjustment for her. But—"

"But what?"

"Oh Lord. I was just about to say that Colin is a great guy and she really loves him. Was I really going to say that?"

"I remember when you used to call him 'the Toad,'" she said, laughing.

"Oh my god. Okay, Colin is not a great guy, but he's great to her. How's that?"

"Sounds much more like you," she said.

"They…get along great." And that was the truth. They were much better matched than she and my father had ever been.

We both navigated toward the river. Funny how that river just sucks you in, regardless. We looked both ways on River Point Road and then crossed it. All the way down at the end of the street, on my right, was the Murdoch Inn, looking lovely in its new blanket of snow. Eleanore had put little electric lights that looked like candelabra in all of the windows. She always takes down the obvious Christmas decorations, but she leaves the candelabra and the greenery around the posts on the front porch until March.

"I want to go down and look at the wreck," Collette said.

"Oh no," I said. "I promised Colin I wouldn't go messing around down there, and I meant it."

She rolled her eyes at me just as we reached the bank of the river. "You've made him a million promises that you never kept."

"Yeah, but I meant this one. Besides, it's dark."

"Come on, Torie," she said. "It'll be fun."

"Fun? What if we slip on the snow and end up in the river?"

"Like that's gonna happen," she said.

"You know, you only snoop around where you're not supposed to—to learn something you're not supposed to know. Not because it's fun. You need to learn the rules to this stuff," I said.

"That's the problem with you, Torie. You never did know how to have fun."

"I beg your pardon," I said. "I know how to have lots of fun."

"Okay, not counting your trips to the zoo with the kids."

I stammered a bit. "I...love snowball fights."

"Oh, okay, like you get to do that more than twice a year."

"I..."

"Yes?"

"You know, the things I enjoy are just different from the

ones you do. I happen to think curling up with a good book is fun. I enjoy going through courthouse records for eight hours immensely. So there.''

She laughed at me. I mean really laughed, all the way from her belly. ''Oh sure, and you like those hay rides, too. Whoo hoo.''

''Hey, you know what?'' I said. ''You can shut up anytime now. And if you don't, I'm going to make you sleep in the chicken coop.''

Collette gave me a serious look. ''I just worry about you. You don't *get out*. See the world.''

''I get out plenty.''

''Yeah, in your safe zone of New Kassel.''

''New Kassel isn't all that safe anymore. It's obvious you haven't been down here too much in the past few years.''

''You know what I mean,'' she said, letting out a deep breath.

''We're just different,'' I said. ''How did we ever become friends anyway?''

''Tommy Barker had put smashed-up worms in my gravy at school and you beat him up,'' she said.

''Oh, yeah,'' I said. Maybe Rachel had just been following in her old mom's footsteps. ''Well, anyway, I go places. I went to West Virginia last year.''

''Year before last.''

''Whatever.''

We were both quiet awhile, just listening to the rush of the river and watching the snow fall. It was dark outside, but there was enough illumination from the streetlights to see. Although when I looked out at the Mississippi, I could not see the Illinois side. Halfway out, it was just pitch-black. In fact, I could barely see the railroad tracks that separated us from the river.

In the silence, I thought I heard something. ''Did you hear that?''

"What?"

"Sounded like somebody moaning," I said.

We both stood completely still, holding our breath, waiting to hear the sound again. When you're trying to hear something in particular, you end up hearing all the things that you never really paid attention to any other time. Like the lapping of the water on the bank, the dog on the next street over barking like mad, the clanking of Charity's gate in the yard across the street.

"Look," she said, pointing downriver. "I think it was just that tugboat."

I looked down the river, and way in the distance was a light on a vessel coming upriver. "No, that's too far away," I said. "That's not a tugboat anyway. That's a barge."

"How can you tell?"

"I can tell by how high the light sits from the river."

"Good Lord, you *do* need to get out of this town. Come up to St. Louis with me," she said. "We'll eat exotic foods."

"And I'll get indigestion."

"We'll go hear some reggae."

"And I'll have an asthma attack from those clove cigarettes everybody smokes at reggae shows."

"Drink some Jaegermeister..."

"Oh, and I'll end up getting killed. Last time I drank that stuff, I was chasing cars in the street."

"I know," she squealed. "That was so much fun."

"Collette," I said. "Stop. I make it up to St. Louis to see the symphony a couple of times a year, and I go to every play of the Shakespeare Company's summer season. We usually go up for Mardi Gras festivities in Soulard. I get out plenty. Just not as often as you."

There was that sound again.

"Did you hear it this time?" I asked, the hair prickling on my arms.

"Yeah," she said, wide-eyed. "I did."

"It's coming from down that way."

"Down by the wreckage," she said.

"Yeah. Come on."

I was four steps away from her when I realized that she wasn't walking with me. "What?" I asked, turning back to her.

"You sure we should go down there?" she asked.

"Oh, *now* you don't want to go down there," I said. "Come on, loosen up. *It'll be fun.*"

"You know, you can be a real bitch sometimes," said Collette.

"So can you," I replied, taking a few steps. "Come on." Reluctantly, she followed behind me.

"Watch your step," I said.

"Don't worry. These shoes are Italian."

"You wouldn't happen to have a flashlight in your purse, would you?"

"No," she said. "Should have known I'd need a flashlight. What about you? Don't you carry a flashlight?"

"My purse is in the car."

"I was joking," Collette said. "You really carry a flashlight?"

"Shh," I said as we crept closer. The crime-scene tape that the sheriff had put up on Wednesday was still there, flapping in the wind. We were about ten yards from it when I remembered something.

"Hey, give me your keys."

"What? What do you want with my keys?"

"Just give them here."

"Jesus, Mary, and Joseph," she said. "Standing on the bank of the river in the freezing snow and she wants my stupid keys. Here!"

On Collette's key chain was one of those little minilights so that you can find a keyhole in the dark. It wasn't big enough to put off any light from this distance. But up close, it might come in handy.

"Shouldn't I go call 911?"

"And leave me here alone? I think not," I said.

We stepped over the crime-scene tape and walked toward the wreckage. "Crap," I said.

"What?"

"There're footprints here in the snow."

"So?"

"So that means somebody is down here. Or was recently."

Just then, the barge came up close to us and flashed its light around in a circle. When it did, I caught a glimpse of something lying over the side of the visible wreckage. "Double crap," I said.

"Hey, where are you going?" Collette called after me.

I took off at a pretty good speed and slid a little as I got to the wreckage. In the darkness, I saw what looked like a body. It *was* a body. About five feet from the bank, lying over the wreckage, somebody was splayed out on his back, his knees and feet hanging loosely in the water. I took Collette's little key-chain light and flashed it on the body. I was still too far away to be able to identify anything.

I stepped a little closer.

"Torie, you crazy woman. What are you doing?" Collette called.

"It's a body!"

"A body," she said. "Then get the hell away from there."

The only way I could get close enough to see it was to step in the water. Oh well, my shoes were just ten-dollar Wal-Mart beauties anyway. It wasn't as if they were *Italian.* I stepped into the water and gasped at how cold it was. I flashed the little bitty light at the man's head and it illuminated the features enough for me to see that it was Jacob

Lahrs. A dark red stain ran down the side of his face—blood, I assumed.

"It's Jacob Lahrs!" I said.

"Is he alive?" she asked.

"I'd have to touch him to find out."

"Well, you gotta do what you gotta do," Collette said.

"Mr. Lahrs," I said. "Mr. Lahrs, it's Torie O'Shea."

No response. He was either unconscious or dead. And judging by how still he seemed, I'd say he was dead. I stepped a little closer, and when I did, I must have stepped on part of the wreckage. My foot sank into it, and I felt wood scraping my skin. A creaking noise was the only warning I got, and not soon enough for me to move. The whole thing tipped and Jacob Lahrs just sort of spilled on top of me.

My foot was trapped in the wreckage and I had a bleeding corpse lying on top of me. I screamed.

Then Collette screamed.

Okay, calm down, I thought. If he was indeed dead, he'd only been dead a few minutes. Somehow, a recently dead body pinning me to the snow wasn't as disgusting as a day-old corpse pinning me to the snow. I had just heard him moaning not five minutes ago, so he had probably died as Collette and I stood up on the bank talking about Jaegermeister and the Shakespeare Company. Rigor had not set in yet, and he was still…fairly warm. Oh God. I was going to puke.

No, I couldn't puke. I was lying on my back, and if I puked, I'd choke and die. And wouldn't that be difficult to explain to my husband. Well, Mr. O'Shea, your wife died when she choked on her own vomit, pinned by a bloody corpse in the snow. Yeah, that would be really stupid of me. I began struggling and moving around, trying to get out from underneath Professor Lahrs. I had to concentrate on the fact that I needed to get free of the wreckage, rather than needing to get free of a corpse. "Collette! Go get the sheriff!"

"What?" she shrieked. "I can't leave you here alone."

"Then get down here and get this body off of me."

"Okay," she said. "I'll be right back."

THIRTEEN

"COLIN! AM I GLAD to see you," I said. His flashlight shone brightly down in my eyes, and in the blinding light, he appeared taller than usual. Of course, that could have been because I was lying on the ground and he was standing over me with one hand on his hip, perilously close to his pistol. I had managed to wiggle out from under Jacob Lahrs, but he was still lying right next to me, because I had yet to free my foot from the wreckage. It had gone through the wood easily enough, but something had caught it, and I could not twist it in the right position to get free.

"What the hell? No, I'm not going to ask that question," he said. "I've learned with you that if I don't really want to hear the explanation, I should just not ask *the damn question!*" he yelled.

"I can explain all of this," I said. "If you could please just help me get my foot free."

"Oh, I can't do that," he said.

"Why not?" I asked, panic rising in my chest.

"This is a crime scene. I can't disturb anything until the CSU gets here."

"Oh, you can't be serious," I said.

He knelt down then and deliberately put the flashlight under his face. He smiled a wicked smile, reminding me of the Joker from *Batman*. "Oh, believe me. I am dead serious."

"Colin! Look, the crime scene is all screwed up anyway.

Mr. Lahrs was up there, and then he was here on top of me, and now he's over there. He's been more places dead than most people have been alive. And…and…my footprints are everywhere. So please help me get my foot out. It's bleeding. And *my ass is freezing!*"

He stood up then and walked back toward River Point Road. I thought for a moment with a sinking sensation that he was just going to leave me there in the snow. I wasn't joking about my butt being frozen. In fact, I was wearing just a normal pair of underwear and a pair of jeans, no thermal underwear or anything. Since my bottom half was in the water, it was getting to the point where I couldn't even feel my butt any longer. I was becoming numb from the waist down. He stood with his hands on his hips, shaking his head back and forth. I could see people starting to gather up on the road.

How embarrassing.

"I thought I told you to stay away from down here. Not that it matters. I should have known better. I tell you to stay away from all sorts of places and you still go there. It's like you navigate to the very places I tell you to stay away from. Hey, Torie," he said, turning around. "Don't you ever go to the North Pole. Not ever. Make sure you stay away from the North Pole. Now with any luck, you'll go to the damn North Pole, and I'll be rid of you!"

"Colin, please. My foot is getting infected as we speak, and I think I may be getting frostbite. Or…hypothermia. That's it. I'm getting hypothermia. Collette and I came down here because we heard Mr. Lahrs moaning. That's it. That's the only reason. I haven't set foot down here since I was here with you on Wednesday."

"You didn't think to call 911 first?"

"Well, Collette did, but I—"

"Well, at least we know which one of Laurel and Hardy has the brains."

"If you'd just let me finish, Colin. I thought that in the time it would take to call 911, whoever was moaning could die. I mean, I didn't know. I thought somebody could be drowning. So I just thought I'd see first, and then if it wasn't something I could handle, I'd send Collette to call 911. I thought time was of the essence," I said.

He stood there a moment. I couldn't judge his expression, because it was dark and the light from New Kassel was behind him. "I swear, Colin, my first thought was to help whoever it was."

"You swear you have not been down here any other time?"

"I swear, cross my heart, and all that garbage. Please, just help me get my foot out of the wreckage. If I scoot down any closer, then my whole body will be soaking wet," I said.

He hesitated a moment, but he finally came forward and pointed the light at the hole where my foot had slipped through. He grabbed hold of my foot and twisted. "Here, if you just turn your foot—"

"Ouch! Jeez, if I could have turned it in that position, I would have gotten free. I don't think feet are meant to turn in that direction."

He played the flashlight across the snow-covered ground. The light fell across Jacob Lahrs, who was now lying face-down in the snow. Then he found a big rock a few feet away. He stood up and walked close to the river, obviously trying to disturb the snow as little as possible. He came back with the rock and smashed the wood around the area of my foot.

"So, what did you see?" he asked. "When you found him."

"Uh…well, it all happened so fast. Basically, he was ly-ing up over the wreckage and there was a whole lot of blood running down his face. My guess is, somebody smashed his head in.''

"How do you know it wasn't self-inflicted?" he asked, giving one final blow to the wood. It crumbled all around and he reached down inside and moved aside a piece of metal that my foot had gotten hung up on.

"Well, if he fell, I wouldn't think he'd be laid out on the wreckage like he was. Anyway, I couldn't really see who it was, so I was stepping in the water to get a closer look, and I ended up stepping on the wreckage. It shifted and Mr. Lahrs fell on top of me.''

My foot was finally free, and I jumped up to get as far away from Mr. Lahrs as possible. I shivered, and it wasn't from the cold. I looked down on my coat and saw the blood on it. "Oh, gross," I said, and took off my coat. I threw it in the snow, as if it were some sort of live organism trying to eat me.

"What?"

"It's Mr. Lahrs's blood," I said, shaking my hands. "Do I have any more on me?''

He flashed the light up and down my body. I found it difficult to stand on my left foot. Little hot flashes of pain shot up my ankle into my shin. "Yeah, you got some on your neck.''

"Oh, oh, oh God. I'm gonna be sick.''

"Just calm down," he said. "You've seen blood before."

"Yeah, but I've never had somebody else's blood on me, for crying out loud!''

"Just breathe," he said. "Put your head between your knees.''

I did as he instructed, and I felt better. I had better things to worry about than puking. Like having frostbite and getting gangrene. Sheriff Brooke flashed his light on the ground. "Walk around this way," he said. "Go up to the Murdoch Inn and tell Eleanore to run you a bath. As soon as you're cleaned up and have on fresh clothes, have Collette take you to Wisteria General. You're gonna need a tetanus shot. Plus, you probably sprained your ankle really good.''

"Why can't I just go home?"

"Well, for one thing, home is a half a mile walk that way. Eleanore's is right there. Plus, I don't think the kids need to see you with somebody else's blood on you."

"Good thinking," I said.

"I am capable of it once in awhile."

"Can I come down now?" Collette called from the road.

"Yeah," Colin yelled. "Come and take Miss Marple to Eleanore's."

Getting up the bank of the river was a joke, since it was slippery with snow and I couldn't use one of my feet. Not to mention that I was shaking and my teeth were chattering from being in the cold water. Collette pulled and tugged, trying to get me up over the bank, but I just couldn't get enough of a hold in the snow and push myself with one foot at the same time. "This isn't working," she said.

"Get behind me and push," I told her.

"I love you, Torie, but not that much."

The CSU pulled up about that time and began unloading equipment. The snowflakes were bigger now; everything was covered with at least six inches of snow. And that meant the footprints and evidence down on the river were quickly being covered up, as well. I just gave Collette a defeated look and sat down. Reluctantly, she got behind me and sort of positioned my butt on her shoulder and pushed. "If I've ruined my shoes, there is going to be serious hell to pay. And just for the record—this is the first time I've ever touched another woman's butt."

"Shut up," I said.

I felt a hand grab mine and start pulling me up as Collette was shoving me. When I got to the top of the road, I found

Elmer Kolbe standing there, smiling down at me. He reached down and helped me stand, then gave Collette a hand as she tried to climb up the bank, which was now a wall of slushy mud. So much for her expensive Italian shoes.

"Thanks, Elmer," I said. "I don't think I would have made it without you."

A few people had now gathered in the area, and Eleanore had come out on her front porch to see what was going on. It was more or less her backyard, after all. With the help of Collette and Elmer, I hopped on one foot to the Murdoch Inn and then up onto the porch.

"Oh my Lord. What's happened?" Eleanore asked.

I held a hand up to her, indicating that I would tell her in just a minute.

"Would you run home and get me a pair of sweats?" I said to Collette. "They're in the middle drawer in the chest."

"Sure," she said.

"Oh, and clean underwear, too."

"Okay, Anything else?"

"Mmm, my purse. If you want to stay with the kids so Rudy can take me over to Wisteria General, that's fine. Or else you can take me and he can stay with the kids. I don't care either way."

"We'll work it out," she said.

I turned to Eleanore, who was in her robe and had her hair up in curlers. She looked weird without all of her makeup and jewelry. She had no eyebrows. All of this time, I never knew she had no eyebrows. She must have penciled them in.

"Eleanore, I'm all yours. Sheriff says to run me a bath," I said. "But you know, I think I'll just take a hot shower instead." I didn't want to be in the same water that Professor Lahrs's blood would be in.

"Of course," she said. "Right away."

Elmer helped me hop my way inside.

FOURTEEN

I WAS CLEAN and dressed in dry clothes. Thank God. Of course, I would never be entirely convinced that little river organisms hadn't infiltrated my body by way of the gashes in my foot. And no matter how many times I'd scrubbed Jacob Lahrs's blood off of my skin, it still felt as if it were there.

My foot and ankle looked like they had gotten caught in a meat grinder. Nothing really bled profusely, but I had large amounts of skin missing in various places. I was about ready to put my tennis shoe on the other foot and leave for the hospital, when the sheriff walked in.

I was seated at the table in the kitchen of the Murdoch Inn, with its array of copper pots and pans hanging from the middle of the ceiling and what seemed like a thousand and one sunflowers scattered about the room. They were everywhere—on the wallpaper, the curtains, stuck to the fridge, and a big silk bouquet of them in the middle of the table.

"What's up?" I asked, putting my shoe on my right foot. My lips were still a little blue when I'd stepped out of Eleanore's bathroom, and I still had a mild case of the shakes. But the hot shower had done wonders to warm me up.

The sheriff nearly knocked one of the pans down as he made his way toward the table. I always forget how tall he is, until something like this happens. He steadied the pan with his hand. "You see the footprints down there in the snow?"

"Yeah," I said. "I saw them when I first went down there. I just thought they belonged to whoever was doing the moaning."

"Looks like there are several sets. A few lead down to the boat, although they weren't necessarily made at the same time. In fact, I think one or two sets were from earlier, because there is more snow covering them than the other set. Only one set leads back up the hill. I think those were Collette's. I can't be sure right now."

"Well, that's good," I said. "Right? You can follow them straight to the perp."

Colin hung his head in thought. "Seems our perp was a little smarter than that. I can only find one set that actually leads away from the crime scene. I think the perp realized he was leaving prints and headed for the river."

"That's it?" I asked. "So, what, is he still in the river?"

"I'm thinking he might have been in the river when you went down there."

I laid my head on the table. "Great."

"I think he just simply walked up the river, or down, as the case may be. Staying close to the edge, of course. And then got out at some point. But the snow will completely cover the prints before we can track them. Who knows how far he walked?"

"You're serious," I said, looking back up at him.

"Yeah."

"Wouldn't he have a bad case of frostbite?"

"Possibly," he said. "I've got word out at the hospitals within sixty miles to call me if they get a patient with wet feet and frostbite, possible hypothermia. But who's to say he'll go to a hospital? Who's to say he won't get on a bus and go to a hospital in another state? Or if he had it all planned out, who's to say he didn't have a car waiting somewhere? All he has to do is cross the river on the ferry down in Sainte Genevieve.''

I thought a moment. Would the perp think to do that? If it had been premeditated, I could see it. But if it had been an act of passion? If it were something the perp hadn't intended to happen, would he think to cross the river and go to Illinois to go to a hospital? I don't know if I'd think that clearly if I'd just smashed in somebody's skull.

''Any sign of a struggle? Like a fight?''

''It's too hard to tell.''

''Do you think it was premeditated?''

''Most likely. In fact, I think the perp waited for him to go down there and then followed him.''

''Can you compare the prints to everybody's shoes in town?''

He laughed at me. ''Okay, let's say for a moment I have those kind of man-hours and I could literally compare every pair of shoes in New Kassel. The snow fell too fast to get a clear visual of the prints. I've got the scene covered with a big tarp now, so no more snow will fall on it, but I think the damage has already been done,'' he said. He paused a moment and thought of something. ''We got pictures of them, but I really think the snow was too heavy. They were mostly obscured by the time we got there. We might be able to narrow it down to the size and type of shoe, based on the photographs. Sneaker, boot, whatever. But I don't know that I can narrow it down to brand or specific treads. And, like I said, I'm not sure what the photographs will even show.''

The throbbing in my foot was becoming unbearable. ''You really think the perp was still down there when I got there?''

''I don't know,'' he said. ''Maybe, maybe not. Lahrs could have been lying there moaning for a couple of hours.''

''In which case, the perp would be long gone.''

"Right."

"Anybody missing?"

"What do you mean?"

"I mean from here. The inn. Jacob's two assistants, or Mr. Chapel from Channel Six news?"

"Newsome is checking on that as we speak."

"I just had a thought," I said. "If the actual event occurred earlier than we thought, it's possible the perp could have already been at a hospital and was released before you ever put out the APB."

"True," he said.

Something didn't set right with me. I wasn't sure what it was, but the thought of some guy walking around in the river for an hour just didn't seem right. It was twelve degrees outside. He wouldn't be that stupid. That was, of course, if the perp was a guy. Could have been a female. Although less likely. Not because women are less stupid, but because the type of crime seemed to fit a man.

"So did you notice anything else while you were down there?" he asked. "Anything at all that you think might be of use?"

"You mean did I see a guy hiding in the river?" I asked, nearly laughing at him.

"Well, I might get lucky. You never know."

"No," I said. "In fact, it seemed like an unusually quiet evening. Everybody was inside early because of the snow. I mean, people tend to go home early on Sunday evenings anyway because of school and work the next day. But it was quieter than normal. Ask Collette what she saw."

"I will."

"I'm sorry, but I was really more concerned with the body."

"Let's get you over to the hospital, get you some antibiotics and a tetanus shot before you get lockjaw," he said. His eyes suddenly lit up. "On second thought, you with lockjaw would be a blessing. You wouldn't be able to open your mouth!''

"You can shut up anytime now. I just suffered a traumatic event, you know.''

THE NEW KASSEL GAZETTE
The News You Might Miss
By
Eleanore Murdoch

I just have one thing to say. This town functions quite nicely on its own, and as soon as outsiders come in, somebody turns up dead. Of course, my husband, Oscar, reminded me that without the generosity of the tourists, we would be in the poorhouse or working the midnight shift at a fertilizer plant. Still, what happened to Professor Lahrs is most distressing. Especially since it happened a few hundred feet from our home. And how much tourism will we continue to have if people get murdered when they come here? Really, we must come up with a plan to screen those who come to spend any length of time in our town. That's all I have to say.

Oh, and the winner of the snowman contest was Davie Roberts. His snowman was a self-portrait. He used some blackberries his mother had in the freezer to give his snowman two black eyes. Father Bingham found this ingenious, and probably felt a little sorry for him, too.

Until Next Time,
Eleanore

FIFTEEN

THE NEXT MORNING, the sun shone brilliantly on the new snow. The sky was a deep, deep blue as I dropped the kids off at school and headed out to Wisteria to see my mother. I'd called Helen Wickland and asked her to take over my tours today, because there would be no way I could climb the steps of the Gaheimer House on my left foot. It was sprained all right, and I could barely walk. It was a good thing that I needed only my right foot to drive. My arm was killing me from the tetanus shot they had given me, and I think there were sections of my rear end that were still numb. Have I complained enough?

I pulled into my mother's driveway about ten minutes later and wondered where the time had gone. Some days when I make the drive out to Wisteria, I notice every little side street and house. Then there are other times that I'm so deep in thought, it seems like I leave New Kassel and then suddenly I'm in my mom's driveway. Which was how it felt today.

I knocked on the door and then went on in. I never wait for her to tell me to come in. The knock was just so she knew I was coming through the door. My mother and I had lived together entirely too many years to become formal with each other now. Besides, she was going to baby-sit for me today, so she was expecting Matthew and me.

"Hello!" I called out. I reached down and took Matthew's coat off, then mine, and tossed them over the chair by the door. I was not walking to the coat closet if I didn't have to. I usually threw my coat over the chair anyway.

"We're in the kitchen," Mom called out.

It's a good thing Matthew can walk now; otherwise, I would have had a heck of a time carrying him in the house. I walked—no, make that hobbled—through her living room and into the kitchen, where she and Colin were drinking coffee and reading the paper. Colin immediately put the paper down. "How's the foot?"

"I'm all right. Just can't put a lot of weight on it," I said, sitting down as fast as I could. "And I have to wear a house slipper, even in eight inches of snow."

My mother smiled at me then, as if I should have known better than to put my foot through an eighty-year-old piece of wood. She held her hands out to Matthew, who instantly climbed up her wheelchair and onto her lap. My mother is a beautiful woman, with a long oval face, large brown eyes, and creamy skin. Her salt-and-pepper hair is nearly the only thing that gives away her age, other than the slight crow's-feet at the corners of her eyes. And you couldn't tell that she was in a wheelchair until she actually pulled away from the table. She had been one of the last polio victims of the 1950s, and it left her without the use of her legs. But that hadn't stopped her from getting married, having me, and cleaning her own house. And then snagging the sheriff. Plus, she is an outstanding cook. Now that I thought about it, maybe that was why I'd dropped all that weight. She had moved out last year.

"Have they got you on painkillers?" Mom asked. She wheeled over to the refrigerator with Matthew on her lap and got out the juice for him.

"Just some large doses of Ibuprofen," I said. "And Amoxicillin four times a day."

"So, you're feeling all right, then?" she asked.

"Yeah," I said. "It only hurts when I try to walk."

"I've got an extra wheelchair in the basement if you want to borrow it," she offered. She handed Matthew his cup of fresh juice. Juice, along with everything, is always better at Grandma's house.

"God no, I'd end up hurting myself worse. Plus breaking everything in the house," I said. "No, I'll just hop from place to place, thank you very much."

"Rudy said one of your chickens got out," she said.

"Yeah, it's the same one over and over. I don't know how she's doing it. I wouldn't be that worried about it, except I'm afraid if the mayor finds her first, she's going to end up on his dinner table."

"That's a legitimate worry," Mom said.

"So...Colin," I said. "Any ideas on a murder weapon?"

"Coroner hasn't said yet. But it's looking like something big and heavy."

"Like a rock?"

"Exactly like a rock. The trauma area on the skull isn't small enough to be something like the butt of a gun or a hammer. It's a big area," he said. "So I'm thinking who-ever it was just picked up a big old rock and smashed him in the head."

"Gee," I said. "That doesn't sound too premeditated to me."

"Still could have been," he said. "The perp might have picked out the rock he was going to use the day before."

"Any idea on suspects?"

"Well, everybody in town," he said. "But if you want to know who had motive, we're not sure yet. Obviously, everybody in the Murdoch Inn is a suspect at this point. Those are the people who would have had access to him, and it's closest to the crime scene."

"Boy, am I glad Collette was staying with me," I said. "Otherwise, she'd be a murder suspect right now."

"That's right," he said.

"So what about the whereabouts of Jacob Lahrs's associates?"

"They say they were both in the inn the whole time. Jeremiah said he hadn't been anywhere all day, except to walk out for breakfast and lunch. They were waiting for Jacob to come back from the copier to go to dinner."

"Were their cars there all day, too?"

"Newsome said that Jeremiah claims his car was there the whole day, while Danny said his had been at the inn since about noon."

"Hmph" was all I said. I was about to ask the whereabouts of Bradley Chapel and his cameraman, when I noticed an old yellowed piece of paper sitting on the table, the edge of it tucked under the napkin holder. There is usually very little clutter in my mother's house. Don't get me wrong—she keeps everything: all of my report cards, half of the papers I did in elementary school, all the programs for every concert. But they are tucked away in plastic containers, and she knows what is in each one of them. So I wondered if the piece of paper was there for a reason. Then when I noticed my mother and Colin both looked at it and then at each other, I wondered even more about it.

"So...what's up?" I asked, forgetting all about Bradley Chapel and his cameraman. It was a really lame way to segue to a different topic, but I couldn't think of anything else.

"I gotta go get an oil change in the Festiva," Colin said. "I'll talk to you guys later." With that, he gave my mother a kiss and walked out of the kitchen and into the garage. It was weird watching my mother kiss the sheriff.

"Okay," I said. "What's going on?"

"Your father called me," she said.

Oh boy. Here we go.

"That's nothing unusual," I said. "You guys talk all the time."

Matthew decided to scoot down off of her lap then, and go watch the fish in the fish tank in the living room. She leveled a gaze on me that said in no uncertain terms she was in no mood to be jerked around. "So, he called you. What about it?"

She said nothing.

"Okay, I went to his house. I was very upset."

"I know you're upset," she said.

"Are you going to tell me I shouldn't have said those things to him? Mom, how would you feel? How *do* you feel about this?"

"I'm not surprised," she said. "I think I knew he had a child out there somewhere, even before he did. I won't lie. When he first told me, it opened up the wound that he'd inflicted years ago when he had the affair. But I also made peace with it years ago, so I'm able to look beyond the hurt."

"Well, good for you," I said. Lord, I sounded like a snotty twelve-year-old.

"Victory," she said in her best "Shame on you" voice.

"What?" I asked. "I'm glad you can move forward, Mother. That's great."

"It took a lot of guts for him to call me," she said.

"Well, at least he *told* you. I had to have some girl knock on my door and drop it on me like Nagasaki," I said. "Do you have any idea how…stupid I felt? I didn't know if I should laugh, cry, apologize, or kick her out the door. I mean, I didn't know what to do."

"Look, I know your father is a chicken. He's never done what he's supposed to when it comes to things like this," she said. "He runs from confrontations. He runs from emotional encounters. He always has."

"So that's it? Because he always has, I'm just supposed to let it go this time. And the next and the next, and he never learns, and he never has to do what's right! It's not fair," I said. "I should have known. He should have told me."

Having a dead body trap me in the snow had done very little to make me forget the pain of all of this, I was surprised to find out. "I can't believe you're taking his side," I added.

"I'm not taking his side," she said. "You misunderstand me. He didn't call me to plead his innocence. He called, first of all, to tell me about your sister, and, second, to tell me that you had gone to see him and what you had to say. But he really called me about Stephanie Connelly."

I narrowed my gaze on her, suspicious. "What do you mean?"

"His concern is not whether or not you ever talk to him again," she said. "For once, he's thinking of somebody else. He wants you to talk with your sister."

I crossed my arms and looked around the room. Anything other than to have to look into my mother's eyes. "Why?" I asked the floor.

"Because she's your sister," she said.

"So?"

"Stephanie very much wants to get to know you. She has no siblings, other than you. She's grown up with only one side of her family. She's missed knowing her grandparents, Torie. Your dad's parents are already gone. You had the pleasure of growing up with them. She didn't. You know what it was like to be loved by Grandma Keith. Stephanie doesn't. But it's not too late for her to meet her aunts and uncles and cousins."

"Dad can introduce her to everybody just as well as I can."

"Victory" was all she said.

"What if I don't want to get to know her? What if I don't want her just to waltz into my world and..."

"And what?" she asked.

I didn't answer. I just sat there with tears perched and ready to fall.

My mother reached across the table and picked up the yellowed piece of paper that I'd noticed sitting there earlier. She opened it and handed it to me. It was a letter I had written in the second grade, when I was eight years old. A letter to Santa. I could barely read the words through my tears.

Dear Santa,
I wold like a Sweet April playland for Christmas and the doll to go with it. And a Mister Patato Hed too. But most of all I wold like a sister. I ask you for a sister every year and I never get one. How come? I wold be vary nice to her and I wold love her and we wold be best frinds.
I have been vary good.

Love, Torie

I had dotted the *i* in my name with a heart.

I swiped at the tears that fell, feeling like a complete heel.

"Is there a reason that Stephanie has to pay for your father's sins?" my mother asked me in her solemn and peaceful voice.

"No," I whispered.

"Then call her," Mom said. "Meet her for lunch."

SIXTEEN

I SAT IN MY OFFICE at the Gaheimer House, tapping my pen on the desk and looking out my window. I had sent an e-mail to Stephanie Connelly and suggested that she meet me at Fraulein Krista's for lunch tomorrow. I could have called her, but then I would have had to talk to her. Call me strange, but I didn't want to say anything to her over the phone. I wanted to see her face when I talked to her for the first time. Well, other than the time I had been rude to her in my office. She'd sent an e-mail back almost within the hour and told me she would be there.

Now I had to be there.

"Torie," a voice said.

I looked up to see Sylvia standing in my doorway. She walked in briskly and sat down in the chair across from my desk. Sylvia is the anti-little old woman. Her sister Wilma had been that greeting card-perfect old lady: round, plump, kindhearted, and a great cook, and I miss her more than words can say. Sylvia, on the other hand, is thin, gnarly, sharp as a tack, and grouchy as a bear with a thorn in its butt.

"What did you need?" she demanded.

I had asked her to stop by my office when she had a moment. "I wanted to ask you about the night of the wreck. *The Phantom.*"

"Sheriff Brooke thinks it has something to do with the death of Professor Lahrs?"

"Well, no, not really. Other than the fact that Professor Lahrs was in town investigating the wreckage, and his body was found draped over it. I mean, in that way it involves the wreckage, but I don't think in any other way," I said.

"What do you want to know?"

"Well, first of all, I was hoping we could take some of the money from the River Heritage fund and maybe put up one of those plaques down by the river, telling about the wreck. But first I need to try to find out exactly what happened."

She thought about it a moment. "I don't see why we couldn't put up a memorial of some sort. Several people lost their lives."

"That's great, Sylvia. Thank you," I said.

Sylvia and I have a love-hate relationship. I love her; she hates me. Well, not exactly. I respect her and, I guess, I sort of do love her because, since coming to work for her, I have learned that there is a lot more to Sylvia than being grouchy. I used to think she was cold and unfeeling, when in fact she has had a life full of tragedy. Hermann Gaheimer had been a man old enough to be her grandfather and she had had a torrid affair with him. When he died, he left her everything, including the Gaheimer House. I had often wondered why he had not left the house to his children, and then one day I discovered that he had been unable to have children. His wife, not knowing he was sterile, had become pregnant by her lover and tried to pass the kids off as his. What I found out was that at one time, Sylvia was warm, generous, and loving. But at some point in her life, she forgot how to live and love, and she shut herself up tighter than a clam.

As far as I am concerned, I think she hates the way I do things but respects the fact that I'm the only one in town who really gives a hoot about the probate records from 1852 to 1877. Who else would care? So in me, she has found a like-minded spirit. Even if I do infuriate her most of the time. It makes for a prickly relationship, one that I'm constantly redefining.

"Second, I'd like to know what you remember about the day of the wreck," I said. She would have been about fourteen at the time, give or take a few years, because I don't know exactly how old Sylvia is. I have this recurring nightmare that someday when she dies, we'll find out that she was about 150 years old. I always wake up screaming from that nightmare.

She glanced at my desk, her eyes skimming over the files and photographs that I had lying out. She stood then and riffled through some things and found a photograph. "That's me," she said. "And that's Wilma standing behind me. You can see her big white bow peeking out from behind her head. Mom had bought us identical bows for Easter the year before."

I had not known that the girls in the picture were Sylvia and Wilma. How many times in the past few days had I looked at this photograph and had no idea it was my boss? It suddenly made me want to have Sylvia label every picture in the house. When she died, how would I identify the pictures? She had no children to recognize the people in the pictures. So unless she labeled them now, the identities of the people in all these old pictures would go with her. I made a mental note to spend a week having her go through pictures with me. Even her private collection.

"That's my brother," she said, pointing to a boy of about seventeen.

In the distance, you could see the wreckage, but only because the photographer had stood at an advantageous place on the front porch of the Murdoch Inn. Although then, the Murdoch Inn had been owned by Alexander Queen and was a private residence. If the photographer had stood level with all the people, one would never have been able to see the actual wreckage behind them.

"So?" I asked. "What do you remember?"

"Lots of things," she said. She sat back down, the photograph still in her hand. "I had been at the Queens' house," she said. "Mrs. Queen was expecting, and I used to take them their groceries while she was bedfast. She paid me a nickel to pick up the groceries and deliver them to her, and put them away, too. If I didn't put them away, I didn't get the nickel. Sometimes she'd give me a cinnamon stick."

I didn't interrupt her, even though it had very little to do with the wreckage. When Sylvia opens up about the past, it's a rare occurrence.

"I was just coming through the kitchen, almost to the door, when I heard...I heard screaming. I went out onto the porch and saw people jumping off of *The Phantom*. Then somebody sounded the bell and the townsfolk came running to the river's edge. I was one of the first ones there," she said.

"So...when the passengers began jumping into the water, could you see anything wrong with the boat? I mean, why were they jumping?"

"The boat was on its side, although not completely," she said. "It was cold that day and the sky was nearly silver. The river was particularly aggressive; the wind was blowing. I remember seeing little whitecaps on the river."

I knew from living in New Kassel my whole life that it took some pretty good winds to make whitecaps on the Mississippi. "Were the winds strong enough to topple the steamer, do you think?"

"No," she said. "I don't really know, but I don't think so. I didn't get to see the boat when it went up the river, only when it came floating back down, derelict."

"Did you see any other boats going up or coming down-river within ten minutes or so?" I asked, remembering that

Jacob Lahrs had said that he thought *The Phantom* might have been hit by something.

"I saw nothing when I walked down River Point Road to deliver the groceries to Mrs. Queen. Now, it took me maybe ten minutes to put away her things. So if another boat was on the water, it would have to have been during the time I was putting away her groceries," she said.

"You think *The Phantom* was loaded flat?" I asked.

"Probably, but I can't be sure."

"I've got a call into some of the historical societies down south to see if anybody has a picture of her the day she left. I think she was loaded flat," I said.

"You are most probably correct," Sylvia replied.

"When did you first start hearing rumors about diamonds?" She cleared her throat and looked back down at the photograph. "Almost right away."

"Whom did you first hear it from?"

"Wilma and I had helped a woman out of the water. She...she was a prostitute. You could tell by the way she dressed and the way she behaved. She all but seduced Doc Hallam when he examined her. She said that she had seen a large case of diamonds in one of the guest's rooms," she said.

"What was her name?"

"Don't know. That's the funny thing. As soon as Doc Hallam checked her out, she simply walked out of town, and none of us ever saw her again."

"Huh," I said, mulling that over in my head. "Did she say what guest's room she had seen it in?"

"I think she might have, but, Victory, it's been eighty years and I really don't remember," she said.

"What else do you remember?"

"Bodies washing ashore."

"Ugh."

"There was a child who said he'd heard the captain fighting with somebody up in the pilothouse," she said.

"Makes me wonder if they could have been physically fighting, as well."

"Possibly."

She was quiet a moment. "You know, the funny thing is, the ones who jumped off into the river, most of those people died. When the steamer stopped in the cove, the whole boat didn't fill up with water right away. People were able to get out. But those who jumped into the water were just ever seen again."

I found it hard to believe that *none* of the people who had jumped in the water were ever seen again. What were the odds that all of them would be lost? You'd think one or two would wash ashore a few miles downriver. I convinced myself that Sylvia was being a little melodramatic, which, in and of itself, was odd. Sylvia was never melodramatic.

"Anything else?"

"Just the bodies and debris washing ashore," she said. "That was a ghastly sight."

She was quiet again, reflecting on something. I assumed it was the floating bodies. Finally, she handed the photograph back to me. "They're buried over at the Lutheran cemetery."

"Who is?"

"The seven recovered bodies," she said. "We couldn't bury them in the Santa Lucia Cemetery, because we didn't know if the victims were Catholic. So Doc Hallam and a couple of the other officials decided to bury them out at the Lutheran church. Down High-way P."

I knew the church she was referring to. It isn't really within the city limits of New Kassel, but it is just a few miles south of town, off Highway P. I was a little astounded by this information, because I had never heard it before. All the years I'd lived and worked here and I hadn't known it.

I felt like the girl in school who knows nothing about the party after the big game on Friday night. How'd I get left out of this juicy piece of information?

"Back then, there was no quick way to get bodies back to loved ones, even if we had been able to identify all of them," she said. "So we just buried them here. What else were we supposed to do?"

"I never knew that" was all I said.

"Well, you don't know everything, Victory," she said. "Contrary to what you may think."

I ignored her; I was used to this from Sylvia. "Did you ever hear anything about the Huntleigh heiress?"

"Only that she went down with the ship. Her body was never found," she said. "Jessica Emeline Huntleigh was her name."

"Why was she on board?"

"She was returning from a holiday in New Orleans," she said. "She caught *The Phantom* in Memphis, because the steamer she'd originally been on had broken down and couldn't take her the rest of the way to St. Louis. Once in St. Louis, I think, she was supposed to take a train back to New York. It's all fuzzy now."

"Talk about bad luck."

"I know," Sylvia said. "She was only a few hours from her destination."

"What was the original steamer that she'd been on?"

"Oh, I think the papers said it was the *Louisiana Purchase*," Sylvia said. "It was one of those luxury liners that rich people took vacations on all the time."

"So, how did we determine that the Huntleigh heiress was actually on board *The Phantom?* If she didn't survive, how do we know she was on board at all?"

"One of her suitcases washed ashore, I believe. And then Doc Hallam received a telegram the next day from Jessica Huntleigh's father."

"But if she switched steamboats in Memphis, how did her parents know she was on *The Phantom?*"

"Well, she wasn't traveling alone," Sylvia said. "That's it—now I remember. Her companion survived and contacted the family."

"And then what?"

"It was like a circus here. For weeks after the boat went down the Pinkertons were here. Mr. Huntleigh had hired them to try to find his daughter. Or her remains."

"With no luck," I said.

"That is correct. Other than her suitcase, nothing was ever found of Jessica Huntleigh."

"Okay," I said. "This is a long shot, but are any of the survivors still alive? Any you would know of?"

She walked over to a filing cabinet of mine and pulled out a file. "This is a list of everybody who was on board," she said. "Judging by how long ago it was and the age of most of the survivors, I'd say you have about a three percent chance of finding anybody still alive. But at least you have a place to start," she added, pointing to the paper.

I glanced down at the list of names. "Is this taken from the manifest?"

"Sort of," she said. "It's from the list of names taken in port in Memphis."

"Jessica Huntleigh is not on here," I said.

"I noticed that, too."

"But she was definitely on the ship," I said. It was more a question than a statement.

"Yes," Sylvia replied.

"This makes no sense."

"Unless she didn't want anybody to know she was on board *The Phantom*," Sylvia said.

"Why?"

Sylvia only shrugged.

"Her companion…" I ventured.

"Yes?"

"Was her companion male, female? Do we know his or her name?"

"Her cousin, Matilda O'Brien," Sylvia said, and pointed to the paper once again.

With that, she left the room. She was finished talking, either because she had nothing else to say or because she was too tired to continue. With Sylvia, you never know. For one thing, she rarely volunteers information. She could have had plenty more to say to me about the wreck. Maybe I just hadn't asked the right questions. That's the way she is. It's almost as if she wants to see how smart I am. Yeah, it's definitely a love-hate relationship.

I dashed off an e-mail real quickly to an associate in Tennessee. We often swap favors with each other. Believe it or not, it is easier to have somebody in a specific area go and look something up for you than it is to write to the courthouses. Not to mention cheaper. So I look up things for him in eastern Missouri, and he looks up things for me in western Tennessee. I had built quite a network of research buddies since getting on the Internet.

Dear Ian,

Could you check the shipping and docking and manifests for a ship called the *Louisiana Purchase* and see if there was a woman on board named Jessica Huntleigh. It would have been January 1919, heading from New Orleans to St. Louis. The ship broke down in Memphis and she switched ships then, getting on a ship called *The Phantom* for the duration of her trip. I'm trying to track her movements from New Orleans. For some reason, she doesn't actually show up on any lists of names for *The Phantom*, but it is widely accepted that she was on board when the boat sank. If you could

just varify that she was on the *Louisiana Purchase,* I
would be forever in your debt.

—Torie

I hit the send key and then turned off the computer.

SEVENTEEN

I LIKE THE FACT that there are still places in Granite County where the two-lane roads are bordered with nothing but trees and pastures. More and more civilization has encroached, and half of the drives I used to take through the countryside are now drives through the land of subdivisions. But the particular stretch of Highway P just south of New Kassel is still country. New Kassel is situated with the Mississippi River to the east and Wisteria directly to the west. To the north are a few miles of woods, until you reach the next town, and to the south is rolling pasture, the occasional woods, and lots and lots of farms.

I was about five minutes out of town when I came to the Granite Lutheran Church on my left. Don't ask me why I felt the need to come out here and look at the graves of the wreck victims, but I did. I suppose it was because I never knew this piece of information before and it bugged me. I am a historian. It's my job to know these things, and yet somehow, I had never bothered to find out, or else this fact had just slipped my notice. Helen Wickland, a few other people, and I had compiled a publication on all of the cemeteries of Granite County a few years back. My only consolation was that Granite Lutheran had not been one of the cemeteries I had traipsed through and cataloged grave by grave. One of the other volunteers had done it. But still, I felt like I should have known the wreck victims were buried there.

Granite Lutheran is a beautiful little church, built of red brick, with four arched windows on each side. Each one of the windows has a blue stained-glass background with a brownish cross in the middle. Rounded oak doors are hung on large black cast-iron hinges and creak when opened. The most beautiful thing of all, though, is its location. Situated on a slight incline, it can only be reached after you cross a creek and covered bridge. Trees seem to rise up behind the church and cradle it, but without smothering it. And today, with the heavy white snow…well, you just couldn't get any more postcard-perfect than that.

I pulled my van into the parking lot and parked away from the church and the few other cars in the lot. These probably belonged to Earl Kloepper, the minister, and maybe his assistant. I got out and grabbed the disposable camera I'd bought at Wal-Mart. I always keep a few of them on hand at the Historical Society, because I just never know what's going to come up. I snapped a picture of the church and the lot from where I stood next to the van.

I wrapped a scarf around my neck, tucked one pants leg down in my boot and the other down in my house slipper, and headed for the graveyard, which is situated to the southeast of the church. I didn't take my crutches because they were a pain in the butt in snow; plus, my foot was getting better. I listened to the snow crunch under my feet as I went, the silence interrupted only by my breathing and the hawk that circled around the trees behind the church. Finally, I reached the cemetery, yanked open the big black wrought-iron gate, and entered.

Before leaving my office, I had looked through the *Granite County Cemeteries* publication that we had compiled. It told me what row the victims were buried in, so I didn't have to go up and down every row. Depending on the size of the cemetery, some could have taken the whole day to cover. Granite Lutheran is a small to medium-sized cemetery, however, so I could walk it and look at every tombstone in about an hour. But still, with my ankle the way it was, and the fact that snow was leaking down into my house slipper, I just wanted to go straight to the victims' graves.

When I shut the gate, I noticed that somebody else had been in the cemetery recently. Well, at least since Sunday night, when the snow had fallen. So sometime in the last forty-eight hours. Could have been the minister, although unless somebody had been buried recently, Earl probably wouldn't have been wandering through the cemetery. I thought no more about it and headed toward the row that had been designated for the wreck victims. The hawk I'd heard earlier swooped down and scared the bejesus out of me. He landed on a tombstone at the end of the cemetery. I noticed the footprints in the snow led down the very same row I was turning into.

I scanned the cemetery and the surrounding woods for another person but saw no one. It felt like eyes were watching me, but that had to be my imagination. I'm fairly impressionable, I'll admit. I turned down the row, and there were the seven headstones, all next to one another, with a paddle wheel carved into each. They simply read: FEMALE. WRECK OF THE PHANTOM, 1919, OR MALE, as the case might be. All seven tombstones were identical, other than designating the deceased as male or female. And somebody else had stood right where I was now, looking down at these same stones, in the last day or so. The footprints turned back on themselves and led out the way they had led in, back to the parking lot.

Snapping two pictures of the tombstones, I listened for any change in the world around me. The hawk screeched from several rows away, a car passed by on Highway P, and my breathing had become more labored from the trudge up through the snow. I snapped a picture of all of the footprints, and one of the church and surrounding area, as well.

All together, I probably took six pictures. And then I ran like hell back to the van.

You'd think as much time as I spend in cemeteries that I would have learned not to let my imagination run away with me. But it happens every now and then, just the same.

Words cannot express how difficult it was to move quickly when only one foot worked correctly. I sort of ran, hopped, leapt, and said, "Ooch, ouch" the whole way.

As I was getting in the van, Earl Kloepper came wandering down the front steps of the church. He is about fifty-five and walks with a pronounced limp, usually with the aid of a cane. It worried me that he was walking down the slippery steps without his cane, so I postponed leaving and made my way toward him.

"Reverend Kloepper," I said. "You need some help?"

He looked down at my slipper-clad foot and laughed. "The blind leading the blind?"

"Well, if we fall, at least we'll fall together," I said.

He made it to the bottom of the steps just as I reached him. "Where are you headed?" I asked.

"Goin' into town to get some salt for out here," he said. "Lotsa traffic lately. The shipwreck, you know."

I walked beside him as we headed to the parking lot, making sure that he didn't fall. "Where's your cane?"

"Left the dern thing at my mother's when I went to see her at the home yesterday," he said. "Gotta pick it up while I'm out. What brings you here?"

"Oh, uh…" I glanced toward the cemetery.

"The shipwreck," he said.

I nodded. "You have a lot of people coming out to look at the graves?" I asked, feeling a little bewildered by how other people in town knew that the graves were here but I hadn't.

"More than usual," he said. "Had some reporters a few days ago. Some townsfolk. Even Helen Wickland stopped out there to see 'em when she was here Monday for the Bingo chili supper.''

Helen had compiled the information on this particular cemetery for the country records, so it made sense that she'd know about the graves. "Well, you be careful, Reverend Kloepper," I said. "It's pretty slick in town."

"I will," he replied.

He waited for me to return to my van and then he started his car. He put it in reverse about the time I was crossing the bridge.

EIGHTEEN

I SAT IN my favorite booth at Fraulein Krista's. I'd come early so that I could be there waiting for Stephanie Connelly. For some reason, if I had arrived and she had already been here, I would have felt awkward. Even though it's my town and my booth, I still would have felt like the outsider. I know, I was just being a jerk. I'd brought some pictures along for her to see. Pictures of Dad growing up, pictures of Grandma and Grandpa Keith, and pictures of me through the years, and my kids. She might not care at all, but if I were in her shoes, I would love it if somebody brought me pictures of my family for me to see.

Just like a scene out of a movie, Stephanie entered the restaurant almost in slow motion. Looking around, her gaze landed on me in the back of the room. She smiled, tucked her hair behind her ear, and walked toward me. I seemed to be in a vacuum as she approached. Suddenly, it was as if there was nobody else in the restaurant and no noise in the universe. I was looking at my sister. *My sister.* It was just too surreal.

She sat down with a swoosh of Estee Lauder and put a package on the table next to her. "Hi," she said.

"Hi."

She noticed my crutches leaning up against the booth. "Did you break your leg?"

"No, just sprained my ankle. But I sprained it really good," I said.

"How'd you do that?"

I thought it would be best if I didn't tell her that I broke it while trying to identify a dead body. It might scare her off. "Slipped."

"Oh," she said.

We both started talking at the same time, both gushing apologies. "You go first," I said.

"No, you."

"I, um, just wanted to apologize for the way I reacted the other day when you came into my office," I said. "I didn't know what to do or say. I felt extremely betrayed. And I acted like a jerk. It took a lot of guts for you to come and see me."

"It's all right," she said, and shrugged. "It's not as if I just blurted it out. I was a little chicken."

"No, it's not all right. I shouldn't have acted that way. I considered nobody or nothing except myself. I mean, you really threw me. I just thought that if my dad had fathered a child, I'd know about it. And there you were, standing in front of me in the flesh, and I didn't even know about you," I said. "I guess it was a real blow to my ego."

"Your ego?" she asked.

"Yeah, I take great pride in knowing everything," I said, and laughed. "Or at least I think I know everything. Then every now and then, something or somebody comes along and proves me wrong, and it knocks me on my butt. That's what I get for having an ego in the first place, I suppose. God's revenge."

She laughed for a minute. "Well, I am very sorry I upset you. But it became pretty clear that Dwight was never going to tell you. And I...just couldn't wait any longer. After my daughter was born...well, she just made me more aware of what was missing in my own life."

"That happened to you, too?" I asked. "I had always wanted a sibling, but it was almost painful not having siblings once I had my own kids and I watched how they interacted. Of course, Rachel and Mary swear they hate each other right now. That's been going on for about two years, but I have faith that it will pass. But, at any rate, there wasn't much I could do about not having siblings. I couldn't just waltz out and create a sibling for myself.''

''Yeah, and I have people say to me, 'Oh, you were an only child? I bet you got whatever you wanted.' They have no idea.''

''Well, for some people, being an only child is probably the best gig in the world. But not for me. Not only was I *not* spoiled but I was lonely, too. What good is your own room if all you want is somebody to be in it with you?''

She just shook her head. ''I know exactly how you feel.''

''The world's a big place,'' I said.

''Sometimes I feel like I'm the only person in it.''

I couldn't have said it better myself. I am surrounded by people all the time. I know the entire town, for pete's sake. But there are times when it's as if I'm the only one of my kind in it.

Krista appeared at our table, beaming down at me. I think my mother had told everybody in town that I was meeting with Stephanie today. ''Torie,'' she said. ''What would you and your...*friend* like to drink?''

''Krista, this is my sister, Stephanie Connelly. Stephanie, this is Fraulein Krista,'' I said.

''It is so nice to meet you!'' Krista exclaimed, and shook Stephanie's hand.

''Nice to meet you, too.''

''I mean, it is really nice to meet you,'' she said. ''We all love Torie. I just want you to know that if you're anything like your sister, we'll all love *you*, too.''

Stephanie laughed at Krista's remarks. And then she said, ''I'll have a Dr Pepper.''

I just stared at her, blinking. "Yeah, me, too." Krista winked at me and went back to the kitchen to get our drinks.

"So," I began. "Tell me about yourself."

"I'm a teacher."

"Really? What do you teach?"

"History."

"History. Of course you do," I said.

"I have a daughter, she's three and a half. I live in St. Louis right now, but I grew up in Arnold."

"That close," I said. "Jesus."

"I know," she said, and looked at her hands. "Oh, I brought some pictures to show you. I bore everybody to tears with pictures. But I love them."

"Funny, I brought pictures, too."

And that was that. We laughed and started showing each other pictures, both of us talking about a million miles per second, and that was the way it went for close to two hours. We talked about our differences, too. Her favorite color is blue, whereas mine is purple. She loves to ski, and I've never even tried it. Our biggest difference is that she actually understood high school algebra and passed it in college. Okay, I passed it, too, but I hadn't understood it.

It seemed everybody and their uncle was just stopping by Fraulein Krista's for coffee or tea or some other little parcel of good-tasting things. It was probably because everybody wanted to see what Stephanie was like and if we were getting along. It's a shame to admit it, but I guess there just wasn't anything else better to do on a Wednesday afternoon than to snoop on me. I made a mental note to berate my mother and her big mouth.

But there was one guest I doubted was here for the sideshow. Bradley Chapel and his cameraman, Kyle, came in and sat down in the booth catercorner from us. Stephanie noticed my attention shift, and she turned and looked.

"Somebody else that you know?"

"Yeah," I said. "Although not all that well."

Stephanie's attention seemed to fixate on her empty glass. In a matter of seconds, it was as if she were someplace else.

"Is there something wrong?" I asked.

"No," she said. "Not at all. A personal matter that keeps popping up in my mind."

"Oh," I said. I would have offered to hear what was on her mind, but I wasn't sure if that would be appropriate, considering we were still in the early stages of our relationship.

"Well, it's been great," she said suddenly. "We had today off for grade day at my district. I've got to get home and actually do some grades."

"Okay," I said. "I'll have copies made of the pictures you asked for."

"And I'll have some made for you," she said, and smiled. She hesitated a moment. "You are exactly like I thought you would be."

"Is that a good thing?" I asked, laughing.

"Yes," she said. "It's a good thing."

"So…" I began, unsure of what to say. "Are we going to see each other again?"

She nodded her head. "I hope so! I want my daughter to meet her cousins," she said.

"Great, maybe you and your family could come down for dinner sometime?"

"We'd love to," she said. "I'll call you."

With that, she picked up her package of pictures and exited. Mr. Chapel happened to see her as she walked by, and he glanced up from his menu and saw me staring at him. I couldn't help myself—I looked at his shoes. They were expensive shoes and looked as though they'd never been worn before. What did he do—wash them?

"Can I help you with something, Mrs. O'Shea?" he

asked. Kyle, who had a ketchup-dripping french fry hanging out of his mouth, turned around and waved.

"You're still in town?" I asked. "Don't you have a life?"

"I'm leaving Friday," he said. "But I'll still be around until I get everything I need for the story."

"It wouldn't be because the sheriff has asked you to stick close by, would it?"

His expression turned from piety to distaste in a millisecond. "What are you suggesting?"

"Nothing," I said, and finished my soda. I stood up to leave.

"Mr. Ketchum had some interesting things to say about exactly what Professor Lahrs uncovered when he was diving," he said.

"Like what?" I asked.

"Well, now that's for me to know and for you to find out."

I was more angry with myself for walking into that than I was at Mr. Chapel for being such an arrogant twit. I grabbed my crutches.

"Good day, Mrs. O'Shea," he said as I walked by.

What I wouldn't have given just to whop him with one of my crutches. But what would that solve? Nothing. "Yeah, whatever."

NINETEEN

I WENT TO MY OFFICE after having lunch with my newfound sister. I had a few things to look up, but I could not stop thinking about Mr. Chapel's last words to me at Fraulein Krista's. I tried pushing them to the back of my mind and began opening the mail that had arrived while I was at lunch. I logged on to the Internet to check my e-mail. There was a response from Ian in Tennessee.

Torie,
Took me several hours to find the records, but I eventually found them in a private collection of a man who collects all things dealing with the Mississippi and the steamboat era! I was beginning to think that I would have to tell you that I'd found nothing. Your girl, Jessica E. Huntleigh, was on board a ship called the *Louisiana Purchase* and switched boats after a two-day layover. However, there was nothing wrong with the *Louisiana Purchase*. It simply docked to let off passengers and then went on its way to St. Louis, and eventually Minnesota—I'm assuming to Minneapolis. So not sure where you got your info or why you think the *Purchase* had broken down, but she didn't.
Let me know if I can get anything else for you.

Ian

I jotted off a quick thank-you, telling him that I owed him big-time, and then put lots of exclamation marks and several smiley faces to drive the point home of just how indebted I was. Then I turned off the computer and thought about what it could mean. Jessica Huntleigh had not switched boats because of engine trouble or anything else to do with the *Purchase*. She had switched boats because she wanted to. But why? And why would her cousin have lied about the reason they switched boats?

After a few more hours of distracted work, I finally decided that it was time to call it a day. I stopped by the Murdoch Inn on the way home. Now, granted, Mr. Chapel could have said those mysterious words to me at Fraulein Krista's just to see how easily I could be manipulated. Well, he would have been happy to know that it worked. But I didn't care.

"Torie! How is your foot?" Eleanore asked as I went into her office.

"It's getting better," I said. "I was wondering if you could tell me what room Jeremiah Ketchum is in?"

"Oh, he's leaving today," she said. "That Jones fella left yesterday. Guess there's no reason to stay if the leader is dead."

"They're all from around here, though, right?" I asked.

"Well, on their registration slips they filled out, I believe they all said they were from around here. Let me check." She pulled out a big book and flipped through it. "Yes, Professor Lahrs was from Hillsboro. That's what—thirty miles from here? Mr. Jones is from Arnold, and Mr. Ketchum is from Sainte Genevieve. So, all within an hour's drive, give or take."

"Good," I said. "Now what room is Mr. Ketchum in?"

"Oh, he's up on the third floor, room 3B."

"Thank you."

As I turned to leave, Eleanore stopped me. "How are you going to get up the steps?" she asked.

"Oh, I can hop," I said. "My foot is much better."

"Oh dear," she said.

And so I hopped up the steps, made my way to room 3B, and knocked. Mr. Ketchum answered after maybe sixty seconds. He looked at me as if he didn't remember who I was, and maybe he didn't. I'd only met him twice, and they were both fairly brief encounters. "Yes?"

"Mr. Ketchum, I'm Torie O'Shea. I was wondering if I could have a word with you?"

"Oh, Mrs. O'Shea," he said. "I…you look different. Come in."

"I guess it's the crutches," I said. I entered his room and noticed that he was indeed in the middle of packing. A large baby blue suitcase was open on his bed, with clothes tucked neatly inside. More clothes were laid out on the large four-poster bed, and on the table by the window was his brief-case, files, and papers.

Eleanore had done this room in sort of Early American style, although the bed was a little too Victorian to fit completely into Early American decor. I love antiques, but I'm not so sure I could own a bed like that. I'd need a ladder just to get into it.

"What can I do for you?" he asked.

"Oh, I was wondering if Professor Lahrs had said anything to you about…well, maybe that he was receiving threats of some kind?"

He smiled at me, but the smile didn't quite reach his eyes. "Playing detective, are we, Mrs. O'Shea?"

"Well, the sheriff is married to my mother."

"So however I react, regardless of my guilt or innocence, it will be reported back to him," Mr. Ketchum said.

"Something like that," I replied. "Look, this really has nothing to do with you. Although I do find it interesting that you assumed I was trying to come to a verdict on your guilt or innocence, when, in fact, all I want to know is if Professor Lahrs received any threats on his life."

He seemed to be weighing something in his mind. Eventually, though, he decided to talk. "Well, I certainly have nothing to hide," he said.

Yeah, that's what they all say.

"So talking with you won't hurt anything," he said. "To answer your question...no. Okay, you can leave now."

I laughed at his quip but ignored it. "Did he act bizarre?"

"When didn't he act bizarre?" Jeremiah said, shoving some socks into the side compartment of the already-bulging suitcase.

"What do you mean?"

"Well, he was either stoned or drunk most of the time," he said. "Therefore, he acted pretty bizarre on most days."

"Even in class?" I asked.

"Definitely in class," he answered. "Jacob didn't want to be a schoolteacher. He wanted to be Jacques Cousteau. Teaching biology at a junior college wasn't exactly the road to *National Geographic*."

"There's nothing wrong with teaching at a junior college," I said.

"Not unless your dream is to be a microbiologist studying life in the sea for *National Geographic*," he said, folding a pair of pants.

"Oh," I said. "So why didn't he become a microbiologist and follow his dream?"

He shrugged. "That, I don't know. But he didn't. This thing with his great-grandfather was supposed to give him his big break."

"What do you mean?"

"Danny Jones was documenting as we went," he said. "I guess Jacob thought he could make a documentary out of it, and of course make some major discovery, submit it to whoever it is you submit those types of things to, and he'd be on his way.''

"Oh" was all I said. I thought for a moment. "What do you mean 'major discovery'?''

He hesitated.

"Oh, don't tell me the diamonds,'' I said.

He said nothing.

"How major would that be?'' I asked. "Everybody already believes they're down there anyway. I mean, that's not much of a 'discovery.'''

A noise came from outside. It sounded like a car crashing. I gave Mr. Ketchum a signal to wait just a minute while I looked out the window. I pulled the curtain aside and saw that a car had backed into a parked car down in the lot below. "Oh man, somebody backed into a blue Cavalier.''

"Blue Cavalier?'' he said. He moved to the window. "That's my car!''

He all but ran out of the room, leaving me standing above the table with his briefcase sitting on it. Okay, I told myself that I would not go through the man's briefcase. That would be a complete and utter violation of his personal rights, and I would not do that. Not to mention that Colin would have my butt in a sling, and I wasn't sure I could walk on crutches with my butt in a sling. But I could look at the papers that were already out on the table.

I glanced down, perusing the papers quickly.

And I was amazed at what I saw. Letters and documents, dated from 1919 to 1922 or so. And signed by the captain of *The Phantom*.

A few moments later, I was down the steps and on the front porch of the Murdoch Inn. Mr. Ketchum stood beside his car, rubbing his head in disbelief. I didn't recognize the car or the woman who had backed into him, so I assumed she was a tourist. She was a small woman, in her mid-forties, and she kept apologizing over and over.

"I know. I heard you say you didn't see the car," Jeremiah said. "But really, lady, it's a big blue thing in the middle of all of this white stuff. How could you not see it?"

I carefully walked over to the car and the steadily growing crowd. "You need me to call the sheriff?" I asked.

Mr. Ketchum rolled his eyes heavenward. "Yes, please," he said. "Great. Just great. First my wallet was stolen…now this. How am I gonna explain this to the deputy?"

Walking around the front of his car, I viewed the damage from the driver's side. His entire back bumper had been shoved up into the trunk. The woman hadn't just hit the car; she'd walloped it. She must have been doing fifteen miles an hour in reverse to do that much damage.

I pulled my cell phone out of my purse and leaned on the hood of the car for support. My foot was better, but there was no point in deliberately putting weight on it if I didn't have to. Something caught my eye on the dashboard. Deputy Miller's voice came on the line.

"Yeah, this is Torie," I said, peering closer to the dash for a better look. "We've got a fender bender out here at the Murdoch Inn."

"Okay, we'll send somebody out," he said.

Thrown haphazardly on the dashboard was a speeding ticket. It wasn't a Granite County speeding ticket—ours don't look like that. And trust me, being the stepdaughter of the sheriff does not make me exempt from tickets, so I would have known one of ours when I saw it. I leaned a little closer to the glass and saw that it had been issued a few days ago. I stood up straight and thought a moment. Then I leaned in for a closer look. It had been issued the same day that Jacob Lahrs was killed. And it looked as if it was Jefferson County issue. That was just to the north of New Kassel.

"Well, Mrs. O'Shea, are the police coming?"

"Yes," I said, pulling my attention away from the dash. "They're on their way."

TWENTY

On Thursday morning, I paid a visit to Sheriff Brooke.

"How stupid do you think I am?" the sheriff asked.

"You know, my mother always told me never to ask questions that I didn't want to hear the answers to," I said. "You might consider her advice."

He sat behind his desk in his brown-paneled and thoroughly depressing office at the Granite County Sheriff's Department. Next to the phone sat a photograph of my mother, taken on their honeymoon, and one of my kids sat off to the right on his desk. On the wall hung one of those posters with all the NFL helmets on it. Indoor-outdoor carpeting just sort of added to the aura of "built in great haste."

"Look—"

"No, *you* look," I said. "I don't have access to everything you do, so I don't know what you found in Jacob Lahrs's room and what you didn't, but I'm telling you, I saw what I saw."

He pinched the bridge of his nose; he was getting one of his Torie headaches. At least that was what he called them. In my opinion, his headaches were brought on because his sphincter muscle was too tight. He sighed and then spoke finally. "We didn't find much. His room hadn't been wiped clean exactly, but the only thing we found was a neatly packed suitcase. Contents of which were clothing, toothpaste, toothbrush, a box of condoms—"

I raised my eyebrows.

"Young, single, male. You never leave home without them," he explained. "His cell phone was in the front pocket. That was it."

"Nothing related to the wreck? I mean, he brought no papers, no nothing?"

"No."

"Professor Lahrs wouldn't come down here to work on a project that could make or break his career and not bring one thing pertaining to it! Look, I know what I saw. I saw a letter written in 1921 by a man who claimed to have been the captain of *The Phantom*."

"Whose name was not Eli Thibeau."

"Right. The name on the letter was William Wade. The captain of *The Phantom* was Eli Thibeau."

"Maybe you misread it."

"No," I said. "I didn't. The letter was written to his wife or his lover or something, and it was telling her that he had taken care of 'it.' Whatever 'it' was. And that they would never have to worry about their future. He mentioned very specifically getting a job for the time being as another riverboat captain. And since nobody would know he was the captain of a boat that sank, he shouldn't have any trouble getting a new job. He signed it 'William Wade.'"

He shook his head.

"What?"

"It just sounds like a bad episode of *The X-Files*. If an asteroid hit the earth, you could find a conspiracy in it."

"That is not true," I said. "And there are no bad episodes of *The X-Files*."

"Right, did you see the episode where the killer mushroom ate Mulder and Scully?"

"I think those documents belonged to Jacob Lahrs and somehow Mr. Ketchum ended up with them."

"All right," he said. "So what? They were associates."

I took a deep breath. "Do you mind if I do some searching on my own?"

He opened his top drawer. "Where's my Tylenol?" Not finding his bottle of Tylenol, he slammed the drawer and opened the other one. No Tylenol there, either. I opened my purse and tossed him a bottle of Advil, which he caught. He swallowed two of them without any water. How do people do that?

"Okay," he said. "I'll ask Jeremiah about the documents."

"Colin," I said.

"What?"

"Do you care if I do some research?"

"What kind?"

"Nothing hands-on, for pete's sake. I'm going to do some digging, look up Professor Lahrs's family tree."

"Fine," he said.

"Don't look at me like that. I'm going to take Collette with me, and we'll report back to you as soon as we find something."

"I wasn't looking at you weirdly," he said, reaching for his throat. "The pill is stuck."

Just then, I heard Collette's voice out in the front office. "Oh, gotta go, Colin. Drink some water!"

I was halfway to his door when I realized I'd forgotten to tell him about the speeding ticket. "Oh, and on the dashboard of Jeremiah Ketchum's car was a speeding ticket dated the day Jacob Lahrs was killed."

Colin swallowed some water and gave me an exasperated look over the top of the cup. "How do you know that?"

"I saw it on the dashboard yesterday."

"And you could tell what day it was issued?"

"Well, yes. I looked very closely," I said.

"Maybe it was for jaywalking," he said with a sneer.

"It was issued in Jefferson County," I said. "You might want to check on—"

"Get out of my office!" he roared.

"Yes, sir," I said, and hobbled to the door.

Collette and I drove up to the main library in St. Louis County on Lindbergh. We stopped for lunch in Kirkwood at Einstein's Bagel, then headed on up to the library. We passed the Huntleigh estates, and that made me think of Jessica Huntleigh and why she had switched boats. Granted, there was no connection between the two Huntleigh families, but it niggled something in my brain. She'd gotten onto *The Phantom* for no apparent reason at all. And that just made no sense. Because the *Louisiana Purchase* was a luxury steamer. *The Phantom* was not.

Once we got to the library and went up to the third floor—luckily, they have an elevator—I gave Collette a list of things to look up, then went about my business with my own list. I checked the 1920 census for William Wade and found him with his wife, Maria, and their infant daughter, Tamara. They lived on Russell in St. Louis. William had given his place and date of birth as Union County, Illinois, 1882, and Maria's was listed as Syracuse, New York, 1889.

"Psst, Collette," I said. "Look for a marriage for Tamara Wade somewhere between 1938 and 1950. Check the city and the county."

"Why am I starting at 1938?" she asked.

"As a general rule, you start looking for marriage records about eighteen years after the wife was born. Tamara was born about 1920, so start around 1938."

She nodded and went to get the proper microfilm roll.

Over the next three hours, I checked out all the personal info on the Huntleigh heiress, as well as everything I could find on Eli Thibeau and William Wade. Collette and I met back at our table about 3:30 p.m. "What did you get?" I asked.

"All right, in November 1941, Tamara Wade married a Robert Thatcher," she said. My spirits sank. Not exactly what I was expecting. "But she got married again, this time to one Maxim Lahrs. Seems that Thatcher was a bomber pilot and died in 1943. So in 1944, she married Lahrs. Which is what we were expecting. Looks like Tamara and Maxim were the grandparents of our dead guy."

"Yeah," I said. "They'd be too old to be his parents. What else?" "Well, once I found out when they got married, I checked the newspapers to see if there was an announcement for the wedding. Sure enough, seems Maxim Lahrs was a colonel and had been home on special assignment when he met Tamara and fell madly in love. So he was getting ready to head back to the war and decided to tie the knot first. Anyway, there was a big write-up about him and the wedding and who all attended. Tamara had one brother, Thomas, who, I figure, was only about two years younger than she was."

"How do you know that?" I asked.

"Because William Wade died in 1922. I don't think he was even around for the birth of his son," she said.

"How do you know he died in 1922?" I asked.

"Because," she said, and handed me a photocopy of the article. "It mentions that Tamara was the daughter of the late William Wade. I checked the obituaries in the paper and found his in 1922."

"You're gonna put me out of business," I said. "Excellent work."

"What did you find?"

"Basically, I've been trying to make connections between Eli Thibeau and William Wade. I found the 1910 census and Eli gave his place and date of birth as Union County, Illinois, 1882. Same as William Wade."

"Yeah, but there must have been thousands of people born in Illinois in 1882," Collette said.

"True, but not in Union County. I'll get back to that in a minute. I also checked on the Huntleigh heiress," I said.

"Why her?"

"Something's been bugging me about that whole thing. Sylvia told me that she had switched boats because the one she was on had broken down. But that's not true. I checked. There was nothing wrong with the boat she was on originally. She just switched boats because she wanted to. Why would she do that?"

"To travel with somebody?"

"That's what I was thinking. And Mr. Chapel asked me a really good question. I showed him a picture taken an hour after the boat sank. The pilothouse was still visible. He said if the pilothouse didn't sink immediately, why didn't the captain survive?"

"You think he did survive and just slipped away?"

I nodded my head. "Now, I'm not saying he deliberately caused the wreck. What I'm thinking is, once it happened, it was the perfect opportunity just to disappear."

"But why?"

"Maybe because he was in love with Jessica Huntleigh, who was engaged to somebody else and was forbidden to marry him," I said.

"You're reaching," she said.

"Am I? I checked on Jessica Huntleigh, and she was born in 1889 in Syracuse, New York. The very same information that Maria Wade supplied on the 1920 census. I think Jessica Huntleigh changed her name to Maria Wade."

"But why would she tell the truth for the census? I mean, she could just as easily have lied."

"True, but you know there is a seventy-two-year seal on census info. Nineteen thirty was just now made available to us. So maybe it never occurred to her to lie, because who was ever going to see it? I mean, who would ever look up Maria Wade anyway? And besides, she probably couldn't imagine that the census would ever be available to the general public during her lifetime.''

"I suppose," Collette said.

I scanned the article on the wedding of Tamara Wade and Maxim Lahrs. Then it hit me. "Photographs," I said.

"Photographs?"

"There have to be photographs of Maria Wade. Jacob Lahrs's family—somebody in his family has to have a photograph. I could compare one to a photograph of Jessica Huntleigh," I said.

"You really think it's possible for a wealthy New York heiress just to disappear?"

"In 1919, in the Midwest? Yes, I do. There were no Social Security numbers," I said. "Back then, I don't think you had to have a birth certificate for anything. Not like nowadays. Once the furor died down over the dead heiress, it would have been possible for her to change her hair and wear inexpensive clothes, and nobody would have been the wiser. Because nobody would have been looking for the Huntleigh heiress in the middle of St. Louis."

"The obituary for William Wade said that he was a riverboat captain—go figure—a businessman, a husband and father. The only child they listed was Tamara, which also makes me think that Thomas wasn't born until after," Collette said. She smiled suddenly from ear to ear. "This is fun."

"Addictive," I said. "Guess what else I found? Or didn't find, I should say."

"What?"

"Prior to 1920, there was no William Wade listed from Union County, Illinois."

"How do you know?"

"Because the 1880, 1900, 1910, and 1920 census records are categorized by what they call a Soundex. A Soundex is a code given to the last name. Like Smith would be *S*, fol-

lowed by three numbers. So no matter what county somebody was living in, you can find them by name. But if your
checking censuses prior to that, you have to know an ancestor's exact county of residence. That makes things difficult, because an ancestor could have moved in the ten
years between each census. With the Soundex system, all
you need is the state. I checked Illinois and Missouri all the
way back to 1900, and there was no William Wade born in
1882 in Union County, Illinois. But in 1900, there was an
eighteen-year-old Eli Thibeau living with his parents in Union County. And in 1910, he was living in St. Louis. By
1920, he was gone, and William Wade suddenly appears.''

"Wow," she said.

"Yeah."

"So what's your theory?"

"My theory is that Captain Eli Thibeau, alias William
Wade, decided with his lover to disappear after the wreck.
And I think that since he knew they would not have her
money to live on, he had to come up with some way to give
her the things she was accustomed to. The captain of a
steamship wasn't exactly a wealthy man. So when he realized the diamonds were on board, he saw what a great opportunity it was: They could disappear and be rich at the
same time.''

"So you think they were going to live off of the diamonds?"

"I think that was the plan. In a letter that William Wade
wrote, he talks about how they'll never have to worry about
their future. I think he's talking about the diamonds.''

"When was the letter written?"

"1921," I said.

"The year before he died."

"Yeah."

"So did he ever get the diamonds?"

"I don't know," I said. "We may need to talk to somebody in the family to get a better feel for whether or not they actually got the diamonds. Maybe that's why Jacob didn't seem concerned about the diamonds, because he already knew his great-grandfather had found them.''

"One thing bothers me, though," she said, scratching her head.

"What's that?"

"If the Wades wanted to keep a low profile and not be discovered, then how did Jacob Lahrs know that his great-grandfather was really Eli Thibeau, the captain of the boat?"

"I don't know," I said.

"That was pretty stupid of him, admitting that Eli Thibeau was his great-grandpa," she said. "Because anybody could have come along and checked to see that Eli Thibeau never married and never had kids. William Wade did, but not Eli Thibeau."

"Yeah, but Jacob Lahrs probably wasn't figuring anybody would ever check," I said. "Wait a minute."

"What?"

I sat down in the chair at our table. "Mr. Ketchum said that Jacob Lahrs was making a documentary of his 'discovery.'"

"Yeah? And?"

"Well, if Jacob was really hoping this documentary would be his ticket out of the junior college and to *National Geographic,* he had to know there'd be a certain number of background checks. Maybe the discovery wasn't about the diamonds per se, or *how* the boat sank, but the whole thing. The whole cover-up. The fact that William and Maria Wade were really Eli Thibeau and Jessica Huntleigh. Finally, the disappearance of the Huntleigh heiress would be solved. And at the same time, he could blow the lid on where the diamonds have been all of these years."

Collette sat down in the chair next to me. "You're brilliant," she said.

"No, just tenacious."

TWENTY-ONE

THE NEXT DAY, I felt just like a kid when it snowed. Suddenly, I wanted to walk everywhere instead of drive, take my own good time reaching my destination. But since I was wearing a house slipper on one foot, I thought it would be better if I drove. I was using the crutch less now, but I still had a bandage on my foot, so it wouldn't fit in my boots.

I was on my way to see Harlan Schwartz. I drove up New Bavaria Boulevard, which is in the more residential area of New Kassel. I heard a car behind me when I was almost to Harlan's. I turned around to see who it was. Sheriff Brooke pulled up alongside me in his squad car. I rolled my window down and he followed suit.

"Hey, Torie," he said.

"What's up?"

"Where you headed?"

"I'm on my way to see Harlan Schwartz," I said.

He looked up the road and thought a moment. "I'll go with you."

"Why? What's up?" I asked again.

"Had a talk with Jeremiah Ketchum," he said.

"And?"

"He gave me everything he had. You were right. The documents belonged to Jacob Lahrs."

"And did he have a good excuse as to why he had Jacob's documents?"

He gestured to Harlan's house. "Let me pull in the driveway," he said. "Hold on."

The sheriff pulled his squad car into the driveway of a small ranch house, and I pulled in behind him. We both got out and stood in the drive, which had been recently shoveled and littered with salt. I hoped Harlan had paid some young kid to shovel it, because if he was out here shoveling at his age, I was going to be really upset.

"Ketchum said that he and Jacob had been poring over the documents at lunch on Sunday. When I had questioned him before, he'd said they'd had lunch and then Jacob walked down to the Corner Bar, while he and Danny went back to the Murdoch Inn," the sheriff said.

"What's that mean? Jacob let Jeremiah take the documents back to his room and said he'd pick them up at a later date?" I asked.

"Apparently so."

"You believe that?"

"Sure," he said. "Although I think it could be just as possible that he killed Jacob Lahrs and then stole the documents. But what are the chances that he'd never seen the documents before? He'd probably seen them plenty of times. I don't think stealing them would be motive enough to kill Professor Lahrs."

"Why *would* Jeremiah kill him? I mean, if he did, what would he gain from it?"

"Well, I thought about all of the info that you and Collette found out at the library. I'm wondering if Jeremiah had decided to take credit for the whole thing."

"Yeah, but what about Danny Jones? And everybody else who knew about what Jacob Lahrs was doing?"

"Then maybe all Jeremiah wants is the diamonds."

"That would be more like it," I said.

I thought a moment.

"What about alibis? Do they have airtight alibis?" I asked.

"Well, Danny Jones and Jeremiah Ketchum backed each other up; they both said they'd had lunch together. Later, Jacob knocked on their doors to tell them he was headed to the copiers and that they'd have dinner when he got back. That was about six in the evening. Nobody saw them after that, but their cars were both at the Murdoch Inn. And then when I went to Eleanore and told her to roust everybody, they were both present and accounted for in their rooms. Now, Bradley Chapel and his cameraman, Kyle, were seen having dinner at the Old Mill Stream. They left between six and six-fifteen. Eleanore said she doesn't remember seeing them come in, but she knew that Mr. Chapel had picked up his messages from Oscar at the front desk by six-thirty," Colin said. "Then you found Professor Lahrs around seven-ish."

"That's everybody?"

"Those are the main suspects. You know, there's always the chance that somebody came to New Kassel just to kill Jacob Lahrs. It may not be anybody we've even met. He's got an ex-wife who's pretty angry with him," he said. "I'm checking her out."

"How do you feel about Chapel? Does he seem all right to you?"

"He's all right," Colin said. "A little overdressed for New Kassel. His cameraman is insane. He runs around in the snow in shorts, and I noticed he never wears socks. I confiscated the film they took of the crime scene, though."

"Really. I didn't know they had taken any," I said, and worked my lower lip between my fingers.

"So," Colin said, looking up at the front of Harlan Schwartz's house. "You here to ask him about the wreck?"

"He's the only one in town who is old enough to remember it, other than Sylvia, and I already got her story," I said.

"Let's go," he said.

I watched for patches of ice on the sidewalk as we walked up to the door, but it seemed to be generously sprinkled with salt, as well. I rang the bell and we waited, watching our breath billow in the wind.

"Oh, your mother said to invite you guys over for dinner next Friday," he said.

"What are you, her messenger?" I asked, a little annoyed.

"No big deal, Torie. She knew I was coming to track you down," he said.

I was about ready to knock again, when the inside door opened and the storm door filled with condensation. Mr. Harlan Schwartz, the second-oldest resident in New Kassel, stood there in a flannel shirt and tan corduroy pants. Opening the storm door, he said, "Sheriff, how are ya?"

"Good, Harlan. Can we come in for just a second?"

He looked at me, then back to Colin, and a faint expression of worry clouded his gray eyes. "Sure. What's this all about?"

The house was small, cozy, and extremely warm. His couch had an old blue crocheted throw over the back of it. Harlan sat down in the recliner, moving as slowly as one would expect. I noticed his walker was sitting over in the corner. He picked up the remote and turned off the television. "Can't believe *The Price Is Right* is still on television."

"What I can't believe is that they show reruns of game shows," I said.

"It's silly, isn't it?" he said in an exasperated voice. "So, what do you know, Sheriff?"

"Harlan," the sheriff began. "We want to talk to you about the wreck. You know, *The Phantom.*"

Harlan waved a hand at Colin. "TV reporter already been here."

"Bradley Chapel?" I asked.

"Yup," he said. "Fancy-dressed fella."

"Well, Harlan, I'd like to ask you some questions anyway," I said. "If that's all right with you."

He shrugged. "I don't care. Nothin' better to do."

"What do you remember? Start at the beginning. Where were you and what do you remember happened first?" I asked.

"Well, I was at the sawmill," he said. "I was takin' Dad some dinner. Mom said he was gonna be working late, so to take him some dinner. I'd just gotten home from school, so I didn't have to get bundled up or nothin'. I already was dressed for the weather. It was cold."

"What time was this?" Colin asked.

"'Bout four," he said. "So I started walkin' home, and the train passed me on the way."

Harlan scratched the top of his head, which had wispy white hair, combed to the side. His lips were drawn thin, like somebody who had worn ill-fitting dentures his whole life. "When I got to town, everybody was a-runnin' and screamin'."

"Wait," Colin said. "If you were coming home by the railroad tracks, then you were walking home by way of the river, too."

I looked at him. Of course. Harlan Schwartz would have been upriver. He would be the only one who could have seen what happened to the steamer.

"That's right."

"So did you see the boat before it sank?" Colin asked.

"I did," he said matter-of-factly. "She was loaded as flat as she could be. But, you know, I wasn't payin' no attention. I looked over at her; then I went back to playin' the game I was playin'."

"What game was that?" I asked.

"I used to take a rock and throw it and then try to outrun it," he said, laughing. "I was a strange kid."

"All kids are strange," I assured him.

"So then next thing I know, I look up and she's a-turnin' on her side. I started runnin' for home. When I came over the hill, I saw her out of control and floatin' into the cove, and people runnin' everywhere."

"Did you hear any rumors about diamonds?" Colin asked.

"No, I didn't," he said. "But I was too busy helpin' Doc Hallam. I saved a little kid. Probably two years younger than I was. I reached in and pulled him out of the water. Then I beat him on the back until he breathed."

"That's amazing," I said.

"Elmer's mother came a-runnin' with some blankets, 'cause we were all worried about the people catchin' their deaths," he said. "The water was so cold. Remember that like it was yesterday."

"I imagine that would be something that would be hard to forget," Colin said.

"I didn't wanna forget it," Harlan said. "I saved a life. Far as I'm concerned, I never did anything that mattered since."

The Talmud says that to save one life is to save the world. I guess it must feel that way, indeed. "Did you talk to any of the survivors?" I asked.

"Sure, after things calmed down. But at the time, we were all just runnin' around in every direction, tryin' to pull people out of the water and get them to safety."

"Did any of them talk about diamonds?" the sheriff asked.

"Not that I heard," Harlan said. "One woman lost her dog, though. Couldn't find him nowhere. He came wanderin' through town the next day."

"What about the Huntleigh heiress? Did you hear anything about her?" I asked.

"Just remember those private detective fellas comin' around afterward, showin' us pictures of her and askin' if any of us had seen her. That's all."

The three of us talked a few more minutes about the wreck in general, and basically Harlan had nothing further to add that we hadn't heard already. He really seemed to be animated by the conversation, though. I wondered if it was the subject matter or if it was just the fact that somebody had bothered to come and talk to him.

"Well, Harlan, we're going to get going," Colin said after a few minutes. "I want to thank you for taking the time to talk to us. If you think of anything else that might seem important, give me a ring."

"Sure will, Sheriff," he said, and started to get up.

"No, don't get up. We can see ourselves out," Colin said.

Harlan waved at us, and then as we walked out the door, he turned the television back on.

When we stepped out to the front porch, Colin looked at me. "Well, there's one witness who says she was definitely loaded flat," he said. "I agree with you. I think when Thibeau turned her so hard, the water just came up over the boat."

"Yeah, but what made him do that?" I asked.

"I don't know," Colin said. "At any rate, why the boat sank doesn't really help me with who killed Jacob Lahrs. That's not my mystery to solve."

I stood there a moment and heard the train in the distance. Harlan Schwartz had seen the train pass him by on the way home. The clouds in my mind parted for a moment and I flashed back to the night Jacob Lahrs was murdered. In my mind's eye, I could see Collette and me walking down the street toward the river and nearly being knocked over by Justin on his bike from hell. And then I remembered.

Standing there with Colette, I had heard the train go by.

"Colin," I said.

"What?"

"I think I just figured out how your murderer got away from the crime scene."

"What?" he asked, confused. "How?"

"The perp's footprints disappeared, but not because he waded through the river to safety. The footprints disappeared because he most likely walked upriver, through a bit of water, and then jumped on the train."

TWENTY-TWO

RUDY'S BOWLING TEAM consists of him, Chuck Velasco, Father Bingham, Tony Vogt, who runs the supermarket, and Colin. Father Bingham is the oldest member of the bowling team and also the best. He averages at least two strikes a game and several spares, whereas Rudy's talent lies in fishing, Chuck's in motorcycles, and Tony's in golf. I'm not sure what Colin's specialty is. He is good at fishing and hunting, although I refuse even to smell any of his deer sausage, much less eat it. So shooting matches are pretty good for him. Why this group of men insist on bowling is beyond me, but they meet every Tuesday night. Could be because the Black Cat Alley is the cheapest place in town for beer—a $1.50 a bottle and $1.00 for draft.

Or maybe it was just because they all want to get away from their wives and pretend that they have some semblance of control in their marriages. Although Chuck's wife had been doing the baker on Tuesday nights while Chuck had been trying to knock down ten pins. They divorced. Very bitterly, I might add.

I usually don't accompany Rudy on his bowling excursions, but once in awhile, I go along and bowl a few games with the kids while he engages in his efforts. This Tuesday, I didn't think it would be a good idea to bowl with my foot just healing, so I let the kids have at it. Matthew just sort of pushed his ball down the lane, and although it would take nearly two minutes for the ball to meet the pins, he was actually knocking down more pins than his father.

"So anyway," Rachel said, "Valerie's mom is letting her go to this lock-in over at the church this Friday and she wanted to know if I could come. I told her that my parents would probably say no because you guys always say no to whatever cool thing it is I want to do."

"You know, that just makes me want to say no," I said. She rolled her eyes. "See."

Mary knocked over three pins and came back to wait for her ball to return.

"Loser," Rachel said under her breath.

Mary made a *W* sign with her fingers, which meant "Whatever," then cocked her head to one side, and nearly dislocated her hip making the sassy body language.

As Mary turned around, Rachel made the *L* sign with her thumb and finger and stuck it up on her forehead.

"Will you stop?" I asked.

"She's such a dork," Rachel said.

"No, she's a kid. You were a dork when you were that age."

"Oh, not nearly as bad as she is. She's embarrassing," Rachel said.

"Back to this lock-in thing. What is it exactly?"

"Well, it's where a group of kids get locked in the church all night long."

"And this is fun?"

"Mom," she said. I never could understand how kids manage to put a diphthong in *Mom*.

"How is that fun? When have you ever done this to know if it's fun?"

"Becky Burgermeister said it's tons of fun."

"Oh, and she's the fun expert. The girl watches the Weather Channel four hours a day," I said.

"She does not."

"You forget her mother is on the Octoberfest committee with me every year."

A loud uproar came from the lane next to us as one of the guys got a strike. They all high-fived and raised their fists and their bottles and bought another round. It was a good thing strikes were rare in their game, or they'd all be alcoholics before it was over.

Rachel pouted. "Okay, so if it's not any fun, it's not any fun. I just wanna go."

"You're up," I said. She rolled her eyes yet again and got up to bowl. Mary sat down in her chair.

"So, Mom," Mary began. "Ashley said I could have her old Game Boy, if that's all right with you."

"Why is she giving away her Game Boy?"

"Because she got a new one," she said.

"Why'd she get a new one? Is the old one broken?"

"No, she just got a new one. Can I have it?"

"How do you know she's not going to want it back?" I asked.

"Mom, please. Just say yes or no."

"Fine," I said.

"Great. Can I go to Disney World with her in June?"

"What?"

"She's going to Disney World and wants to know if I can go."

"Did her parents say it was okay?"

She nodded her head, as if she really knew the answer to that question, her blond hair bobbing up and down.

"They probably don't even know about it," I said.

"They do, too. I swear," she said, and held her hand up. "She said her mother said she could take whoever she wanted. And I'm the one she wants to take."

"This week," I said.

"Mom." There was that diphthong again.

"Ashley's parents have four kids. Why would they want

to take another one with them if they didn't have to?'' I asked.

"Oh my gosh!" Mary suddenly exclaimed, forgetting all about our Disney World conversation. "There's Justin McKinney!"

I looked around the bowling alley and, sure enough, there was Justin McKinney. Before I could say anything, Mary was down off of her chair and running over to Justin's lane to speak to him. Rachel knocked down eight pins and was quite proud of herself. Matthew came over and sat in the same chair that Mary and Rachel had been in before. His feet just barely came to the end of the chair. He smiled, showing those completely adorable dimples.

"What do you want?" I asked. "Aren't you going to ask me for something?"

"Uh na keekoo," he said.

"Of course you want a cookie," I said.

"Where's Brat?" Rachel asked.

"She saw Justin McKinney three lanes down," I said.

And then I remembered. Justin McKinney was the one and the same kid who had barreled through town on his ten-speed the night we found Jacob Lahrs's body.

"Oh God," Rachel said. "His sister Meaghan is here, too. Hide me."

"What? What have you got against Meaghan?"

"She makes my life miserable," she said with great exasperation. "She's, like, Miss Perfect."

"I've noticed that the Miss Perfects in school usually grow up to be Miss Nobodies in real life," I said. She just looked at me as if I were the stupidest thing on the planet. "Okay, fine. You don't have to talk to her, you know."

"Oh, right. If I don't say something, then tomorrow at school she'll ignore me."

"So?"

"So, if she ignores me, then all the popular kids will ignore me."

"Rachel, there're what—forty kids in your entire grade? How many popular and nonpopular kids can there be?"

"You just don't get it," she said.

"Okay, then just go over and say hello. Then you've said hello and done your bit."

"I can't do that."

"Why?" I asked.

"Because then it's like I've got nothing better to do than to say hello to her. You know, like I'm groveling. She'll probably ignore me."

"You know, Rachel, you make my head hurt," I said.

"Whatever."

"Stay here and watch Matthew, then, okay? I need to speak to Meaghan and Justin's mother."

"Oh, that's perfect," she said, elated. "Then I can't go and speak to her because I'm baby-sitting. Mom, you're a genius."

I didn't want to think about how she'd come to that conclusion. "I'll be right back" was all I said.

I walked down three lanes. June McKinney saw me coming before I got there and waved me on over. She was about forty, with blondish hair and sparkly green eyes. She wore khakis and a sweater with pinecones all over it. "Torie, how have you been?"

"Oh, pretty good."

"I heard about your foot," she said. "Does it hurt?"

"Not too much anymore. Is Mary bothering you?"

"Oh, not at all," she replied.

Yeah, right. What a polite and sweet woman, I thought. "Hey, I wanted to ask you," I said, leaning toward her. "Did you know Justin was out on his bike the Sunday before last in that snow? I wouldn't normally say anything, I figure that's the parents' business. But it was dark and icy, so I thought I should bring it to your attention, if you didn't already know.''

She wasn't the least bit shocked by what I'd said. ''I know he was out. We grounded him for the week. I have told him time and again not to be out on the bike after dark, especially when the weather is bad. And here he was out after dark, in the snow, and on the very night somebody got his head bashed in!''

''Yes,'' I said, pondering that a moment. ''He was, wasn't he?''

''Sometimes I think the brain doesn't develop until you turn twenty-five,'' she said.

I laughed at that, agreeing with her. ''Well, has…has he been acting funny since then?''

''What do you mean?'' she asked.

''I mean, you don't think he saw anything, do you? Pertaining to the murder?'' I asked. ''I tell you, he was flying by me on that bike.''

''Probably because he knew he was going to get in trouble for being out so late,'' she said.

Or because he'd just seen a guy get his head bashed in and it had freaked him out a tad.

''Yeah, you're probably right,'' I said. ''Well, I have to get back to our game. I just wanted you to know he was out.''

''I appreciate that,'' she said.

''Mary! Come on, we have to finish our game and get Matthew to bed,'' I said.

She stomped her foot, clearly unhappy with being pulled away from Dreamboat Justin. Finally, she walked toward me, and Justin's eyes met mine. In that moment, I knew that he had seen something that night. A silent positive message was hidden there beneath those dreamy green eyes that Mary always talked about. And they were just begging for somebody to ask him about it. Some kids are like that. They want desperately to tell something to an adult, but only after you go through the motions of prying it from them.

"It's your turn to bowl," I said to Mary as we walked away. I dropped her off at our lane and then went to the next lane to speak to Colin. As soon as I entered the Sacred Circle of Terrible Bowlers, Chuck held a hand up to me.

"We love you, Torie, but you're not allowed," Chuck said.

"Oh, shut the hell up, Chuck. I need to speak to my stepdad, if you don't mind," I said.

Colin leaned back in the chair and sort of looked at me upside down. "What do you want?"

I leaned down so that nobody else could hear what I had to say. "You need to interview Justin McKinney about whether he saw anything the night Professor Lahrs was murdered."

I pulled away, and he raised his eyebrows in the form of a question.

"I forgot to tell you. He was out that night. He nearly ran over me and Collette, and he was riding his bicycle like a bat out of hell. As if he'd seen something he shouldn't have," I said.

Instead of answering me, he yelled at Tony, who had just rolled the ball in the gutter. "Aw, what was that? You bowl any worse, I'm gonna have to arrest you!" he yelled.

"Colin," I said. "Did you hear me?"

"Yeah," he said. "I'll check into it."

TWENTY-THREE

ON THURSDAY, I decided to go visit Danny Jones. He had appeared fairly levelheaded, and so I thought maybe he could give me some insight into the relationship between Jeremiah Ketchum and Jacob Lahrs. I was, of course, judging that solely on the fact that he hadn't tried to get liquor illegally that night at the Corner Bar. What can I say? It made a good impression on me.

He attended the Granite County junior college, which was about a half hour south of New Kassel. I did my morning tour at the Gaheimer House—yes, my foot was feeling much better—and told Sylvia I would be back for the one at two o'clock that afternoon.

It hadn't warmed up enough to melt all of the snow yet. But it was off the roads and the sky was a deep azure, in stark comparison with the snow white of the ground. The green of the conifers peeked out from under the heavy snow, reminding us all that eventually everything would return to green.

I enjoyed the ride down to Granite County Community College. I passed through several towns that were no more than a four-way intersection with maybe a gas station, a church, and a grocery store on the corner. All were little hamlets, whose names might appear on one of the more comprehensive gazetteers but not on an average map.

Just before arriving in the town of Rosefield, I spotted a dairy farm off to the right, dotting the landscape with its black-and-white cows. As I came around the bend, a valley sprang forth; in it lay Murphyville and Granite County CC. It was a perfect little dell, like something the Teletubbies would visit. I passed through three stoplights, made a left, and parked the car.

The secretary at the administration building wouldn't give me any information about what class Danny Jones was in, saying that was against the rules. But Colin had let it slip that on Thursdays Mr. Jones only put in a half day, so I was just going to find his car and wait by it. Not a difficult thing to do, since I had casually asked Colin what sort of car Danny Jones drove, and he'd told me he owned an old beat-up Chevette. They don't even make Chevettes anymore. It was probably his mother's old car, from when she was in college.

I drove up and down the lanes until I found a white Chevette, decorated with an unbelievable amount of both rust and bumper stickers. The stickers held eloquent phrases: MEAN PEOPLE SUCK; MY OTHER CAR IS A BMW; and, my favorite, JESUS IS COMING. LOOK BUSY. There were several other bumper stickers pertaining to bands that I had only a peripheral knowledge of. In other words, I knew they existed, but I wouldn't know their music if I heard it: Insane Clown Posse, Limp Bizkit, and Alien Ant Farm. Maybe he wasn't so levelheaded after all.

I got out of my car and circled his, peeking in the windows for no other reason than that I'm nosy. You find out a lot about a person by what the inside of his car looks like. With mine, you know I have kids, because of the car seat, the forty-odd Barbie shoes—none of which match, by the way—and the mess of school papers. One could tell I had a dog, too, by the nose smudges on the passenger-side window. I know, it's terrible, but I guess my car-cleaning fairies are always on strike.

What Danny Jones's car said to me was that he was

young, single, and considered himself hip and cool—and that he used his car as a laundry basket. The guitar picks in the little coin holder told me he was a musician, and a serious one, too, judging by the *Rolling Stone* and *Guitar* magazines and the catalog for Danelectro that I found on his passenger seat. He preferred Taco Bell to McDonald's, but he had a definite thing for shakes from Steak-n-Shake. I learned all that just from peeking into his car windows.

Mardi Gras beads hung from the rearview mirror. Studying his dash, I saw old parking stubs for concert events, a melted, half-eaten Snickers bar, and lots of dust bunnies.

"It's not for sale," a voice said.

I jumped and squealed.

When my heart had calmed down enough that I didn't feel as if it were going to run away, I managed a smile. "Mr. Jones, you scared the bejesus out of me."

"I see that," he said. "You down here just scoping out the shittiest cars in the parking lot, or did you want something with me in particular?"

I took a deep breath and swallowed. "I, uh…I came by to speak to you."

"What about?"

"Mr. Ketchum said some fairly unusual things about Jacob Lahrs, and I just wanted a second opinion."

"What do you care?"

"Uh…Collette. My friend Collette is doing a story, and I told her I'd help her out by doing some interviews. We just want to profile what type of person Jacob Lahrs was." That sounded good, I thought.

"Professor Lahrs was great," he said, setting his books on the hood of his car. "He was my favorite teacher."

"Mr. Ketchum said something about Jacob having a substance-abuse problem."

Danny smiled and fished around in his huge pockets, which were situated on the sides of pants that were two sizes too large. He found his keys and held them in his hand. "Professor Lahrs loved to party. He liked to drink. But I never saw him drunk in class or under the influence of anything harsher than alcohol."

"Why do you think Mr. Ketchum would say otherwise?"

Danny looked around the parking lot, his dark eyes landing on nothing in particular. He shrugged then. "I think...I think Mr. Ketchum was jealous."

"Of Jacob Lahrs?" I asked. "Why?"

"He's an old fart, you know. He is in his forties, and here Professor Lahrs had this really cool thing that was gonna get him out of the community college before he turned thirty, and Mr. Ketchum would still be here."

"What's so bad about teaching at a junior college?" I asked, ignoring the "old fart" comment about a man in his forties. I mean, I'm not forty yet, but it isn't too far off.

"Nothing's wrong with it," Danny said. "But if you want to be something else and this is what you're settling for, it can be a bitter pill."

I said nothing, so he went on.

"Being president would suck if you wanted to be king," he said.

"In other words, having to settle was the problem."

"Exactly. From what I understand, they both had settled for something they didn't want. Only Jacob was getting ready to do something about it."

"How much do you know about what they were working on?"

"All three of us were working on the same thing," he said, correcting me. "I get the feeling you know what it was."

"It wasn't how the wreck happened, was it? Were you guys going to blow the lid off of the Huntleigh mystery and retire on your laurels?"

Danny Jones looked at his feet. "Yeah, well. That's all

over now,'' he said, grabbing his books off the hood of the car.

"Why?"

"Because we still don't know where the diamonds are. Jacob had an idea of where they were, but evidently it was a semipublic place and he couldn't just go and get them without some hard evidence.''

He unlocked his car door then, but I stopped him. "Wait," I said. My head was spinning. Jacob Lahrs didn't know where the diamonds were? What did he mean by that? That could only mean one thing. That William Wade had never retrieved the diamonds. They really had been missing all this time, and they still were.

"I have to get to work, Mrs. O'Shea," he said.

"Of course, the letter mentioned about them not having to worry about the future. He was going back for the diamonds, but he died before he could.''

"Mrs. O'Shea?" Danny asked, a puzzled look crossing his face.

I hadn't realized I had been speaking out loud.

"Just one more question," I asked, ignoring him. "What were you guys celebrating that night at the Corner Bar?"

He hesitated a moment. "On a dive, Jacob found the case the diamonds were supposed to have been in. The case was shut but not locked. They were all gone. Not one single diamond left in a closed case. It confirmed to Jacob that somebody had taken the diamonds off the boat before the wreck.''

I thought about that a moment as Danny Jones opened his car door. It was clear that he thought I knew more than I did, so I just played along.

"That's it? That's what the celebration was about?"

"More or less," he said. "He'd also found a few personal items that had belonged to his great-grandparents.''

"Eli Thibeau and Jessica Huntleigh.''

An admiring smile crossed his face. "The rumors about you are true," he said. "Jacob said more than once that if you weren't so anal, he'd bring you on board."

"'Anal'?" I asked. "I am not anal."

"I have to go, Mrs. O'Shea."

"Sure," I said, thinking about what he'd said. "Hey, where do you work?"

"Camelot, the music store," he said.

"Where's that?"

"Wisteria," he replied.

"Have a good day," I said.

He shut the door, started the car, and pulled out of the parking lot. I got in my car, fairly satisfied with the way the interview had gone. Well, except for when he'd called me anal.

TWENTY-FOUR

LATER THAT EVENING, I was sitting at the kitchen table, peeling an orange and mulling over the things that Danny Jones had told me, when Rudy walked into the kitchen from the garage.

"Honey, do you think I'm anal-retentive?" I asked as Rudy got himself a glass of milk out of the refrigerator.

"You're entirely too much of a slob to be anal," he said without even thinking. He turned around and smiled at me.

"Jerk," I said, tossing an orange peel at him. "I'm being serious."

"So was I. Hey, don't hit me. Okay, maybe you are. I'm not sure how you want me to answer this question."

"Just tell me what you think," I said.

"Oh, so you want my opinion. I thought you wanted one of those 'Tell me what I want to hear or you're dead' type of answers. I didn't know you wanted a real answer." While he thought a moment, I was entertaining ways to mutilate his body without getting caught. Finally, he gave a big sigh. "All right. Do you realize that you buy a bag of ChexMix and eat only the corn Chex? And you buy a bag of Gardetto's and eat only the pretzels. You leave the rest of the stuff for us to eat. There's something wrong with that."

"Yeah, but that's not anal. That's neurotic."

"Can I quote you on that?" he asked.

I whizzed another orange peel at him. "Hey, hey, watch the milk," Rudy said.

He came over and sat down at the table with me, brave man that he was. His brown eyes were warm and caring, even if they were twinkling with mischief. It was amazing how a decade and a half of marriage had not diminished his cuteness. Okay, there were times I could throw more than an orange peel at him, and this might end up being one of them, but it was as if the cute things got cuter and the irritating things got more irritating. Which was good, because if there wasn't that balance, I'd probably have tossed him out the window by now.

"Why?" he asked.

"Why what?"

"Why do you ask if you're anal?"

I said nothing.

"What—did somebody say you were anal?" he asked.

"No," I said.

A smile broke across his face, causing those appealing little crinkles to form at the corners of his eyes. Of course, on women, those are considered crow's-feet, and not desired in the least. On men, they are quite attractive. Why does it seem as though Mother Nature has it in for women?

"You're lying," he said. "I can tell by the way the corner of your mouth twitched."

That's the other thing about being married for years— your spouse learns all of your secrets.

"Well, it doesn't matter what anybody else thinks," I said, although not really believing it. "Unless more than one person thinks it, and then there's power in numbers to consider."

"Well, let's see," Rudy said. He stole a slice of my orange and made an exaggerated expression of concentration. "No, I'd go more with OCD than with anal."

"Are you saying I'm obsessive-compulsive?"

"You check the stove three times before we leave the house."

"So? It might be on."

"But after you've checked it once, you know it's not on."

"But somebody could have accidentally bumped it," I said.

"Okay, you double-check all the seals on the food you get from the store."

"That's just common sense."

He gave me that "Get real" look. But I was holding my ground on this one.

"If I'm an hour late from anywhere, you're convinced I'm dead."

"Again that's neurotic, not obsessive-compulsive."

"All right, you check your food at the restaurant for spit from the cooks. You won't sit on a public toilet without putting down a paper cover; nor will you open the rest room door without a paper towel, because somebody else may have opened it without washing her hands!"

"That's just germ-conscious. With germs, you have to be on the offensive," I said.

He threw his head back and laughed. "Honey, you may not be anal, but you're not normal, either."

I pouted a little, my lower lip protruding.

"It's all right," Rudy said, smiling brilliantly. "You're my little neurotic, obsessive-compulsive, slightly anal-retentive angel."

I banged my head on the table. The phone rang, interrupting my thoroughly depressing conversation with Rudy. He answered it.

"Torie, it's Colin," he said.

I held my hand out for him to place the phone in it, not taking my head off the table. "What?" I asked.

"Well, hello to you, too," Colin said.

"Just get to the point," I said.

"Justin McKinney did see something that Sunday night," he said.

I sat up, noticing that I now had orange pulp in the bangs of my hair. "What did he see?"

"Well, actually, he heard something. He heard two guys fighting and then one of them calling out in pain. Then he turned on his bike and got out of there," he said.

"Did he hear what they were arguing about? Could he recognize the voices?" I asked.

"He heard one say something like 'You're not going to get all the credit.' And then the other said 'I worked my ass off on this project,' yada yada yada. Justin was pretty sure both were men's voices. So I think we can probably safely say that whoever killed Professor Lahrs was a male."

"Jeremiah Ketchum?" I asked.

"I'm going to check into who else was helping with the project, someone who maybe never made an appearance in New Kassel," the sheriff said.

"What do you mean?"

"Well, I immediately assumed that the argument was with Jeremiah Ketchum or Danny Jones, but thinking about it, I'm not sure," he said.

"Why?"

"Because their cars were at the Murdoch Inn through the whole ordeal. That still leaves the question of how they could have left the crime scene and gotten back into the Murdoch Inn by the time you found the body and I came around asking questions. Plus, they had fairly tight alibis," he said. "I'm not saying it's not either one of them, but I'm going to look into some other people who may have had a motive."

"Speaking of cars," I said.

"Yes? You going to tell me how your visit with Danny Jones went?" he asked.

"How did you know I went to see Danny Jones?" I asked.

"I'm not the sheriff for nothing, you know."

I thought about that a minute and had a vision of the sheriff following me around, snooping on me. Disturbing, to say the least.

"Uh…it went fine, but I learned something interesting."

"What?" he asked.

"Danny Jones's car is dirtier than mine," I said. Rudy gave me an exasperated look.

"Really?"

"Yeah," I said.

"What else?"

"Well, he really played down Jacob Lahrs's chemical dependency, and he claimed Jeremiah was just jealous. Oh, jeez, I almost forgot—the three of them found the diamond case in the wreckage, with the lid shut and the diamonds gone," I said.

"Which means what, exactly?"

"Well, at first I thought that William and Maria Wade had made off with the diamonds and lived happily ever after with them. But now I don't think so. I don't think William ever got a chance to get the diamonds, for whatever reason. Danny seemed to think that finding the case empty meant the diamonds made it off the boat and that Jacob knew where they were hidden, but because it was a fairly public place, he couldn't just go and get them."

"What do you think?" he asked.

I looked over at Rudy and shrugged. "It's possible," I said. "Was there anything in any of the documents that Jeremiah had that gave away the secret location?"

"Not that I could determine," he said.

"By the way, how's the ex-wife thing coming? You know, you mentioned that Jacob had an ex-wife."

"Haven't had time to talk with her."

"It might be important."

"Torie, I'll get to her," he said. "I've been doing other things, like checking up on forensics and fighting the rest of the crime in Granite County."

"Okay, okay," I said. "Don't be so crabby."

"We'll see you guys tomorrow night."

"Huh? Oh yeah, dinner. Okay, see you then."

THE NEW KASSEL GAZETTE
The News You Might Miss
By
Eleanore Murdoch

The Meyersville Lions clobbered the New Kassel Kings in Tuesday night's varsity basketball game. Father Bingham would like for me to express how it's not very sportsmanlike for the parents to throw chairs at the referee.

Still no fairies have been returned to Tobias's garden. He warns that whoever the culprit is, warts will begin to grow on your face, and your hair will fall out. I'd return them if I were you.

Arthur Burgermeister has reported that he and his wife, Carol, had a baby boy last night. Nine pounds, four ounces. The bouncing, bawling boy is bald and carries the name of Junior. This is the couple's second baby, first boy.

And I want to thank all of you upstanding New Kassel citizens who have been calling our reporter friends to task on their manners. Fraulein reports the incidence of flatulence has greatly diminished.

Until Next Time,
Eleanore

TWENTY-FIVE

THE NEXT DAY, I was on my way to work at the Gaheimer House when I saw Kyle, the Channel 6 cameraman, sitting on the curb of Jefferson Street. Why he'd chosen to sit in the snow, I'll never know, but then, why he never wore socks would probably remain a mystery to me, as well. I thought about asking him, although it really wasn't any of my business. But then, when has that ever stopped me?

"Don't you own any socks?" I asked.

Kyle turned around and saw me standing above him.

"I hate socks," he said. "My mother said she could never keep them on me, either."

He stood up and glanced around, looking sort of embarrassed. His shoulder-length hair was scraggly. I like long hair on guys, as long as it is clean and pretty. Kyle's was not pretty. It looked as though he hadn't shaved in a few days, either. He wore his Kurt Warner jersey with great pride, though. Not so much as a smudge anywhere on it.

"Your butt's wet," I said.

He gave me a blank expression.

"From sitting in the snow," I added.

"Oh," he said, and wiped at his derriere.

"You want to come in for a minute? It's warmer than sitting on the sidewalk." I gestured to the Gaheimer House, which he looked at in a curious manner. "I work here."

"Oh," he said. "No, I'm just waiting for Bradley."

"For what?"

"There's some footage he wants me to shoot."

"Oh yeah? Where?"

"Out at some cemetery."

The hair pricked on my neck. "What cemetery?"

He shrugged. "Out in the country somewhere."

"Do you have to cross a covered bridge to get there?" I asked.

"Don't know, haven't been there before."

"Is it Lutheran?"

"Yeah," he said, snapping his fingers. "That's it."

I nodded my head knowingly. "You sure you don't want to come in and wait? I can get you some coffee. Tea?"

"No," he said. "Thanks anyway."

Sheriff Brooke pulled up to the curb at that moment, and Kyle looked around nervously. A flight-or-fight expression played across his face, and for some reason, I found that funny. I waved to Colin as he got out of the car. He glowered at Kyle, who shrank back, as the sheriff had intended for him to do. I remembered that glower. And I remembered how it used to work on me.

"What's up?" I asked as he headed toward me.

"You got a VCR in there?" he asked, pointing to the Gaheimer House.

"Mmm, maybe. Come on in," I said.

We left Kyle standing on the side of the curb with a wet butt and no socks, waiting for Bradley Chapel to arrive. Colin and I walked through the parlor and then down the hallway to my office. After taking my coat off, I set my purse on my desk and booted up my computer. "Want something to drink?"

"Coffee," he said. He sat down and I went out to get it.

Sylvia was standing in the kitchen, taking a pie of some sort out of the oven. "Good morning, Victory," she said in the most noncheery fashion she could muster. Her salutations are always gruff and sound like required statements.

I poured Colin his coffee and set the pot back on the stove. "Do we have a VCR here?"

She gave me a rueful expression, and I almost wished I hadn't asked. "What would I need a VCR for?"

"I just asked, Sylvia."

"I think there is one out in the shed," she said.

I stopped by the soda machine and got a Dr Pepper. Entering my office, I said, "Sylvia says there is a VCR out in the shed. You can go get it if you want. But beware that the only television in the house is some thirty-year-old thing in the kitchen. I'm not sure if it will have the right hook-ups."

Taking a drink of the coffee I gave him, he handed me a videocassette and smiled. "I guess I'll go out to the shed."

While he was gone, I checked through the papers on my desk and then logged on to see if I had any e-mail. I had the usual requests from people looking for info on their ancestors, grandparents or great-grandparents who had lived here at one time. I saved them all to answer later, then went about reading the others.

There was an answer to an e-mail I had sent out earlier to the historical society in Arkansas. It read:

Dear Mrs. O'Shea,
In reply to your question about the diamonds and the Hills diamond mine: The mine has been defunct for close to twenty years or more. We checked the list of names that you gave us and found that Samuel Higgins mined close to forty pounds of uncut diamonds. The case he would have carried them in would indeed have been marked clearly "Hills Mine. Hills, Arkansas." And most likely, it would have been made of some sort of metal. So it looks as though Samuel Higgins was the one carrying the diamonds on board *The Phantom.* As to your other request, I am attaching a jpeg file,

which is a photograph of *The Phantom* when she was in port. However, I can't be sure that the photograph was taken on the same run when she sank. If I can be of further assistance, please let me know.

Carol Klein

I opened the file and up came a photograph of *The Phantom,* with the crew and passengers posing along the railings. She was definitely loaded flat, even if it wasn't the same run as the one when she sank. Maybe it was Eli Thibeau's habit to load her as full as he could.

I sat back and tapped my pen on my lip. My gaze landed on a sticky note on my telephone from Sylvia. It read: "Torie, do you have all the info together for the *Phantom* memorial?"

When would I have done all of that? Most of the things I wanted to say for the memorial plaque, I already knew. I even had a photograph of the boat, thanks to Carol Klein, showing what the steamer looked like before it sank. I thought about what Kyle had said out on the sidewalk—that they were going to go shoot some footage out at a cemetery. A Lutheran cemetery. He had to be talking about Granite Lutheran. And I supposed it made sense that Bradley Chapel would want footage of the tombstones of the seven dead passengers of *The Phantom.* If I were shooting a documentary or a spot for the news, I would want the tombstones as part of my footage.

I think he and Bradley Chapel have struck a bargain.

Those words sort of meandered in and out of my head without form at first. And then I remembered. I had sat in the booth across from Krista and we were talking about how Bradley and Jacob Lahrs had struck a bargain because Jacob was letting Bradley film his dive. What if Bradley had decided that he wanted the story of Jessica Huntleigh and Eli

Thibeau? He was probably smelling Pulitzer for breakfast, lunch, and dinner.

"I worked my ass off on this project"—that's what Justin had heard one of the men say the night Jacob Lahrs was murdered.

I logged off the Internet and stared at my computer screen for a moment. I flipped through my Rolodex and found the number for Baxter Monument Company. They were the closest and largest monument company in Granite County. What's more, they were family-owned and had been in business since 1901. I dialed and waited for somebody to answer, tapping my pen on the edge of my desk the whole time.

Tom Baxter answered the phone. "Baxter Monument."

"Tom, this is Torie O'Shea over in New Kassel," I said.

"Yeah, hi, Mrs. O'Shea. What can I do for you?"

Tom knew who I was. I'd called him many times to ask for his assistance. "I need you to check and see if you guys made the tombstones for the seven unidentified bodies of *The Phantom* wreck in 1919."

"Well, it may take a minute, since they were unidentified. I'll have to check by year," he said.

"It happened in January, so it should be at the very beginning," I said.

"You know, I think we did do them. For some reason, I think I remember my grandpa talking about it. Let me check, though."

"Thanks."

While I was waiting, Colin came in and motioned for me to come to the kitchen. He must have found the VCR and actually gotten it hooked up. I handed the tape back that he'd given me earlier. "Hang on just a second," I said to him.

He nodded and went back to the kitchen. In a moment,

Tom Baxter came back on the phone. "Yeah, Mrs. O'Shea. We sure did do the tombstones."

Normally, monument companys have information like next of kin, surviving family, that sort of thing. Not all monument companies keep records like this, but a lot do. In fact, such records often contain the name of the funeral home and the cemetery, and sometimes even a clipped obituary. I had found the names of all of one of my ancestor's brothers and sisters that way. And once I had found the burial place for another ancestor, someone I'd looked for high and low. Turned out he'd been buried in the next county over. Funeral home and monument records are a great, albeit often overlooked, source of genealogical information.

But in the case of the seven unidentified bodies of *The Phantom,* I wanted to know only one thing. "I'm doing a memorial for *The Phantom,* and I'm trying to come up with different tidbits of information. You know, how it affected the town, et cetera, and I was just wondering who paid for the tombstones." I said to Tom.

"Uh...William Wade."

I almost choked on the cap to my pen. "D-did you say William Wade?"

"Yeah, William Wade. And he picked them up," Tom added quickly.

"What do you mean?"

"Well, the records indicate that he picked them up. So I'm assuming he placed the stones on the graves himself. Not an unusual thing to do back then. Especially since these particular tombstones were made out of limestone and pretty lightweight."

I knew exactly what he meant. Those old limestone monuments all but melted in the elements. Nowadays, the stones are far too heavy for the average person just to pick up and place on a grave without any help.

"Thank you, Tom," I said. "Thank you very much."

I hung up the phone and wandered in a daze into the kitchen, where Colin was waiting for me. He took one look at me and could tell I'd just made an amazing discovery.

"What?"

"It can wait. Show me what you've got."

"You look like…well, you look like you've just been hit with a brick," he said. "Are you sure it can wait?"

"Yes, but not for long, so show me what you've got."

"Well, it's more like what I don't have," he said. He pushed the play button and footage of the Murdoch Inn came on. "This was taken by Kyle, Bradley Chapel's cameraman, the night of the murder. You'll notice the Murdoch Inn and its parking lot."

"Yeah," I said.

"This is Jeremiah Ketchum's car," he said. "That's Danny Jones's car, and this is the Channel 6 van. They are all present and accounted for. Now, if you'll notice the snow—"

"What about it?"

"There's the same amount on all of the vehicles," he said, stopping the tape and then rewinding it. "Meaning all three of those vehicles had been in the same place since the snow began. Which was about four that afternoon. Maybe four-thirty."

"What's that mean?"

"It means that if any of those three men killed Jacob Lahrs, he managed to get away from the crime scene and find a way back to the Murdoch Inn, undetected, without using his own vehicle," he said.

He let the tape continue to roll, and I saw all the commotion as Elmer and Collette tried to pull me up the bank of the river. I could just see the top of my head bobbing up over the snow-covered embankment, and then I'd slip back down. I saw Collette get behind me finally and push, and I was up. It was weird watching myself on video footage. It was one thing to be filmed when you knew about it, but it was strange watching footage of myself that I hadn't known was being shot. It was almost like having an out-of-body experience.

"Now, what news did you have?" he asked.

"Wait a minute," I said. "What about that ticket? If the cars were there all day, then how did Jeremiah Ketchum get a ticket on that day?"

"Good question," he said. "I'll check first thing when I get back to the office and see what Duran came up with on the ticket. Now, what did you find out?"

"Well, Kyle mentioned this morning that he and Bradley Chapel were headed out to the cemetery to film the tombstones. Then just now, I was poking around, trying to find different tidbits of information about the wreck and how it affected the town. And I just wondered who had paid for the tombstones of the victims. So, I called the monument company and asked."

"And? Torie, what did you find out?"

"Well, I had expected it to be one of the richer patrons in town—you know, like Mr. Gaheimer, or maybe a charity organization like one of the Rotary clubs or something."

"Torie. What did you find?" he asked again, exasperated.

"I think I know where the diamonds are hidden."

He dropped the remote control for the VCR. *"What?"* he said, bending over to retrieve the remote.

"William Wade, also known as Eli Thibeau, paid for the seven monuments. Why would he do that?"

"Because he felt guilty, since he was the captain of the boat?"

I shook my head. "I don't doubt that was part of it. But he also picked them up and erected them himself. I think that's where he hid the diamonds. For whatever reason, we may never know, but I think that's where the diamonds are.''

Colin picked up his radio. "This is Brooke. Have a car meet me at Granite Lutheran Cemetery." With that, he headed down the hallway.

"Hey, wait," I said. "I'm coming with you."

"No, you're not."

"I'll stay in the car," I said.

"You're not going," he said, twirling around to face me.

"Look, I found the darn things."

"*If* they're there."

"Whatever, I found 'em, and I'm going."

Rolling his eyes, he motioned for me to follow him. "Okay, but if I so much as see one hair on your head outside of that car, I'll throw you in jail."

"No big deal," I said. "You've done that twice already."

"Fine, then this time I'll just shoot you."

TWENTY-SIX

RIDING IN the front seat of the sheriff's official car was pretty cool. It was a lot like riding in a fire truck, this exotic place that is normally off-limits. "Ooohhh, what's this button for?"

"You touch that button and I'll break your finger."

I withdrew my finger quickly and looked around. "Is that gun loaded?"

"Of course it's loaded. You think the bad guys are going to let me take time to load it?"

"No, guess not."

Colin picked up the radio and contacted the other squad car headed out to the cemetery. "Yeah, Duran. Wait on the other side of the covered bridge for me to arrive. I don't want to interrupt Mr. Chapel if he's about to incriminate himself."

"'Incriminate himself'?" I asked.

"You said that Danny Jones and Jeremiah Ketchum didn't even know where the diamonds were, right?"

"Yeah?"

"So then if we get there and Bradley Chapel is hacking away at the tombstones and takes the diamonds, that's not going to look too good on his part, now is it? How would he know the diamonds were there if Danny Jones and Jeremiah Ketchum didn't even know?"

"You know, sometimes you're all right," I said.

"Like I need your approval."

"You do, whether you admit it or not," I said. "If I'm not happy, my mother's not happy, and if mother's not happy, then you won't be happy. It's simple family dynamics."

"There's the Channel 6 van," he said, ignoring me. He pointed beyond the covered bridge to the parking lot of the church. We pulled up along the road, a few feet before the turn to the covered bridge. Normally, we would have been able to pull all the way off the road, but the snow kept us from doing that. When the snowplows had gone through and cleared the roads, the snow naturally went to the sides, creating a three-foot-high wall. So we were sort of stopped in the middle of the road.

"You stay here," he said.

"Colin," I said, whining. "I can't even see the cemetery."

"My heart bleeds for you, Torie. Really it does." With that, he got out of the squad car and went to meet up with Deputy Duran. The two crossed the covered bridge on foot and then headed up the road toward the church. From where the squad car was situated, I could not see them as they wound around the front of the churchyard to reach the cemetery. Lord knew how long they were going to observe before moving in.

Colin had left the keys for me—in case of an emergency, I assumed. I thought a moment about turning the engine on so that I could listen to the radio. But I had a feeling this car was booby-trapped, and I just wasn't going to take the chance of turning on the sirens by accident and warning Bradley and Kyle that we were there. So I tapped my foot and hummed a song by Dido.

It seemed like twenty minutes had passed when Deputy Duran came walking back across the bridge and motioned for me to come. I got out of the car, half-afraid that this was a test and Colin was going to bark at me from behind a tree and carry me off to jail. But I got out anyway. "Colin says he wants you."

"Okay," I called to him.

Deputy Duran waited for me to get to the bridge and then walked alongside me. A few years older than I, Duran used to be the all-star quarterback for Meyersville High. Funny, Deputy Newsome used to play football, too. Anyway, Duran once belonged to a motorcycle club with Chuck, but he'd quit a few years back, after a really nasty accident left him with a broken leg and a hole in his skull.

"What did he find?"

"We waited behind the tree and watched, but all they were doing was filming video. Doesn't look like they were up to anything else," he said.

Just as we reached the cemetery, Earl Kloepper came walking from the church, his gray hair combed straight back. "What's going on, Deputy Duran?"

"Come on out to the cemetery, Earl. Colin's probably going to want to talk to you."

The three of us walked to where the sheriff, Bradley Chapel, and Kyle stood in front of the seven tombstones. "Earl," the sheriff said. "I need permission to do something."

"What's that?" Earl asked.

"I need to move these seven tombstones," he said. "But I promise if they are destroyed in the process, the Historical Society will pay for new ones. Right, Torie?"

"Right," I said, not knowing whether we would or not. Knowing Sylvia, though, she would pay for new ones. She may be an old biddy sometimes, but she's generous about things like this.

"Duran, go get a shovel."

Bradley Chapel peered at me with curious eyes. I nodded to him, and he nodded back. "Are you ever going to tell me what this is all about, Sheriff?" he asked.

"Kyle," I said. "You might want to start filming."

I took my cell phone out of my pocket and dialed Collette's work number. After three rings, she answered. "Hey, it's Torie. I know you probably can't get here in under an hour, but you need to come out to the cemetery at Granite Lutheran. Bring a camera."

"Hey!" Bradley said as I hung up the phone. "You can't do that. She can't do that!"

"I always thought journalism was a dog-eat-dog world, Mr. Chapel. The way I see it, Collette did a lot of footwork on this. She deserves a good story, too," I said.

He punched the sky with his fist and made a very unhappy sound.

"So, Mr. Chapel, how much did Jacob Lahrs tell you, anyway?" I asked.

"I don't have to answer your questions," Mr. Chapel said.

"Answer her," Colin said.

"I don't have to answer yours, either. I want my lawyer."

"Fine. Kyle, stop filming," the sheriff said. "Go on home, both of you."

"No, no, wait," Bradley said, flailing his hands all about.

Deputy Duran, out of breath, came back then with a shovel. He handed it to Sheriff Brooke, who waited until Bradley Chapel began to talk.

"Jacob told me that he was onto something big. That he could solve the mystery of the diamonds and the Huntleigh heiress all in one fell swoop. He agreed that if I filmed for him, he would give Kyle and me credit on the documentary he wanted to make," he said.

"Meaning you'd give up exclusive rights to the story?" Deputy Duran asked.

"It wouldn't do much good if I had only half the story," Bradley admitted.

"I thought Danny Jones was documenting," I said.

"He was," Bradley said. "But he didn't have access to our good equipment, nor had he had the years of experience that Kyle has. So Jacob asked if we'd film."

"You wanted the story for yourself," I said.

"Of course I wanted the story for myself. What self-respecting journalist wouldn't? I'd probably get a book deal out of it," he said.

Duran, Colin, and I just stared at him.

"Hey, no. I know what you're thinking. I did not kill Jacob Lahrs. I wouldn't do that, man. I hate blood."

"It was dark," I said. "You wouldn't have seen any."

"Look. After I heard he was dead, I did plan on going on with the story. I am guilty of trying to steal his documents from Jeremiah Ketchum," he said. "But nothing else. The race is on, Sheriff Brooke. You have to understand. Now that Jacob is dead, it's down to me and Jeremiah. Whichever one discovers the truth and turns it in first wins. There's no place for seconds in journalism."

"You're in third," I said. "Collette and I already know the secret. We did it the old-fashioned way. Not by stealing somebody else's work, but by going to that good old institution known as the public library."

"What are you talking about?" he asked.

"Colin," I said, and nodded.

Colin took the shovel and wedged it underneath the edge of the first tombstone. With very little trouble, he pulled out the part of the stone that was in the frozen ground. He had only dug down about a foot when he found something. In the dirt was a burlap bag. My gaze met Colin's and anticipation crackled in the air. Even Kyle knew something was up, for he concentrated his camera lens on the burlap bag, moving around me to get a better view. Colin picked it up and unrolled it. Then he dumped part of the contents out into his hand. A mound of uncut diamonds piled up in his palm.

Nobody said anything at first. We all just sort of held our breath and blinked several times. Then Bradley Chapel broke the silence.

"I'll be a son of a bitch!" he yelled.

"Watch your language. You are on sacred ground," Earl snapped.

"Diamonds," I whispered.

"Well, the legend was true after all," Earl said.

Colin put the diamonds back in the bag and handed it to me. Then while he went to work on another stone, Duran started on the third one. All the way down the row they went, turning over one tombstone after another, until all seven revealed a burlap bag full of uncut diamonds underneath.

My head was spinning. It was true, all of it. This was definitive proof that William Wade had indeed been Eli Thibeau. There was nobody on board *The Phantom* named William Wade, so how would that person have the diamonds if he wasn't Eli Thibeau? And his wife, Maria Wade, Jessica Huntleigh, was the heiress whose body was never recovered from the wreckage. The heiress whose family mourned her loss by naming a hospital after her in New York and putting up a monument befitting a queen on the family property. She had simply become Maria Wade, wife of an ex-steamboat captain and businessman, and slipped into anonymity forever. I had to wonder, since Eli Thibeau/William Wade had died just three years after the wreck, if she had ever regretted her decision. Had she ever wanted to go crawling back to her family in New York? Would she have given up her identity and life of privilege if she had known her happiness as Mrs. William Wade would have been so short-lived?

If anybody had the answers to those questions, it would be Jacob Lahrs's grandmother.

"I don't understand," Bradley said. "How did the diamonds get here? Who put them there? And why?"

"That's for me to know and you to find out," I said.

Colin laughed a little, but he quickly tried to conceal it. Bradley Chapel looked as if he'd just swallowed a jawbreaker whole. Well, that was what he got for being so snotty to me at Fraulein Krista's.

"Should we put the tombstones back now?" Deputy Duran asked.

"No," I said. "I want Collette to get pictures."

Half an hour later, Bradley Chapel and his cameraman were sitting on the front steps of the church when Collette pulled up in her maroon sports car. She stepped out, dressed in a navy suit and matching pumps. An associate with some camera equipment got out on the passenger side. They walked up to the cemetery, and the first thing Collette said when she reached me was, "This better be good, because I just got mud all over my pumps."

I handed her a burlap bag, which she opened, then looked inside. She reached in and pulled out a handful of diamonds. Her head snapped up and she looked at me. "Th-the diamonds?"

"Yeah," I said, and pointed to the graves. "They were hidden beneath the tombstones."

"Oh shit," she said. "Oooh, guess I shouldn't cuss on church property. Sorry."

"Get pictures quickly," Colin said. "I want to get the tombstones back in place and get the diamonds into the evidence room."

Collette's photographer took still photographs of all of the graves and the seven bags of diamonds. Finally, he took a few shots of Collette and the people standing all around. Then Duran and Colin put the tombstones back upright, which the photographer got shots of, too.

"I don't think we damaged any of them," Colin said.

"Unbelievable," said Earl.

Collette looked at me quizzically.

"I'll explain later," I said.

"Man, I wish I had some pictures of the gravestones before you guys started digging," she said.

My gaze traveled to Bradley and Kyle, who were still sitting on the steps of the church, looking as if they had just lost their best friends. I guess that for a reporter, losing a story is the equivalent of losing a friend. I doubted seriously that they would be good-enough sports to share with Collette. Which was a shame. If they could collaborate, they would probably have a better story than Jeremiah Ketchum would have. Then I remembered the disposable camera that I had in the glove compartment of my car.

"Oh, I took some pictures out here the other day," I said.

"You did?" she asked.

"Yeah. They won't be the greatest quality in the world, since they were taken on one of those six-dollar disposable cameras," I said.

"That's all right," she said. "I'll take them."

"Want some lunch?" I asked her. "I'll explain everything then."

"Sure," she said, looking at her photographer, who nodded, indicating that lunch sounded good.

After putting the last tombstone back in place, Colin came and stood next to me. "You know, this still doesn't tell me who killed Jacob Lahrs."

"I know," I said. "Is Bradley Chapel off the suspect list?"

"Why? Just because he didn't know the diamonds were here? No, he's not off the list."

"You know what I'm thinking?" I asked.

"I never know what you're thinking, Torie. And I'm happy to keep it that way."

"I'm thinking that the other day when I was out here to

look at the graves…somebody else had just been here. If
that person knew the diamonds were here…''

"Yeah?"

"I'm wondering if that person is our killer."

TWENTY-SEVEN

DINNER AT my mother's house was the greatest thing in the whole world. I couldn't believe that we'd eaten like this every day when my mother lived with us. Today, she had prepared a Cajun fifteen-bean soup, which had, well, fifteen kinds of beans in it. I didn't even know there were fifteen kinds of beans in the world. Then the main course consisted of ribs, which Colin had barbecued. He's just like Rudy. A little snow or cold weather isn't enough to stop them from using the barbecue pit. Then there was some sort of home-made bread with cheese baked in, asparagus, tomatoes—which my mother must have paid a fortune for, good to-matoes being rare in January—and baked potatoes. Then for dessert, she hit us with buttermilk pie. If I were to go swim-ming in a lake today, I would sink all the way to the bottom.

"I'm so proud of you two," Mom said.

"Who?" I asked.

"You and Colin. You two went through the entire meal without talking shop. Not once," she said.

"We were too busy stuffing our faces," I said. "Give us time."

Mom doesn't believe in cleaning up the dishes right away. She likes to sit and visit with her company. Which is something I learned from her. Most of the time when I have company over, I do the cleaning after they've left. My mother's motto: Company does not pay for their meal by cleaning up.

"Have you seen Stephanie since Fraulein Krista's?" Mom asked.

"No," I said. "She did call and leave a message at the office on Tuesday. Said she wanted to make plans to get together."

"I know you told me all about her," she said. "But you haven't elaborated. Which is odd, to say the least. You always elaborate, even when I desperately want you not to." Everybody laughed, because it was true. "Do you think you guys will develop a relationship?"

I gave a moment's thought to that. Stephanie seemed like a sweet girl, and she wanted the same thing I had always wanted. Why shouldn't we continue to see each other? "Yeah, I think so."

"Yippee!" Mary squealed. "I can't wait to meet my new aunt."

"Oh, I meant to tell you," Rudy said. "She called yesterday, too. Said she really needed to speak with you."

Well, that news left a feeling of foreboding in my chest. I barely knew her. What would she "really" need to speak to me about? I thought about it a moment and then brushed it off. "Guess I'll have to call her tomorrow."

Matthew was still in his high chair, so I cleaned him up and then let him down to wreak havoc in Grandma's house. Colin excused himself and came back with his new fishing pole to show Rudy.

"Rachel," Mary said. "Can I listen to your CD player?"

"Oh, let me think," Rachel said in a sappy voice. Then she changed into Mr. Hyde in nothing flat. "No!"

"Rachel, you are the biggest snot," I said.

"What? She'll break it if I let her have it."

"All you had to say was no. You didn't have to be so hateful."

She rolled her eyes and stormed off to the living room,

where I heard the television click on. Mary finished the last of her milk and then smiled and said, "She's got PMS."

Everybody at the table whooped with laughter, while Mary just smiled, quite pleased with the reaction she got. I could hear Rachel in the living room, swearing that she was going to move to Canada as soon as she was eighteen.

"Go play," I said to Mary.

Colin and Rudy talked about their fishing poles and what sort of bait to use for what kind of fish. Of course I didn't understand why they didn't just use a worm. Worm equals fish. That's what I was always taught.

My mother and I pretended to hang on their every word, but finally I could take it no more. "You know you can go to the store and buy whatever kind of fish you want. Probably a lot cheaper than all the money you've got tied up in that equipment."

"Yeah," Rudy said. "And you could pay somebody to trace your family tree, rather than do it yourself."

"Okay, point taken," I said, laughing. Still, a worm and a hook would have worked just fine in my book.

A few more minutes went by and then, Colin couldn't hold it any longer. "If Jacob Lahrs's killer was at the cemetery the same day you were," he said, "why didn't he just take the diamonds then?"

I shrugged. "I don't know."

"Maybe there were people there," Mom said. "And he thought he'd get caught."

"Right," I said. "There were some cars in the parking lot when I pulled in. Earl was probably inside."

"So then why hasn't he gone back for them?" Colin asked.

Mom and I both shrugged.

"Maybe he hasn't had the chance. Maybe he's worried that the place is under surveillance," Mom said.

"Sure," I interjected. "Whoever it is has waited this

long, so maybe he figures he'll just wait until all the hoopla dies down and then he'll go get them."

"But he didn't plan on you finding them first," Mom said.

"Oh well," I said. "Those diamonds belong to somebody else anyway."

"Who?" Colin asked. "Have you found out who they belong to?"

"Uh-huh. I got an e-mail from the historical society down in Arkansas. Evidently, the Hills Mine kept a log of who mined what. One of the names matched one of the names on the passenger list of *The Phantom*," I said.

"Who was it?" Colin asked.

"A man named Samuel Higgins," I told him.

"Was he a survivor?"

"Unfortunately, no. His body was never recovered. This is purely speculation, but I can't help but wonder if when he realized the boat was going down, he went to get the diamonds and then drowned as a result."

"Very possible," Colin said. "After all, Billy Zane's character ran around the *Titanic* trying to shoot Leonardo DiCaprio as the ship was going down. I mean, I don't know about you, but if the ship was sinking, I wouldn't worry about anything but getting off the boat and making sure everybody I loved was off it, too."

"True. But people are stupid. And some people are greedy," I said.

"And some people are stupid and greedy," my mother chimed in.

"I think it's a ridiculous notion, too. But stranger things have happened," Rudy added.

"I'm going to see if this Samuel Higgins person had any children. I want to return the diamonds to the rightful family. If he didn't have any family at all," I said, "then I'm not sure what to do."

"Forensics came back with the footprint info from the Lahrs crime scene," Colin said. "It's just as I suspected. They can tell me the prints were probably a sneaker, probably size eleven or eleven and half, but they can't be more specific about the brand. Still, I've got warrants to find out which of our suspects has a big foot."

"Let's say Jeremiah Ketchum has a big foot. That doesn't mean he's the killer. Could just be coincidence that he and the killer have big feet," I said.

"I know," said Colin. "But it's something."

"If I were a murderer and I'd killed somebody in the snow, where I knew my footprints would be left," Rudy said, "I'd throw my shoes in the river as fast as I could. Then all the technology in the world couldn't connect my shoes to the scene, because I wouldn't have them anymore."

"Yeah, there's always that," Colin said. "*If* our killer thought of it."

"What about the footprints at the cemetery?" I asked.

"Should have those results back on Monday," he said. "There were a few things found at the crime scene, but you know Jeremiah Ketchum, Danny Jones, and Bradley Chapel were all down there around the wreckage so much, so who's to say these things weren't dropped at an earlier date? Forensics is having a field day trying to decipher what was there before and what was dropped the night of the murder. They have to determine each object's exact placement in the snow."

"What types of things did the CSU find?" I asked.

"Well, one of the things was a guitar pick."

"A guitar pick?" I asked.

"Yes," he said. "It was red and had an alien's face on it."

"You do know that Danny Jones is a musician," I said. "I saw guitar picks all over his car."

"When were you in his car?" my mother asked.

"I wasn't *in* his car," I said. "I was outside looking in."

"I'll make a note to ask forensics to bump that one up. If there's a print on it, and it had the right placement in the snow, we could have our killer."

"Well," I said, stretching. "I'm going to go visit Jacob Lahrs's grandmother."

"Why?" Colin asked.

"Torie," Rudy warned.

"I'm going with Collette. If she's going to do this story right, then she's going to need an interview with the family. Think about it. Jacob's grandmother is the only one who can really tell us about her mother, Jessica Huntleigh," I said. "I can't help but wonder if anybody else in the family knows what Jacob knew."

"Be careful," Mom said. "She may not know who her mother was, and you could greatly upset her."

"I know," I said. My mother always worries about me upsetting somebody. "But Collette's going with or without me, so I figure I should go along and judge the reactions."

"Oh, yeah," Colin said. "And manipulate the conversation, and snoop around, and—"

"Yeah? So?" I asked, my face flushing.

"At least she has the decency to blush," my mother said.

"Just be careful and call me the minute you get back. I want to know what you find out," Colin said.

"Okay," I agreed. Colin has learned that people often give different answers to certain questions, depending on whether or not you wear a badge. Sometimes he lets me question somebody in a casual sort of way, and then he'll go and interview them on his own. Then we compare notes. Quite often, the answers are different, or even just our impressions.

I'd venture to say that if pressed, and he had to answer honestly, he'd admit that I'm not such a bad stepdaughter after all.

TWENTY-EIGHT

COLLETTE DROVE a little too fast for my taste. But she does a lot of things too fast for my taste. I guess if one is going to own a little maroon sports car, one should drive it like a sports car and not like a station wagon.

The town of Pevely sits between Highway 61-67 and I-55. I remember when I-55 was built, back in the early seventies. I was a kid at the time and was quite impressed with its two lanes heading south and two lanes heading north, separated by a large grassy median. Once you get up to Arnold, it becomes eight lanes, four on each side. Then later, as a teenager, I realized that if I wanted to, I could take it all the way to Memphis. That made it the coolest of all highways to me.

Highway 61-67 has a different history altogether. It starts as Lemay Ferry Road up in St. Louis—four lanes, separated only by a yellow line. Then it becomes Jeffco Boulevard in Arnold, and in Festus, it is called Truman Boulevard. It takes a wide detour around Wisteria and continues on south as just Highway 61, and southwest as 67. It had originally been called "Cow Dung Alley," the path the farmers used to take to get their cattle and crops up to St. Louis. I'm not sure when, but at some point in time, somebody got the brilliant idea to pave it and give it a more appealing name. It had been the only way north and south along the Mississippi, until I-55 was built in the seventies.

Pevely, where Jacob Lahrs's grandmother lives, manages

to snuggle in between the two highways just perfectly. Although to get to her house, we had to go to the western outskirts of town—under the Highway 55 overpass and down Highway Z, which is no more than a two-lane country road.

"I've never understood why they call these kinds of roads highways," I said, gripping the armrest. Collette didn't slow down to any noticeable degree on this road, and it made me a wee bit nervous. There was no shoulder, no sidewalk, just two lanes of blacktop winding around sharp curves and up and over hills.

"I know," she said. "Whoever named them highways needs to be dropped into Los Angeles or Atlanta on a Monday, say around five or six in the evening. *Then* they'd know what a highway is."

I shivered at the thought of all of those cars in Los Angeles. And all of those people. None of whom would be more than a passing face to another driver. A nameless individual, whom you'd never see again, unless you happened to find yourselves in the same traffic jam. To have to live like that would be the equivalent of a prison sentence for me. Collette can say all she wants about my not getting out enough. She can say that I just want to stay in my "safe" walls of New Kassel until the sun comes up. It seems pretty clear to me that she's the one who's hiding. She is hiding in the crowds of people, where she can be the person she imagines she is, rather than the person she actually is.

"So, do you want to hear about the guy I met last week?" Collette said. She had the look of a satisfied cat.

"Does the *guy* have a name?" I asked.

"Steve," she said.

Steve. The last Steve she had gone out with was a professional hockey player. When she found out that his two front teeth were fake, she ran into the arms of…Clarence, the real estate broker. No missing teeth there.

"Okay…what about him?"

"Oh my God. We're talking arms of steel. Rippled abs, fast hands, beautiful eyes…"

"Sounds like Superman," I said.

"I hadn't thought of that," she replied. "But the analogy could work."

I couldn't help but laugh.

"He's a drummer."

"A drummer," I said, letting the word hang in the air as if it were a disease. I have nothing against drummers. I dated a drummer once. "What band?"

"The Bloody Virgins."

"Jesus, Collette," I said.

"What?"

"The Bloody Virgins? What kind of band is that?"

"Mmm, death metal, I think."

"You don't even like death metal."

"I didn't say I liked his music. I said I liked his arms and hands, and abs and eyes. And oh, a few other things, too!"

"How did you meet him?" I asked, afraid of what the answer would be.

"A bunch of us girls went out after work."

"And a death-metal band happened to be playing a happy-hour set?"

She laughed. "No, silly, our happy hour sort of went on until one in the morning. And we switched bars several times, too, and at the last one, there was Steve."

She spoke his name as if it were liquid butter. "Okay, wait," I said.

"What?"

"You can't go into your latest…endeavors right now. Although I'm sure they are worthy of a chapter in the *Kama Sutra.* Jacob Lahrs's grandmother lives on this next road up here," I said.

"Where?" she asked. "This one?"

"No, the one on the right."

She turned down the gravel road and looked at me as if I'd committed a cardinal sin. "You never said anything about a gravel road."

"So you'll have to wash your car," I said. "A small price to pay for a great story."

"Oh, I totally agree," she said. "I just…I dunno."

"Did you forget that there are gravel roads still in existence?" I asked.

"Yeah, I guess so."

"Right here," I said, pointing to the house on the left. Well, it was the only house that was visible, except for one way down on the right. The house was a large two-story affair with a wide front porch. Empty flower buckets hung from the porch at three- or four-foot intervals, waiting for spring, when Tamara Wade Lahrs might plant petunias or pansies in them. A bird house and bird feeder were off to the right, situated close to a large cedar tree. Across the gravel road were several cows, contained by a barbed-wire fence.

I braced myself as we got out of the car, because I knew what was coming. Collette took her sunglasses off and looked across the road. "Cows?" she said. "Cows!"

"Yes," I said. "Otherwise known as cattle. You know, where milk comes from. Or did you think it came from the store?"

She shot me a look that said I'd better shut up or I'd be dead.

"The world is not covered in concrete, Collette."

"Yeah, well, it should be," she said.

I couldn't help but laugh at her. We walked up to the front porch and looked around for a doorbell. I found none, so I opened the storm door and knocked. An eighty-year-old woman answered the door. I knew her age because of

the census records we'd found at the library. She wore her
gray hair cut short. Her snappy hairdo gave her the appearance of a woman much younger.

"Yes?" she asked.

"Hello, Mrs. Lahrs. My name is Torie, and this is Collette. We'd like to talk to you about your grandson, Jacob."

The expression on her face went from politeness to sor-
row at the mere mention of his name. "I don't want to talk
about it," she said.

"Mrs. Lahrs, I live in New Kassel. I spoke with your
grandson just the day before he was killed," I said. "We
want to know who killed him as much as you."

"Are you the police?" she asked.

"My stepfather is the sheriff," I said. "I work for the
Historical Society, and sometimes I assist him on cases that
involve a historical aspect."

Her gaze darted from my face to Collette's, then back to
mine. Clearly, she was unsure what to do. "I don't think I
can help you."

"Mrs. Lahrs," I said. "I know what your grandson was
working on."

"What he was *really* working on," Collette added.

Mrs. Lahrs's gray eyes narrowed a bit.

"May we come in?" I asked.

"For a few minutes, I suppose," she said, and moved to
let us pass.

The living room was spacious. An old Kimball upright
piano stood in the corner, almost like the one I owned. The
furniture was probably twenty years old, but it showed no
obvious wear. Brown-and-blue plaid upholstery added a
warm color to a room otherwise devoid of it. Cream-colored
carpet, white walls, and white lace curtains surrounded us.
I took a seat next to Collette on the couch and Mrs. Lahrs
sat in a neighboring chair.

"I don't know what you think I can tell you," she said. "Jacob was a spirited child. Very special."

"How many grandchildren do you have?" I asked.

"Thirteen," she said, smiling. It had been her most unguarded moment so far.

"Mrs. Lahrs," Collette began. "What did Jacob tell you about his work?"

"He was a teacher at the college," she answered.

"No, I mean, his extracurricular work. The project he was working on in New Kassel," said Collette, clarifying her question.

"It had something to do with…the wreck of that steamer," she answered.

"Your grandson's associate told me that the captain of the steamer was Jacob's great-grandfather," I said. A dark expression played across Tamara Lahrs's face. "And Jacob didn't seem upset that I knew. I suppose Eli Thibeau could have had children before he died, and therefore Jacob could have been descended from one of them. But Eli Thibeau did not have any children before he died. He did what most men can't do: He had them after he died. In other words, he had them once he became William Wade. Now, Jacob knew that this information was a matter of public record. He knew all I had to do was go and look at the census records and I could find out the truth."

I remembered Danny Jones's words: *Jacob said more than once that if you weren't so anal, he'd bring you aboard.*

Collette and Mrs. Lahrs looked at me, waiting for my next words.

"I think he wanted me to know. I think a part of him wanted me on board his project. And if he had lived long enough, he might have actually asked for my assistance."

She was quiet a moment. I had no idea if any of what I'd just said was true. There was no way I would ever know if

Jacob had given me that piece of information for a reason. It was pure speculation. But I'd felt on more than one occasion that it seemed odd for him to have told me that Eli Thibeau was his great-grandfather, knowing I could find out the truth. If it helped Tamara Lahrs open up to us, it was worth the slight deception.

Tamara stood and went to the bookcase behind her. She pulled out a photo album and opened it. "This was my mother. You can tell by the photograph that she was Jessica Huntleigh," she said.

Collette nearly jumped into my lap to get a better look. Tamara handed me the album, pointing to a good-quality studio portrait, probably taken in the late twenties. It was Jessica Huntleigh all right. "Oh my Lord," I said.

There were other pictures of Jessica through the years, with her two children and without them. Some of them were taken from a distance or with poor lighting, so it was difficult to see the resemblance. But there was no denying the studio picture. I wondered if she'd had the picture taken as some sort of private declaration.

"She is buried at Shepherd of the Hills, off of old Highway M, under the name Maria Wade," she said.

"It's all true," Collette said to me. "Everything we suspected."

Tamara Lahrs looked at me questioningly. "We did quite a bit of research before coming here. We had our suspicions about Jessica Huntleigh," I said. "Did your mother ever try to contact her family once Eli died?"

Tamara nodded her head. "During the Depression. When things got so bad, she felt she had no choice but to try to contact them. She did it for me and my brother. She thought…they could help out—financially."

"And what happened?" I asked.

"At first, they didn't believe it was really her. After ten years, it was too much, even for her mother to believe. But she sent them photographs and told them things in letters that only she could have known. Her mother believed her, eventually. But there was no happy reunion.'' There was a sadness in Mrs. Lahrs's voice. ''Her mother told her that if she could help us, she would. Simply because Jessica was her daughter. But she told my mother that if the reasons were true about why she had faked her death, the family could never fully welcome her back. She would disgrace them all. Not that it mattered.''

''Why not?'' I asked.

''Evidently, by that point, her father had lost most everything in the stock market crash of 1929. He still had his land, but nobody was buying. Her family could not help her,'' she said.

''But...aren't the Huntleighs a wealthy family now?''

''Yes,'' she said. ''The family moved to Europe, where they had a chateau and land and a house full of antiques and gold. My grandfather was a shrewd man. He found a way to rebuild his empire. And then they came back to the States.''

''That must have been so devastating to your mother,'' I said.

''She killed herself,'' Tamara said, as calmly as if she were noting the weather outside.

''She what?'' I asked.

''After my brother and I were safely married, she locked herself in her room and just stopped living. She willed herself to die.''

''Oh, Mrs. Lahrs,'' I said. ''She was probably ill and just never told you.''

''No,'' Tamara said. ''She went to bed and only got up to go to the bathroom and answer the door. She stopped eating. It took her two months to die.''

My mother's words came back to haunt me: *and you could greatly upset her.* I firmly believe we never give our mothers enough credit. How often do we just dismiss what they say, only to find out that they know what they're talking about? I wondered then if my children would ever discover how brilliant I am.

"Mrs. Lahrs, I am so sorry," I said. "I didn't know."

"My mother led a life more tragic than a Shakespearean character," she said.

Wealthy girl gives up everything to be with the man she loves, penniless steamboat captain, who dies, leaving her destitute. Then her family refuses to help her, and she wills herself to die. Yup, tragedy on the grandest scale.

"When did you discover the truth?" Collette asked.

"During the Depression, Mother told me that her family had lots of money. I had asked my mother on several occasions how come we didn't have any grandparents. She told me that my father's parents were dead, and that hers lived far away and didn't speak to her anymore. But she never once hinted that her parents were the Huntleighs," she said. "I didn't find out they were the Huntleighs until after she was dead."

"How did you find out?" I asked.

"The same way you did," she replied, leaning back in her chair. "After she was dead, I suddenly wanted to know everything about her. Funny how I didn't think to ask what school she'd attended. What her mother's maiden name was. Just didn't seem important until I couldn't ask it."

"I've heard that more than once from my clients," I said.

"I started going through Mom's papers and such. She had no birth certificate. No diploma. Nothing prior to her marriage to my father. Then I noticed the same thing about my father. There was nothing. No photographs of either of them before 1919, no papers, nothing. Of course, the 1910 census wasn't available to see back then, so I couldn't check their whereabouts. I'm not even sure it would have occurred to me then anyway."

"How did you find out, then?" I asked.

"Well, what my mother did have were newspaper cuttings about this family in New York, the Huntleighs. Tamara and Chester Huntleigh. She must have had four dozen clippings, with pictures. I immediately thought that these must be the 'wealthy' parents she had spoken of. And the resemblance between my mother and my grandmother was profound. And of course the name—Tamara," she added.

Collette and I exchanged wondrous glances.

"It was enough for me," she said. "So I began researching what had happened to Jessica Huntleigh. One of the papers had an article about the sinking of *The Phantom*, and showed a photograph of the Huntleigh heiress. It was my mother."

"So when did you realize that Eli Thibeau was really your father? That he had become William Wade?" I asked.

"I didn't. It was my grandson Jacob who figured that out. I had no clue why my mother had chosen to walk away from her life of comfort," she said. "She had quite a few letters from my father, William Wade. And he spoke of certain things in them, like 'the diamonds' and 'the wreck.' A place called New Kassel. But he never once hinted in those letters that he'd been on board the ship, too. Only once did he mention that he had been the captain of a boat that had already sunk."

"So how did Jacob figure it out?" I asked. "Did you tell him you thought your mother and Jessica Huntleigh were the same person?"

"Not at first," she said. "He started asking questions about our family history for a school project he had to do. He was about eighteen at the time. So I did the usual thing. I was elusive and tried to fend off his questions by saying things like 'What do you want to know that stuff for?' Then I realized I was doing exactly what my mother had done to me. I was keeping his history from him. So I finally told him what I suspected. I'd never told anybody else, though.''

''What was his reaction?'' Collette asked. We both had been hanging on every word she said. Her story was so sad, so tragic, we couldn't help it.

''He became obsessed. He asked for all the research I had, which wasn't much. He wanted all the documents pertaining to my parents, and then he went about trying to prove that Maria Wade was Jessica Huntleigh.''

She looked out the window a moment, as if everything was playing before her eyes in the here and now.

''Jacob began researching *The Phantom*,'' she said. ''He found a photograph of the captain, Eli Thibeau, and noticed a marked resemblance to the few photographs I had of my father, William Wade. He was convinced they were one and the same.''

I knew what came next. ''By this point, the census records were available for 1910 and 1920,'' I said.

''Jacob realized that William Wade didn't exist before the 1920 census,'' she said. ''It all fell into place.''

''But what about the diamonds?'' I asked. ''I know that in one letter your father wrote to your mother, he mentioned that they didn't have to worry about the future. I'm assuming now that he meant the diamonds, but when I first read the letter, I wasn't sure. Why did your father have to hide them? Why didn't he and Jessica take them with them when the steamboat sank?''

''What Jacob gleaned from the personal letters was that my father and mother couldn't carry the diamonds with them because they were very bulky. And they were afraid that if they were stopped and the diamonds were found on them, it would all blow up in their faces. So they buried them. But when Dad went back to get them, there was an investigator looking for the diamonds, as well. So Dad was going to go back for them after everything had cooled down.

Only he died without ever having a chance to get back home and tell my mother where they were,'' Tamara said.

''That's terrible,'' Collette said.

If I had had access to all of the documents and letters, I might have been able to figure that out days ago. But I had only gotten a peek at just that one letter. It all made sense now, though.

''So how did Jacob find out exactly where they were?'' I asked.

''I guess the same way you did,'' she replied.

I know the shock must have registered all the way to my toes. ''How do you know that I found the diamonds?''

''Channel 6 news had a tape of you and the Granite County sheriff uncovering the diamonds. You were there, too,'' she said, pointing at Collette.

''Oh, great,'' Collette said. ''He beat me to it.''

''Yeah, but he doesn't have the same info you do,'' I said. ''Don't panic.''

''What about Matilda O'Brien?'' I asked. ''She knew that your mother switched boats in Memphis to be with Eli, or William, or however you want to refer to him. She had to have known, because there was nothing wrong with the *Louisiana Purchase*. Why did she cover for your mother?''

''I called and asked her that about ten years ago, shortly before she died.''

''You did?'' Collette asked. I'll admit, I was equally surprised at the gutsy move.

''Well, at first she wouldn't speak to me because she didn't believe who I was. See, she, too, thought my mother had drowned when the steamboat sank. She saw no reason in soiling my mother's good name. The scandal would have been disastrous. So Matilda O'Brien never told anybody. She's the one that made up the story that the *Louisiana Purchase* had broken down. She had to come up with some reason why the two of them had switched boats.''

Collette rubbed her forehead and took a deep breath. "May I have a glass of water?" she asked.

"Of course," said Mrs. Lahrs.

"So how did your father die?" I asked her as she stood up.

"He was still a steamboat captain at that point, although he was going by the name William Wade. I think somebody recognized him. One of the deckhands said that there was a struggle and that my father fell into the paddle wheel."

What could I say to that? I mumbled a completely inadequate "Sorry," then looked around the room like an idiot. "While you're getting her a drink, I'd like to use your bathroom. Is that all right?"

"Sure, it's down the hall to the right."

I handed Collette the photo album that I'd been clutching and headed down the long hallway to the bathroom. On the way back, I stopped to look at the photographs hanging on the wall. Tamara Lahrs didn't have an abundance of pictures, but the few she had spoke a thousand words. Four eight-by-tens hung in a row in matching oak frames. The subject of each photograph was a family group, a mom, a dad, and various children. I guessed them to be the families of her four children. One child had six kids, two had three, and the first one had only one child. I studied them, trying to find a boy who resembled Jacob Lahrs. It looked as if he was in one of the middle groupings, and that he had two sisters. The eyes were the same.

Tamara Lahrs came to the end of the hallway and smiled. "My children," she said.

"Which one is Jacob?" I asked.

"That one," she said, pointing to the boy I had picked out. "He spent two years in the marines. His father had been in the service, so I think he felt pressured to join."

I smiled at her and then studied the other groupings. As I looked at the first photograph, a chill danced down my spine. It was the photograph of the family with the one child. A little girl.

"Who is that?" I managed to ask.

"That's my daughter by my first husband," she said.

"Your first husband," I snapped. My mind reeled. What was his name? I knew it. It was on the tip of my tongue. The bomber pilot who had died in the war. I had forgotten all about him. "Thatcher. Robert Thatcher."

She looked taken aback at first. "How did you know that?" she asked.

"As I said before, we did a lot of research," I said. It's disturbing to some people just how easily and how much I can find out about their families without their help.

"Yes, that's my daughter Julia."

Mother: Julia Anne Thatcher.

My knees wobbled and I felt sick to my stomach. "And this?" I asked, pointing to the little girl in the picture. I knew who it was. I knew the face. I'd seen it just a week ago in a bunch of photographs.

"Oh, that's my granddaughter Stephanie," she said.

Stephanie Anne Webster Connelly.

Mother: Julia Anne Thatcher.

"Are you all right?" she asked.

"I've got to go," I said, heading back to the living room. "Collette, we need to go."

"But…"

"Thank you so much, Mrs. Lahrs, for talking with us," I said.

"You're quite welcome," she replied. "Are you sure you're all right?"

"I think I've got a touch of the flu," I said.

"Mrs. Lahrs," Collette said. "With the help of Torie's research, I'd like to go ahead and do the story that your grandson started. When I get to the point where I need photographs, would you be so kind as to let me copy yours?"

Tamara Lahrs shook her head, unsure of what to say. The whole time my stomach was burning and bubbling, to the point I thought I was going to hurl right there on the lady's pretty cream-colored carpet. "I don't know," she said finally.

"I'll dedicate the story to the memory of Jacob," she said.

"Collette—" I said. My face was red-hot.

"Just a minute," she snapped at me.

"As long as I get to read it first," Mrs. Lahrs said. "I get to approve it."

Collette weighed this and finally decided it was worth the trade. "All right," she said. "I'll let you read the story and approve it, and if I don't print what you read, you can sue me. In exchange for copy of photographs and documents."

"Okay, I suppose that would be all right."

"Thank you," Collette said.

As we stepped outside, I took a deep breath and felt the cold air hit my hot face. Collette grabbed me and kissed me on the cheek. "Whoo hoo! I got the story of a lifetime. I get to blow the lid off of the Huntleigh heiress! Soon to be known throughout America as 'the Huntleigh scandal.' I couldn't be happier. I don't even care that there are smelly, disgusting cows over there swishing their tails and crapping all over the place. The world is beautiful!" she said. "What the hell is the matter with you?"

"Get me home," I said.

"Sure thing. Torie, you look like you saw a dead person."

"No, did that once this month already."

"Torie, what's up?"

"My sister. Stephanie Connelly."

"Yeah, what about her?"

"She is Jacob Lahrs's cousin," I said.

"Yeah, so?" she said, getting in the car.

I sat in the front seat and stared straight ahead at the dashboard.

"Oh," she said. "You think she was involved somehow?"

"That's what I'm afraid of."

TWENTY-NINE

I SAT ON MY front porch, all six feet by six feet of it, staring out at the river and the dirty old snow. That's the downside of snow. Eventually, it turns brown. The sky was gray and heavy, as if it were about to fall. The weatherman had predicted more snow, which was fine with me. It would cover up the brown stuff, and then I could pretend that it would be white and beautiful forever and forget all about the layer of deflowered snow beneath it.

I could not, however, pretend it was a coincidence that Stephanie Connelly and Jacob Lahrs had come to New Kassel the same week. Every time I buried myself in some activity, thinking Stephanie was gone from my mind, a question would scream at me from some dark corner of my mind. Had Stephanie deliberately befriended me so that I would be more likely to help Jacob if he asked me to?

Well, she had another thing coming. Of course I suspected her of something. What, I don't know. But I knew there was something going on. I believed that. But how could she have known how my mind would work?

I hadn't slept all night. At some point, while Rudy snored and the furnace clicked on and off, the sun had come up and the chickens had begun to cluck. I don't think I had closed my eyes longer than a few seconds. Stephanie had called twice yesterday, and once last night. She had called again this morning, and all four times, I'd refused to speak to her.

It's not that I didn't want to speak to her. Oh, I wanted to speak to her all right, but I wasn't ready yet. Just in case there was some chance that this was pure coincidence, I wanted to make sure that I didn't say the wrong thing. And in order for that to happen, I needed to put some time between my discovery and a conversation with Stephanie.

But I never got that chance. Stephanie Connelly, my newly found sister, pulled her car in my driveway. She got out in a hurry and rushed up the sidewalk. "Torie, you have got to let me explain."

"Explain what?" I asked, cool as a cucumber. Okay, some might say I was flippant and distant. I preferred to think of it as cool.

The expression on her face was priceless, sort of a combination of confusion and relief. It didn't last long, though. "Well, if you don't already know, then now's the perfect time to tell you," she said.

"I'm listening."

"I am Jacob Lahrs's cousin," she said.

"Yes, I know."

"But you just—I'm confused," she said.

"So, tell me, Stephanie." I stood up. "Was it your idea or Jacob's idea to contact me?"

"It's not like that," she said.

"Then tell me what it *is* like," I replied, losing my patience.

"Jacob knew you were my sister, from the first time he ever stepped foot in this town," she said. "He and I were about the same age, and so we were always pretty close. At Christmas one year, he took me aside and told me everything he had discovered about our family. When he was finished, I told him that it was so ironic that my half sister lived in the very town where my great-grandfather's steamboat had sunk."

"To say the least," I said, crossing my arms.

"I saw it in a different light. I took it to mean that I was destined to meet you, that our paths would definitely cross," she said.

"You didn't have to have a great-grandfather wreck a steamboat and bury diamonds in a cemetery in my town to make our paths cross, Stephanie," I said. I turned to go inside. "All you had to do was show up."

"Just hear me out!"

Exasperated, I turned to face her. A part of me, the stubborn part that came from my father, made me just want to say, Forget it. Go away; leave me alone. No matter how sincere she was, no matter how much sense she made, no matter how much that little voice in the back of my head said to listen and believe, that streak of stubbornness ran through my blood and made me want to turn around and go in the house without another word. My dad got his stubbornness from his grandmother. He used to say that his grandma Keith was so mean and stubborn that she would raise hell and then stick a prop under it.

I don't know if I'm that bad. But right then, I was feeling none too charitable.

"A few years later, Jacob asked me if I was ever going to contact you. I told him I wanted to but that I hadn't gotten up enough nerve," she said. "I asked him why he wanted to know that, and he said because he thought you would be a great help to him. He had heard about how you assisted the sheriff sometimes, and, in general, knew of your reputation. He thought you could help him locate the diamonds."

I rolled my eyes. She knew about everything. Even the diamonds.

"But Jacob was pretty sure he knew where they were, without enlisting your help," she said. "Then the river got so low…"

"And then you decided to contact me," I said. "Why didn't you just tell me you were Jacob's cousin?"

"Because I thought you would think I was just doing it to help Jacob. You might have thought he wanted a favor or something, and I didn't want that. I wanted you to know that I wanted to meet you on my own, not because Jacob might need your help," she said. "So when he told me he was coming to New Kassel to dive through the wreckage, I knew I had to make my move."

"Why?"

"Because I was afraid you'd find out on your own that you had a sister. Jacob kept telling me that you would be able to make the connection if given the right information. And I just didn't want you to find out about me that way," she said.

I stood there looking at her, trying to judge if she was telling the truth or not. We must have been ten feet apart from each other during the entire conversation, me on the porch and she on the sidewalk. It started to snow then, and I couldn't help but laugh. I love snow. So does Stephanie. I wondered if this was some sort of otherworldly sign for me to trust and believe her. Okay, it might be corny, but that's what I felt.

"I swear to you, Torie. Jacob was not the reason I contacted you."

"Well," I said. "When I tell the sheriff, he's probably going to want to know if you had an alibi for the night Jacob was murdered. He's rather thorough."

She smiled, her hazel eyes nearly disappearing. "I was at home with my husband and daughter, playing Monopoly, of all things."

"Oh, and we know how long Monopoly can take. You must have been there all night," I said.

"At least three hours, but I always lose my patience and quit early."

"So do I," I said.

She laughed at yet another similarity between us. I turned to go in the house, then remembered something. "How did you know I'd made the connection between you and Jacob?"

"Well, I had made up my mind to tell you about Jacob and me a few days ago. But then Granny called and told me that you and your friend had been to her house. I knew if you'd looked at any of her pictures, you would make the connection. Then when you wouldn't take my calls, I just knew you had found out," she said. "And that you'd jumped to the wrong conclusion."

I raised my eyebrow at her.

"Not that you jump to conclusions all the time or anything."

"Hmph" was all I said. As I reached for the door, she spoke once more.

"Do you believe me?" she asked.

"Yes," I said. "I believe you."

"Then everything's okay?" she asked.

"Everything's fine," I said. "I'll call you."

As I walked in the house, I couldn't help but think about how strange it was to have somebody else initiating a confrontation. I was usually the one who did that.

I had jumped to conclusions about her. I had immediately thought that there was more to her making contact with me than met the eye. Maybe because she also jumps to conclusions, she just assumed I would, too. Lord, Stephanie was even beginning to identify and pounce on my faults. Yup, she was just about a regular member of the family. There was only one initiation she had yet to go through.

NEW KASSEL GAZETTE
The News You Might Miss
By
Eleanore Murdoch

How much snow are we expected to endure? For anybody else experiencing those winter blues, how about purchasing a ticket for the Valentine's dance, sponsored by the Knights of Columbus?

You can take your sweetheart, take somebody else's sweetheart, or find a lonely heart under the red lights and soft music.

I am pleased to say that the New Kassel Kings made a respectable comeback in last night's home game. Unfortunately, there still seems to be a parent or two who think the chairs on the sidelines are to be used as confetti.

It seems as though some of the furor is dying down over the steamboat wreckage. No pun intended to poor Mr. Lahrs. Our town is returning to normal, and slowly the faithful tourist is replacing the reporter and news cameras. I've decided that New Kassel is our home first, and our commodity second. Even if Oscar and I did make a few extra bucks this month from all these visitors.

Until Next Time,
Eleanore

THIRTY

THREE DAYS LATER, I was seated at my desk in the Gaheimer House, munching on some crackers and drinking a Dr Pepper, when the phone rang.

"Gaheimer House, Torie," I said.

"This is Mr. Lawrence Belfer," a voice said. "I am returning your call."

Lawrence Belfer was the only person on *The Phantom* passenger list that I had been able to find alive. He lived in Idaho, and I had called twice and left messages for him. "Mr. Belfer, I am so glad you called," I said. "I'll make it quick, since I know this is a long-distance call for you. From my messages, I guess you realize that I'm interested in *The Phantom*," I said.

"Yes," he replied. "What did you want to know?"

"How old were you when it sank?"

"Nine and a half," he said.

"Where were you located on the steamer when it started to go down?"

He hesitated a moment. "Right outside the pilothouse."

"Mr. Belfer, what caused the boat to sink?" I asked.

"Captain Thibeau was in the pilothouse," he said. "He was talking to another man about selling his boat to him in exchange for some jewels or something."

"Diamonds?"

"Could have been," he said. "Can't be sure. Was a long time ago. Anyways, the other man didn't want to buy the boat. Captain said he had to sell it. He had to get out of the business 'cause he was wanting to get married.''

I blinked. ''You're sure that's what he said?''

''Well, maybe not in those exact words, but that's what it sounded like to me. And they was yelling really loud. The fight got bigger and louder, and then they started throwing punches. Next thing I knew, we were driving hard for the Illinois bank; then the boat went back the other way, and the wave we'd caused clipped us in the front.''

''In other words, the water came up over the bow of the boat?''

''Yes,'' he said. ''Then it turned, and everybody started screaming.''

Mr. Belfers and I spoke a few more minutes about what he'd been doing with his life since the accident. He asked what my interest was, and I told him that the drought had exposed the wreckage and newfound interest had come of it. We then said our good-byes and I hung up and stared at the phone, realizing that the argument Captain Thibeau had had was probably with Samuel Higgins. While I was staring at the phone, it rang again. ''Hello?'' I said.

''Hi, it's Collette.''

''Hey, how's it going?''

''Wonderful,'' she said. ''Steve and I are going to Argentina in a week. I'm going to get away from all of this snow and cold and lie on the beach and, well, you know.''

''Great. I'm sure you will have tons of fun. Take lots of pictures.''

''I will,'' she said. ''Oh, and pictures are what I'm calling you about.''

''Oh yeah?''

''Yes, I need those pictures that you said I could have— the ones of Granite County Lutheran and the cemetery. I'm not going to have the story finished for a while, but I wanted to get my visual material together so that I know what I've got and what I still need to get.''

"Sure thing,'' I said. "I dropped them off for developing yesterday. There were still a few pictures left on the camera, so that's what was holding me up.''

"Can I come down for lunch and we can go get them? I want everything in place before Steve and I leave,'' she explained.

"Sure, come on down.''

Forty-five minutes later, Collette showed up in my office with little boxes of Chinese food. "Knock, knock,'' she said.

"Hey, come in. Oh, you're a goddess. You brought lunch.'' As soon as I smelled the food, my stomach started growling. There isn't a place in New Kassel that has Chinese food. The closest one is over in Wisteria, and it's owned by a sixth-generation Texan. So Collette often brings Chinese food when she visits me.

"I'm a goddess for lots of reasons,'' she said. "Bringing Chinese food is not one of them.''

"It is in my book.''

"Whatcha working on?'' she asked.

"Well, I just got off the phone with a *Phantom* survivor. He said he heard the captain having an argument with a passenger. Seems he wanted this particular passenger to buy his boat in exchange for some jewels, possibly diamonds, because he was wanting out of the riverboat business. Supposedly, the captain told the passenger he was getting married. And I checked the census for Samuel Higgins, the guy who had mined the diamonds originally,'' I said.

"Oh, the *original* owner of the diamonds.''

"Right. I think he was the one the captain was arguing with.''

"Makes sense. What did you find?'' she asked as she

opened the big box of rice and scooped some out on a paper plate.

"Well, it took me two days, because the Hills Mine records stated that they thought he was from Iowa. So I spent a whole day looking through the Iowa census records, only to find out he was from across the river, over in northern Illinois. Um…Rockford."

"How'd you find that out?"

"I got frustrated and started checking the surrounding states," I said.

"Hey, I got you that mushroom garlic stuff you like so well," she said.

"Oooh, good, pour it on. Anyway, in 1920, he had seven kids."

"Seven? Jeeeesus," she said, licking her fingers.

"Yeah, and if this is the same passenger that the prostitute was talking about…She said she saw the diamonds in a passenger's room. What was she doing there?"

"This guy just couldn't get enough, huh?"

"Oh, he's nothing. I have an ancestor who had twenty-two kids," I said.

"By the same wife? Surely not."

"Yes, same woman. Sixteen single births and three sets of twins. Had her first kid at eighteen and her last at forty," I explained.

"I would have shot him," Collette said.

"I would have castrated him first. And I even like kids," I said, laughing.

She handed me a plate of rice and garlic mushroom sauce. "Egg roll?" she asked.

"Please. So anyway, I gave the list of Higgins's children to Colin, and he's going to try to run them down and see if any are still living. If not, it's on to the next generation."

"Can't you do that?" she asked. She took a bite of her teriyaki chicken and sighed. "God, I love Chinese food."

"To answer your question, yes, I could track them down. Well, the guys at least. Girls are a little trickier."

"Why?"

"Because they get married and change their names, and so often on documents, they're listed just as Mrs. Smith, or whatever the husband's name is. You know, no identity of their own."

"Men are pigs," she said. "Except for Steve."

"Gee," a voice said. "Guess that's my cue."

I looked up to see Colin standing in the doorway. He was off duty and was wearing jeans, a blue sweater, and his parka. His face twisted into what looked like pain, but I soon realized he had smelled our lunch. "Mmm, is that Chinese?"

"Want some?" Collette asked.

"Hell yes," he said. He came into the room and began scooping up rice. "You know that your mother hates Chinese food."

"I know," I said, and winked at Collette.

"You want garlic mushroom or chicken teriyaki?"

"Yes," he answered and held out his plate. I laughed at him. Obviously, my mother had not allowed him any Chinese food in awhile. Oh, well. Guess every marriage has to have a bump in the road somewhere along the line.

"Oh, and here are the pictures," he said, handing me an envelope.

Colin had volunteered to go and pay for the pictures, since he would need copies of the ones of the church and cemetery for his report. He sat on the edge of my desk and tore into his lunch. "You got egg rolls, too?"

Opening the envelope, I couldn't help laughing again. The first couple of pictures were of a fish that Rudy had caught. He had insisted that I take a picture of it because it was the biggest fish he'd ever caught. I didn't mind taking a picture of it, because that would keep him from increasing the size of the fish when he told stories about it years from now. "Oh, here's that bass Rudy caught." I handed the picture to Colin.

He whistled. "That's a beauty."

It was ugly. A bass is just an ugly fish.

I flipped through a few more pictures of Rudy smiling at the fish. Next were pictures from the chili cook-off we'd had at the Knights of Columbus Hall. Eleanore's recipe had won. There was a shot of Sylvia standing in the kitchen, waiting for her tea to steep. And finally, I got to the pictures of Granite County Lutheran Church.

Handing them to Collette, I named them as I went. "That's the picture of the footprints," I said. "Don't ask me why I took that. I was just snapping pictures. And here's the one of the woods. And there are the tombstones. That's the church from where I'd been standing in the cemetery. This is the one of the church that I took from the parking lot while I was standing next to my van."

"These aren't too bad," Collette said. "I mean, they're kind of grainy. But what can you expect from a disposable camera?"

"Let me see," Colin said.

She handed him the pictures, which he tried to look at with one hand because he didn't want to set down his plate of food. "Oh, Torie," he said. "I almost forgot."

"What?"

"I heard back from Jefferson County on the ticket that Jeremiah Ketchum got," he said, handing me back the stack of pictures. "He got a speeding ticket at seven-fifteen on the night Jacob Lahrs was killed."

"What?" I asked, almost choking on my rice. "But then that means he wasn't in his hotel at the time of the murder. We figured the attack was between six and seven in the evening."

"In broad daylight?" Collette asked.

"No, not broad daylight. It gets dark at about five. With the snow and overcast sky, it was already pretty dark that day," I said.

"What time did you find the body?" Collette asked.

"Well, now that I really think about it...the train goes by at seven on the nose. By the time we walked and talked, it was probably about seven-fifteen or so."

"Is that enough time for Jeremiah to have hopped on the train, gotten in his car, which he would have had waiting somewhere, and driven back to the Murdoch Inn?"

"Don't forget he went at least ten minutes up the road, because he got the ticket in Jefferson County," I said. "I don't know. What do you think, Colin?"

"It might have been enough time, because you figure I didn't get there for another ten minutes after you guys found the body. By the time we knew what was going on and actually got Newsome in the Murdoch Inn to start checking on the guests there, oh it had to be at least seven-fifty or so. I think he had enough time."

"My gosh, Jeremiah would have been slipping into the Murdoch moments before we were trying to get my big butt up the hill," I said.

"*If* it was Jeremiah," he said. "He denies it was him. Says his wallet was stolen."

"Do you believe him?" Collette asked.

"He didn't cancel any of his credit cards or anything until the day after he claims it was stolen," Colin said.

"You don't act like it's a big deal," Collette said.

He shrugged. "I got two witnesses."

"What?" I asked. I started flipping through the pictures. "What do you mean you have two witnesses? Two witnesses to what?"

"I've got the officer who issued him the ticket," he said. "The officer said that the man he pulled over didn't have his driver's license on him. Said he'd lost it. But the officer also said that he'd be happy to come down here and take a look at a picture or a lineup. He said he would remember him, since Jeremiah, or whoever it was, was doing eighty in a fifty-five zone.''

"In a hurry to get back to the Murdoch Inn and establish his alibi," I said. But it still didn't make sense to me. The amount of snow on his car in the parking lot proved that it had been there the whole time. He couldn't have had his car parked somewhere else, waiting for him to jump off of a train. But before I had the chance to mention this, Collette spoke up.

"And the other witness?" she asked.

"The other witness is the one who rented him the car," Colin said.

My head snapped up. "He *rented* a car?" That would certainly explain why his real car had been at the Murdoch Inn the whole day.

"Showed up on his credit-card statement, and it matches the license number given on the ticket. Jeremiah Ketchum was driving a rented car at seven-fifteen on the night Jacob Lahrs was killed."

"But he denies it," I said.

"Totally," the sheriff said. "Said his wallet was stolen and he knows nothing about a rental car or a ticket."

"You know, he did mention that his wallet had been stolen the day that woman rammed into his car in front of the Murdoch Inn," I said.

Colin just shrugged.

"But he had to know about the ticket. Why else would it turn up on the dashboard of his car?" I asked.

Colin gave me a "There you have it" expression.

"You realize that if he really is the one who rented the car, it's premeditation," I said.

"Yup," the sheriff replied.

"What if he's telling the truth?" Collette said. "Is the car-rental clerk reliable?"

"He's a guy in his mid-thirties," he said. "He seemed trustworthy."

"Did the rental car show up in the video footage from Channel 6?"

"No," Colin said. "And believe me, I checked. But he could have easily parked it one street over and walked back to the Murdoch Inn. With all of the people going in and out, we wouldn't have paid any attention to a set of prints leading into the Murdoch Inn from up the road."

"True," I said.

Upon closer inspection, something in one of the photographs caught my eye. I stopped eating and held the picture up closer so I could see better.

"What is it?" Collette asked.

"Maybe Jeremiah Ketchum is telling the truth," I said. "Maybe his wallet was stolen. And maybe somebody planted the ticket in his car."

"I dunno," Colin said. "I guess it's possible, but I think you're reaching."

"Maybe not," I said, staring at the photo.

"Why do you say that?"

"Because Danny Jones was the one at the cemetery, checking out those seven graves the day I was there," I said. I handed the photograph to Colin, pointing to the telltale item. "That's Danny Jones's car."

"How can you be sure?" Collette asked.

"Rusty white Chevette with the 'Jesus Is Coming. Look Busy' bumper sticker," I said.

"Yeah, but so what?" Collette said. "I thought you said Danny Jones and Jeremiah Ketchum didn't know where the diamonds were hidden."

"I said that *they* said they didn't know where the diamonds were hidden. That doesn't mean they were telling the truth. What if Danny Jones did know?''

"How would he know?" Collette asked.

"From Jacob Lahrs," I said.

"But why would Jacob Lahrs tell Danny and not Jeremiah? Why would he tell either one of them, for that matter?"

"Nobody said he voluntarily told Danny where the diamonds were. You do remember that his head was bashed in. Think about it. Maybe Danny beat it out of him."

Colin's eyebrows creased and he finally set his plate of food down.

"Did the guitar pick at the crime scene turn out to belong to Jones?" I asked.

He picked up the phone, staring at the photograph of Jones's car the whole time. Then he dialed a number and waited a moment. "Yes, this is Sheriff Colin Brooke of the Granite County Sheriff's Department. I was wondering if you had the fingerprint results back on item…" He pulled a notepad out of his pocket and flipped it open. "On item P one forty-five, from crime scene NK seven sixty-one."

A moment went by and he said nothing. Then finally he said, "Thank you." He placed the phone back in the receiver and looked at Collette and then at me. "It's a match. It belonged to Danny Jones. And it was dropped there sometime during the latter half of the snowfall. They can't be more specific yet."

"Do you really think this photograph proves something?" Collette asked.

"I think it proves that Danny Jones knew where the diamonds were," I said. "What's more, Danny was nowhere to be seen when I was there. Which indicates to me that when I showed up, he ran and hid. He was probably in the woods, watching me the whole time." Chills ran up my back as I remembered the day in the cemetery and the peculiar feeling I'd had of being watched.

"You really think that's what the killer wanted?" Collette asked. "The location of the diamonds?"

"Sounds like a good motive to me. The killer gets the diamonds and the story. So he's rich and looks like a genius at the same time. Perfect chick magnet," Colin said.

"'Chick magnet'?" I asked. "Colin, you have to stop watching those cop shows."

"Maybe Danny Jones found out about the diamonds the same way you did, Torie," Collette said. "But what if he didn't know the diamonds were there and he just went to the cemetery for some other sort of research? Like Bradley Chapel and Kyle were doing the day you guys called me down there."

"Then why hide from me? The picture proves he was there. If he was just there to get a few photographs for the story or whatever, then why hide when I pulled up? Why not just stand there and talk to me? That would be the normal thing to do, right?" I asked.

"That's true," she said. She looked up at Colin. "What do you think?"

"I was so sure it was Jeremiah Ketchum," he said.

"What if Danny Jones was the one who stole Jeremiah's wallet? He would have had ample opportunity," I said.

"Ooooh, Torie. Your mind works in wicked ways," Collette said.

"I don't know," said Colin.

The phone rang and all three of us jumped. Nervous laughter bounced around the room as I answered the phone. "Gaheimer House, Torie," I said.

"Mrs. O'Shea," a voice said.

"Yes."

"This is Danny Jones."

"Danny…" I said. "What a…what can I do for you?"

Collette and Colin both came around the desk, Collette on my left and Colin on my right, each wanting to listen in on the conversation. Well, Colin was the sheriff, so I switched ears and let him listen.

"I need to speak with you."

"All right," I said. "I'm not very busy right now. What do you need?"

"No, I need to speak to you in person," he said.

Colin shook his head no.

"All right," I said. Colin threw his hands up in frustration. "What's it about?"

"I need to explain some things and ask you some questions about what Jacob had written in his notes. I think you're the only one who can help me," he said.

"Okay. When?"

"This afternoon?"

"Sure."

"Umm, let's meet out at the Lutheran church," he said.

Sirens went off in my head. Any other time, I would have asked why he couldn't meet me at a restaurant in town. Or at my office. But clearly he had picked the Lutheran church deliberately. If I let on like I suspected something, he might disappear and never be found.

"Oh, that's a lovely spot," I said, hoping I sounded convincing.

"Three o'clock."

"All right, see you then." I hung up the phone, my hands shaking.

"What the *hell* was that?" Colin bellowed.

"He wants to meet with me at the Lutheran church. Call your deputies, Colin. I think your killer is about ready to knock off the one person he thinks can nail him."

"Who?" Collette asked.

"Me," I said. "He saw me that day. He knows I have pictures of his car parked in the lot."

"Torie," she said. "He could hurt you."

"That's why Colin is going to call in the troops. Right?"

"Torie," he said. "Your mother will kill me."

"Can't be helped. I'm the bait. You know all those fishing things you're always talking about with Rudy? Some fish like only certain bait. And this time, I'm it."

THIRTY-ONE

Now I KNEW what it felt like to be a worm on a hook. Well, I didn't have a sharp pointy thing jabbed in my gut exactly, but otherwise, I could empathize. I stood in the middle of the parking lot, waiting for Danny Jones to arrive. Colin's deputies were positioned inside the church. Newsome was up in the bell tower and Duran was just inside the door. Miller was up in the loft part of the covered bridge, and Colin himself was in the woods. I was covered. One false move and I'd have four country boys coming to my rescue. But I still didn't much like waiting for a killer, thank you very much.

Just as that thought entered my head, the Chevette pulled across the covered bridge with a clatter. Danny came to a stop next to me and turned off the engine, which knocked, sputtered, and finally was silent. Danny got out of the car. He was wearing a big green plaid shirt and black pants made out of parachute material. His brown eyes looked worried. Okay, I knew he was supposed to be a vicious killer, but he seriously needed to work on his wardrobe.

"Mr. Jones," I said, "what's this all about?"

"I want to know if you'd go to the sheriff with me," he said.

Not what I expected. "Why?"

"You know the sheriff really well, don't you?"

"He's married to my mother," I said. "I know more about him than I ever wanted to know. Why?"

"Then he'll believe you," he said.

"There's something I have to tell you, Danny. Believe it or not, the sheriff does not always believe the things that I have to say," I said. I looked around, nervous. The glint of Duran's gun up in the bell tower calmed me. Somebody was there. Somebody was watching. Somebody would save me if I needed saving. "In fact, he can be quite stubborn. What is it you want me to tell him?"

"I think I know who killed Jacob," he said.

"Really," I said, trying to look surprised. "Who?"

"Jeremiah," he said. "But I think he's going to try to pin it on me."

I said nothing, waiting for him to speak.

"The day you came down to the college," he said, "you were looking at my car so funny. And I knew then that you knew I had been here after the murder."

I didn't tell him that I had only just made that discovery. I let him continue to think that I had figured it out earlier. "So?" I asked.

"When you found the diamonds, I knew you would think that I had been here to get them. Or that I knew where they were," he said. "And that would make me suspect number one. But, I tell you, I did not kill Jacob."

"What were you doing here, then?"

"Earlier, on the day Jacob was killed, the three of us were eating dinner. Jeremiah got up to go to the rest room," he said. "Jacob told me that if anything ever happened to him that the tombstones at the Lutheran church would prove all of his theories."

"The diamonds," I said.

"No, I don't think that's what he meant," Danny said.

I studied his face for a second. The snow fell all around, accumulating on us as we stood there. He didn't look like a killer. But then, that didn't really mean anything. Jeremiah Ketchum didn't necessarily look like a killer, either. But

Danny was so young, and I'm usually a pretty good judge of character. "What do you think Jacob meant?"

"I'm not sure," he said. "But I'm sure I did not kill Jacob."

I thought about it a moment, and then it dawned on me. Jacob must have found out that William Wade had paid for the tombstones. Which Jacob had taken, as I had, as confirmation that William Wade was indeed Eli Thibeau. Along with photographs of the two, that was enough proof. Maybe that was what Jacob had meant by the tombstones would prove his theories. "So why were you here that day?"

"I just came to look. I thought if I could come and look at them, then maybe I could learn whatever it was that Jacob had known," he said. "But all I found were tombstones of unknown dead. Then you showed up."

"Why'd you hide?" I asked.

"I don't know," he answered. "I was just so creeped out by all of it. As I was on my way out of the cemetery, I heard your car coming. So I ran to the parking lot and hid in the Dumpster over there until you and the minister left. When I saw you, I thought maybe there was something to what Jacob was saying. I thought if you saw me…I don't know."

He shoved his hands in his pockets and looked around. The breath billowed from his lips as he shrugged at his own indecision. "I'm afraid now that Jeremiah is going to pin this on me."

"How can you be so sure it's Jeremiah?" I asked.

"Because it is," I heard a voice say. I turned around and saw Jeremiah Ketchum standing just under the awning of the covered bridge. Deputy Miller was right above him. It took all my willpower not to look up. Not that I would have seen Miller even if I had looked. He was safely hidden. But I didn't want Jeremiah to realize he was being watched.

Somehow, I was more scared now that Jeremiah was here

than I had been when it was just Danny. Which made no sense at all. A killer is a killer.

My gaze flicked to Danny, whose hands were now out of his pockets and twitching in a nervous fashion. He was ready to take flight. *Don't run, kid. Don't run.* I knew if he ran, he'd be in more trouble than if he didn't.

"Mr. Ketchum," I said in my best Scarlett O'Hara voice. "Whatever are you doing here?"

He laughed. "Mrs. O'Shea, they broke the mold when they made you."

"I've been told that before, believe it or not."

Panic settled in my gut as I realized that the sheriff and the boys didn't know what was going on. Would they realize which one was the bad guy? Did I even know which one was the bad guy? In my gut, I thought it was Ketchum. Danny's explanation of why he'd been here and then hidden from me sort of made sense in a stupid teenager sort of way.

"What brings you here?" I said in a more serious tone.

"You, and Danny. I've been following Danny for days."

"You have?" Danny said.

"Why?" I asked.

"I was watching to see if he sold out to the reporter."

"Mr. Chapel?" I asked.

"No, no, the pretty one with the sexy name. Collette," he said. Something in the way he said her name made my skin crawl. "It didn't take me long to figure out that Bradley Chapel couldn't tell his butt from a hole in the ground. But Collette…well, she's pretty bright. And then she had the enigmatic Mrs. O'Shea on her side. I knew it wouldn't be long before you two would have everything figured out. But there were still lots of things you didn't know, and lots of documents you didn't have. And I thought Danny was going to get scared and sell out to the enemy."

My mind was reeling. Sell out? If we found the information on our own and had the whole story, what could

Danny give us? Collette had put together the story of a lifetime without their help. What could Danny have to tell us that could hurt Jeremiah and help our story at the same time? I snapped my head around and stared at Danny, who was looking quite unsure at the moment.

"Danny," I said. "How exactly do you know that Jeremiah killed Jacob?"

"Because it was his idea," Jeremiah said.

"What?" I asked.

"He looked up the train schedule," Ketchum said. "He figured out that if we killed Jacob at precisely 6:50 p.m. a train would come by a few minutes later and I could jump the train to get away. He had a car waiting for me up in Sulphur Springs. What I didn't know is that dumb shit over there had rented the car in my name, and with my credit card."

"Oh, I don't think he was so dumb," I said, looking at Danny Jones with newfound admiration and shock. How could I have been so gullible a few moments ago? He definitely wasn't the naive teenager I thought he was. "Think about it. He knew that when they ran your credit card, it would show up, and suddenly your alibi wouldn't look quite so solid."

"You're the dumb shit," Danny said. "You had to go and get a speeding ticket."

"I am not going to go down for this alone!" Jeremiah said. Suddenly, he pulled a gun from his coat pocket, and I freaked. I started screaming, and Danny grabbed me from behind, placing his hand over my mouth and sticking something sharp against my stomach. My situation wasn't the greatest. I was being held at knifepoint by one psychopathic killer and had a gun pointed at me by another. Sweat broke out along my back and I had to fight to remain calm.

"You gonna shoot her?" Danny yelled at Jeremiah.

"Wife, mother of three. Upstanding citizen and all that crap. Think about it, Jeremiah."

"If I have to go through her to plant a bullet in you, that's fine with me," Jeremiah said.

Danny moved and put his arm around my neck, so that I was staring down at his elbow. All he had to do was tighten his grip and he could either strangle me or break my neck. But the truly terrifying thing was that I was his human shield. And somehow I believed Jeremiah when he said he'd put a bullet through me to get to Danny.

"Colin! Help!" I didn't realize I had opened my mouth and screamed. I just sort of heard it from someplace deep inside me. Blood pounded in my ears and my thoughts raced. Could I get away from Danny? If I did, would Jeremiah shoot me before Colin and the gang had a chance to shoot him?

"Drop it, Ketchum," Colin said, emerging from the woods. "You're surrounded."

Ketchum looked to the ground, shaking his head and laughing. "Ooooh, Sheriff. Isn't that what they say in all the movies?"

"You really are surrounded, you jerk," I said.

A blank expression crossed Jeremiah's face. His nose and cheeks had turned red from the cold, the snow was falling in heavier flakes, and now the wind had picked up. Danny twisted from side to side, moving me with him as he did so, trying to locate the deputies. I could feel his grip on me tighten as his panic mounted.

"Ketchum, don't do anything stupid. You know we can track you in this snow," the sheriff said. "Plus, if you're out too long in this, you could die of exposure."

"Gimme your keys, Danny," Jeremiah said.

"Don't be stupid," the sheriff yelled. "Lay down your weapon."

Jeremiah stepped closer to me and Danny, closing the

space in seconds. An expression of regret played across the sheriff's face. Was he upset that he hadn't shot Jeremiah when he had the chance? The sheriff and I have had our differences, but I could honestly say that if Colin could spare a human life, he would. He couldn't have known that Jeremiah would make this move.

"Come on, Danny. Let's get in the car and go," Jeremiah said. "You and me."

I couldn't see Danny's expression, because he was behind me. But I could feel him hesitate.

"Let's walk Mrs. O'Shea to the car, get in, and drive. They won't shoot us if we have her for cover," Jeremiah said.

"Don't listen to him, Danny," I said. "Think about it. Once you guys are five miles down the road, he'll shoot you dead and leave you for the crows."

I looked all around in every direction I could manage. Colin stood there, his feet apart, pistol aimed, ready to fire. Miller was up in the top of the covered bridge, the barrel to his rifle showing. I couldn't see the church behind me, so I wasn't sure if Newsome had come out or not.

Danny started dragging me toward his car. "Danny, don't. He's gonna kill you!" I shouted. I was afraid to struggle too much, because I was sure Danny would just snap my neck.

"Shut up!" Danny said, and tightened his grip around my throat.

"You're a fool," I said.

"Shut up! Shut up!"

Danny opened the driver's side of the car. Jeremiah hunched down so that nobody could get a clear shot at him and got in the car. Then Danny dived into the car and threw me to the ground. My ankle twisted in the process, the same one I'd injured before, and I slid in the snow.

In a blur, Colin and Deputy Newsome circled the car.

Danny tried to start it, but it wouldn't turn over. That twenty-year-old Chevette wasn't a very reliable getaway car. I heard one shot fired and then lots of shuffling and running and "Get down! Face in the snow! Don't move!" I wasn't sure, but it sounded as if Deputy Miller actually said, "Don't move, sleazeball."

None of it much mattered to me. I lay on my back in the snow, looking up at the sky, unable to move from shock. Hot, searing pains shot from my ankle up my shin, but I just lay there. From this position, the snowflakes looked black as they fell from the sky. And then I heard a voice.

"Are you all right? Torie? Are you all right?"

I blinked and realized that it was Colin speaking.

I turned my head slightly to look at him.

"Are you all right?"

"Yeah," I said. "I'm fine."

No, having Hugh Jackman lick your toes is fine…

"Okay, no, I'm not fine. I'm…not bleeding."

Colin laughed. "Can you move everything?"

I shook my head back and forth.

"No? What can't you move?"

"My left foot."

"Again?"

THIRTY-TWO

A FEW DAYS LATER, I sat in my mother's living room with my foot propped up on a pillow. I was thumbing through a *Reminisce* magazine I'd found in a rack next to the couch. My kids were playing in the other room, Rudy was out in the garage with Colin, and my mother was cooking. Fried chicken, hash-brown casserole, homemade biscuits, salad, baby peas, chunky applesauce from Fraulein Krista's, and, my favorite, a Red Velvet cake for dessert. I was in heaven just smelling it.

The doorbell rang, and I yelled, "Come in."

My father entered the living room, his demeanor hesitant. His big QT mug was in one hand and a single red rose in the other. He saw me lying on the couch and waved. "Hey, Jalena," he said into the kitchen. My mother answered him, and he made his way toward me. Whatever differences I have with my father, I will say that I love the fact that he and my mother made peace and are friends. He is often a guest at dinner, and he is never excluded from holiday events or birthdays. They actually get along better now than they ever did. My opinion is that my dad is a little jealous that my mother has found so much happiness with Colin, but he would never show it. I can see it, though, in the way he looks at them. Like maybe he is seeing what could have been his if...well, if he'd been a different person.

As much as I hate to admit it, Colin never seems to be bothered by the fact that my dad is around. Which says a lot about Colin. He acts as if it's a perfectly natural thing to have his wife's ex-husband over for dinner.

Dad knelt down next to me and handed me the rose. "How's the foot?"

"Hurts," I said.

"You know, you're not Angie Dickinson."

"Dad, you're showing your age. *Policewoman* hasn't been on in twenty-five years," I said.

"Okay, well…you're not Buffy whatshername," he said.

"The Vampire Slayer?" I asked.

"Yeah. What kinda last name is Vampire Slayer?" We both laughed a little too forcefully. "Are you changing careers on us?"

"Hey," I said, palms up. "Stranger things have happened."

"Like the fact you have a sister?"

"Yeah, who would have ever thought that would happen?" I asked.

"Do you forgive me?" he asked, looking around the room. He has never been good at making eye contact, especially in emotional confrontations.

"I forgive you for fathering a child," I said. "I'm still working on the fact that you didn't tell me."

He nodded. "I deserve that, I guess."

I peered at him cautiously. He never admits guilt. Any minute, I expected his skin to melt off and Pa Ingalls to be sitting there. This was definitely a family bonding moment from somebody else's family. It felt odd.

"I love you," he said.

The breath caught in my throat. I must have been twelve the last time I heard those words from my father. I knew what it took for him even to think about them, much less actually verbalize them. Tears welled in my eyes as I looked at his aged and weathered face. I saw a man who had lived far too much in the years allotted. And I saw a father, some-

one often unable to give what is required, but a father nonetheless. I guess you never know where somebody is coming
from, unless you walk that person's path. What to one person may seem like an impossibility may seem like the only
way out to another. And our decisions are based on what
we encounter along that path.

"I love you, too, Dad."

"I didn't upset you, did I?" he asked.

"When?"

"Just now," he said.

"Huh? Oh, no. My foot is really hurting," I said, and
swiped at a tear.

Just then, the doorbell rang again. I thanked God for the
impeccable timing. "Come in!" I called.

The door opened and in walked Stephanie Connelly, followed by her husband, Michael, and her little girl, Julia.
Dad looked at me quickly, his eyebrows raised. "We invited
them for dinner," I said.

It was his turn to have tears in his eyes.

"For the first time in my life, I will have my whole family
at the same dinner table," I said.

He squeezed my hand and then went over to Julia and
picked her up. "Hi, Julia," he said.

"Hi," she said, and hugged him. It was obvious they'd
seen each other before but weren't overly comfortable with
each other yet.

"Take your coats off and just set them there on the
chair," I said. "The chair is our unofficial coatrack around
here."

I got up off the couch and grabbed my crutches. I intro-
duced myself and shook Michael's hand. He was tall and
lanky, and his hands were too big for the rest of his body.
His smile was genuine, though, and I liked that. Dad brought
Julia over to me. "This is your aunt Torie," he said.

"Nice to meet you," she said in a tiny voice. Blond hair

hung loosely around her shoulders, and it was clear from first glance that she had inherited our hazel eyes.

"It's nice to meet you, too," I said. "Are you always this shy? You'll never last around my Mary."

My mother wheeled into the living room then and waited at the doorway. Stephanie suddenly appeared nervous. I grabbed her hand and walked her over to my mother. "Stephanie, this is my mom, Jalena."

"It's...ah...so nice to meet you," Stephanie said, an uncertain look on her face. Her anxiety was understandable. I suppose some might think of her as the daughter of the enemy. But she didn't know my mother. Even if my mother still held a grudge, she wouldn't have directed it at Stephanie.

"The pleasure is all mine," my mother said.

With that, Stephanie seemed to relax and take a deep breath. When she did, she couldn't help but smell dinner. "Oh my Lord. What smells so good?"

"Stephanie, my dear, you are about to go through an initiation you'll never forget: Dinner at my mother's," I said.

"And it can be painful," Rudy said, coming in from the kitchen.

"I think I'll gladly suffer," said Stephanie.

Another knock at the door made everybody look around with questioning expressions. Since my dad was the closest to the door, he opened it. Collette was standing there in her fur coat, and her suitcase sat on the front step.

"Steve went to Argentina with the lead singer of another band," she said, making her way into the living room. "Oooh, did Jalena cook? Hi, I'm Collette. Where do I put my coat? Can you believe he did that? The nerve of him. You don't mind if I stay for dinner, right?"

"Of course not," I said.

Everybody made their way into the dining room, but I

held back a moment, thinking. I thought about how I had jumped to conclusions and assumed Stephanie's contacting me had been because of her cousin, instead of for her own reasons. Even if it had been for just a second, I'd still thought it. I'd had no reason to. No reason other than the fact that I hadn't been able to accept at face value my sister and what she brought into my life. I had immediately thought that she'd had an ulterior motive. Perhaps that New Year's resolution about being more tolerant and understanding had been just words. I'd spoken the words and thought that would make it so. And on my first test of the year, I had failed. Hopefully, I would get better.

And I thought of Jacob Lahrs, who had been killed by both of his partners. When it came down to it, Danny had wanted the diamonds and Jeremiah had wanted the prestige of a great story. Danny, of course, had lied. He had been in the cemetery that day to retrieve the diamonds and was later to split them with Jeremiah Ketchum. Jeremiah had beaten the location out of Jacob, just as we had surmised that day in the office. When I showed up in the cemetery, Danny realized that, regardless of its secluded location, there was always somebody there. And he had no idea how much digging he would have to do to find the diamonds. He just couldn't take a chance on being interrupted by somebody. Even if he could have gotten away without being caught, the location would have been a bust. Somebody would have figured out that there was something hidden there. He would have had to wait until all the hoopla was over.

So, even though he hadn't actually delivered the blow that killed Jacob, Danny had planned the whole thing, and I hoped he would see as much jail time as Jeremiah.

Of course I wished that Jacob Lahrs had not been murdered. But Collette would benefit from his misfortune. For the story of what happened to the Huntleigh heiress was now hers. After the trial, she could have access to any of the footage that Danny Jones had taken while documenting Jacob's exploration of the wreck. But she might not need it. She had a pretty good story without it. And in typical Collette fashion, she would do it up good.

"Hey, Torie," Dad said. "Are you coming?"

"There won't be anything left to eat if you don't get in here!" Rudy called.

I hopped into the dining room and saw all the adults piled around the table, and the kids sitting at the little table that Mom had set up for them. My heart swelled as I looked at all of them. This was my family. Even Sheriff Colin Brooke.

HARLEQUIN®
INTRIGUE®

WE'LL LEAVE YOU BREATHLESS!

If you've been looking for thrilling tales of contemporary passion and sensuous love stories with taut, edge-of-the-seat suspense—then you'll love Harlequin Intrigue!

Every month, you'll meet six new heroes who are guaranteed to make your spine tingle and your pulse pound. With them you'll enter into the exciting world of Harlequin Intrigue— where your life is on the line and so is your heart!

THAT'S INTRIGUE—
ROMANTIC SUSPENSE
AT ITS BEST!

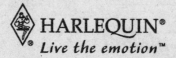

HARLEQUIN®
Live the emotion™

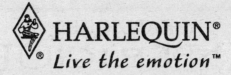

HARLEQUIN®
Live the emotion™

Upbeat,
All-American Romances

flipside
Romantic Comedy

Harlequin Historicals®
Historical,
Romantic Adventure

HARLEQUIN®
INTRIGUE
Romantic Suspense

HARLEQUIN®
HARLEQUIN ROMANCE®
The essence of
modern romance

HARLEQUIN®
Presents
Seduction and passion
guaranteed

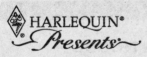
Emotional,
Exciting, Unexpected

Sassy, Sexy, Seductive!

V Silhouette®

SILHOUETTE Romance®

From first love to forever, these love stories
are fairy tale romances for today's woman.

V Silhouette® Desire®

Modern, passionate reads that are powerful and provocative.

V Silhouette® SPECIAL EDITION™

Emotional, compelling stories that capture the intensity
of living, loving and creating a family in today's world.

V Silhouette® INTIMATE MOMENTS™

A roller-coaster read that delivers romantic thrills
in a world of suspense, adventure and more.

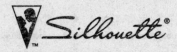